Simon Linter

Let Go

SPLINTER PUBLISHINGS

First published 2016 by Splinter Publishings

First published in paperback 2016 by Splinter Publishings

This edition first published 2016 by Splinter Publishings
Splinter Publishings, Vällingby, Sweden.
www.splinterpublishings.com

ISBN: 978-91-982368-4-2

Printed by Book Printing UK
Remus House, Coltsfoot Drive, Peterborough, PE2 9BF

Thanks to Willie Nelligan and Andrew MacPherson for your editing skills and spotting things I missed.

Thanks to Matthew Starnes for your suggestion.

1.

I love this company. I love its energy, its buzz, and its quest to better the lives of everybody in the world. We don't just sell products and services, we sell life changers. It's not a bold statement when you use them and know how incredible they are. I am the CEO of this fantastic company, and I love every day I spend at work. I love being in the thick of things, being at the heart of it all, feeling the pulse of a major corporation pump. The real heart of this corporation is, of course, each and every employee who works to keep it running like a well-oiled machine. You might call me biased, but then again you don't work for this magnificent company that sells miracles. You haven't had the experience of working for us, or maybe, just maybe, you haven't even tried one of our products. If this is true then you haven't lived. You haven't lived like I have, working for the best corporation in the world. You heard me. *The best.*

GOD! I love this company! After all, they gave me the opportunity to work for them and here I sit, on the eighth floor, in my plush office with all the mod cons to do my job. I never have a boring day, and right now I am thinking about our quarterly conference in a week's time. I'm not in the least bit nervous about it. My fantastic PowerPoint presentation features jumping arrows, a roller coaster, an airplane that moves across the screen, and at one point, a music video, especially made for the occasion. Oh, yes. The stops have been pulled out with this presentation and they needed to be. I have heard the rumours of nervous employees and I know that that situation needs to be defused. Yes, ok, the share prices have dipped over the last month or so but that's no reason for the employees to be worried. It's just a natural occurrence at this time in the fiscal calendar, or at least that is what Freddy Hardcastle, our finance director, had assured me before he retired. The share prices are a lot higher since I took over and are a testament to my hard work and diligence. The dip has been caused by a recession, they say. People aren't spending, they say. The markets will pick up soon, they say. I believe them. They are educated, well-balanced, insightful people in the finance department. When they crunch the numbers, they know what they are talking about because they have been through our training program like every employee has. They are experts in company ethics and uphold our slogan 'Making Miracles Materialise'.

It rolls off the lips: 'Making Miracles Materialise'.

Wonderful slogan.

Wonderful new logo.

A wonderful advertising agency designed it and was worth every penny of the two hundred thousand pounds paid for it, even if it ran way over schedule, but we, as a company, had to get our corporate image right. If we had failed to get that right then the share prices would have dipped even further. Not that the share prices are in any way linked to our corporate statement and logo. Just forget I said that. Anyway, I've spoken too much about the expected natural dip in share prices.

I haven't even introduced myself have I? I introduced this fantastic organisation, but I didn't introduce myself. I always do that. My name is Mark Gallacchi and I have worked for this great company for four years. I started as a trainee and worked my way to the top, which just proves what can be achieved here if one puts one's mind to it. I am twenty-nine years old, which makes me the youngest CEO in *the* company's history, a feat I am proud of. I have been married to my wife Janey for just one year and live in a large house with our newborn daughter, Jane. My work usually keeps me tied up until the late hours with meetings and conventions and its regrettable that I can't spend more time at home, but this company is so demanding to work for. I wouldn't change anything for the world. Well, actually, there is one thing I would change. The sub-directors.

Yes. The sub-directors.

What can I say about them? They have been a thorn in *the* company's side and a thorn in my side. They challenge us here at *the* company's headquarters situated in London. They try to help us with every aspect of what we do, and they try to speak some sense into us when we have dropped the ball. "Try" being the operative word. They operate within *the* company's building but I'm not sure where they are located. I have never met them in person, and don't know what they look like, but they certainly put us in our place. They say the drop in the share prices has created *the* company's own black Friday called black Wednesday. It was the day the stock prices were announced so they deemed it appropriate to keep the word black. I, however, will announce, at the conference that there is no such thing as a black Monday, a black Tuesday, or any other kind of black day because black does not fit in with our corporate identity and corporate aqua blue. It doesn't represent our colourful approach featured in all of our marketing and in all of our in-house material. I will reassure the employees that there is nothing to fear from the descending jagged line on a bar graph. The dips are as natural as hills in the countryside. And if that isn't enough for the employees, then I have something else that will boost their morale, galvanise them, lift their spirits and make them leave the conference hall with can-do attitudes.

It's almost 13:00 and I have talked more than I should. I need to shut down my MacBook Pro, turn off my mobile phone and limit all distractions because my assistant, Lisa Johansson, will be here soon to help start to write my book about *the* company and my journey within it. The employees need to be told that anything is possible in the same way our corporate message speaks to our customers. They will be inspired to read about their very own CEO and how he is one of them. They'll get to know me as Mark and not as Mr Gallacchi, not as boss, not as CEO. When they read my rise from bottom to top within the hierarchy, they'll be inspired and want the same to happen to them. They'll be more focused, work harder and will leave their reservations and fears at the glass lift doors—no—at the silver sliding entrance doors. In fact, I want them to leave all negativity at home before they come to work. Negativity will only serve to bring us down as a company.

Ah! Here's Lisa at my glass door, clutching her laptop, peering in to see if I am busy. I wave at her to come in.

'Hello, Mr Gallacchi, Are you ready?'

'Yes. We have an hour or so?'

'Thirty minutes.'

'Thirty minutes? I thought it was an hour.'

'I have an emergency meeting to go to. I'm really sorry. It's the sub-directors. They want to discuss the dip in share prices.'

I have never met anybody as efficient and hard working as Lisa Johansson, an immigrant from Sweden. She knows how to multi-task and could out-multi-task me if the truth be told. She's always dressed impeccably too. The power suit, tied back blonde hair, nice shoes and only a sprinkle of make-up. She's pretty, so it's not as if she needs to wear any at all.

'Can you cancel? We really need to start work on this. I'm promising everybody that the book will be ready by December as a Christmas present.'

'It's the sub-directors.'

The subs. It's always the subs. This time, they will have to go without Lisa.

'Cancel it.'

'They won't be happy.'

'Cancel it and tell them that I have said so. As CEO of this company, I get to have the last word and my last word is cancel.'

'Yes. Ok. I will email them now.'

The air in my office becomes stale when more than one person is in it, which is why I have walked to the window and opened it. The noise from the traffic on the busy London street below filters in. The office may have the latest in air conditioning, but it still doesn't stop it from feeling warm on a summer's day. My office has been equipped in a more than adequate way for me to do my job. I am surrounded by thick modern soundproof glass that allows all my conversations to remain in the room. I have the latest electronic desk that can be adjusted so I can either sit, stand, or even lower it down to the floor to store it. This is good for blood circulation and stops thrombosis. My ergonomic chair may not look as if it sets the office on fire, but it has been guaranteed to help reduce the effects of kyphosis. A designer lamp hangs from my ceiling and has been replicated all throughout the building. No expense was spared for the employees. A happy employee is a good employee.

Lisa looks as if she has sent her email. I have

prepared what I will say to her and have made as many notes as I could before this meeting. I really had to turn the clock back four or five years and remember who I was and where I was when I first started working here. It's been a fantastic journey and long may I continue to serve *the* company that I regard as being my second family.

'Ok. Do you just want to talk and I can take notes?' asks Lisa.

'Erm, yes, yes. That sounds ideal, Lisa. I guess, I should start at the beginning.'

2.

I threw my mortarboard up and it span towards the clouds. Three long years of studying philosophy had come to an end and I couldn't have been happier. My parent's beaming smiles and their exuberant clapping told me that they were proud of me. I was the only one in my family to see my education right through to the end, and now I could go out into the world and face the prospect of work.

Work.

It was a four-lettered word that I dreaded. Sure, I had worked here and there to support my studies, but I didn't consider that *work* work. It felt as if my mortarboard had just hit the ground when I started to look for *work* work. The local paper always carried a job section on Mondays, and the Internet seemed to be a field with jobs ready for harvest. I thought it would be a doddle. A walk in the park. As easy as breathing.

I was wrong.

International Headhunter.

PR Account Executive.
Telesales Executive.
Project Co-coordinator.
Telesales.
Telesales.
Telesales.

It seemed as if every single job advertised required previous experience, and as a fresh graduate, it was something I didn't have. I didn't even know what some of the job titles meant. I had studied philosophy but hadn't philosophised about employment at the end of it. I asked myself what my perfect job would be and I envisaged myself as a journalist at first, finding stories within the hustle and bustle of the busy city. Then I thought university lecturer, but for that I would have had to return to the university that I had just left and study for a further x amount of years. I could have become a psychotherapist but there weren't any jobs in the paper listed with that job description. So I started applying for jobs marked "trainee", "junior" and "no experience necessary as training provided". If I could bag one of those jobs, I could work and keep looking until something better came up. I sent off, perhaps, ten job applications a week and played the waiting game.

I waited.

I waited a week. Nothing.

I waited two weeks. Nothing.

After waiting three weeks. Two rejections.

After a month, I felt as if the world was against

me. I had heard next to nothing from the endless job applications I had sent off. Not even an interview. I started to feel paranoid about my CV and thought there could have been something wrong with it. I had followed the advice of an article I had read online and I had laid it out exactly to the letter. According to the website, it was the perfect CV.

"This CV will get results fast," they said.

"A one page CV is enough," they said.

"Only list what is relevant," they said.

I had started to question their advice, and was about to redesign my CV, when a phone call stopped me in my tracks. It was from a company. They wanted to interview me about the job I had applied for. I was hard pressed to remember what the actual job was due to the number of applications I had sent out but, of course, I agreed to meet them and double-checked who they were and what the job was afterwards.

Junior Trainee Analyst.

I remembered the job advert. The name of the company stood in bold letters in an aqua blue square with the slogan "Making Miracles Materialise". I didn't know such a company existed that could make miracles materialise, but I knew I had an interview with them. If they stuck to the words in their bold slogan, I would walk away with the job.

The interview was set for 2 p.m. on a Monday, in September, in the middle of London. The weather was bad. Really bad. The rain ran down the street like a waterfall and blocked drains allowed the water to collect and form reservoirs. It was difficult to know how to dress for such an occasion consideringthe weather. I only had one suit to my name and an unwashed tie that had been worn for numerous weddings, christenings and funerals. I ran a roll of sticky tape over my suit to remove the dust and dirt and made it look presentable. If I kept my jacket on during the interview, they would not notice the state of the crumpled tie with a tea stain on the tip. I slipped on my pair of loafers that only needed a quick wipe with a cloth.

After looking at myself in the mirror, I was struck with the realisation that I had nothing to show the company. I didn't have a portfolio; I just had my degree certificate. I didn't know if that was something they needed to see but I took it with me anyway. I figured that the job was for a trainee position and therefore no experience was necessary. I packed my certificate into a plastic folder, grabbed my dad's large umbrella from the stand in my parent's hallway and braved the weather.

When I found the company's building in the city, I looked up at the large logo on the side of the building. It matched the one on the job advert but on a grander scale, made out of metal and lit underneath by four powerful lamps. It reminded me of a lighthouse. The beacon of London.

I shook my umbrella free from raindrops, walked through the silver sliding entrance doors, towards the glass lifts and pressed a button with a triangle on it. The button glowed fluorescent green at first and changed colour. Green to blue to red to yellow. Although part of me thought it was tacky, another part of me was impressed. When the lift reached the ground floor, a small group of men in suits, clutching mobile devices to their ears, stepped out and brushed past me whilst ignoring me. I didn't care for their attitude, but I rose above it, stepped in the lift and pressed 5 for reception. A glass door with the logo of the company revealed itself as the lift doors opened on the fifth floor. The word 'reception' had been etched onto the glass in a frosted style. I looked through the glass door at the reception, which was manned by two women behind a wooden curved desk painted orange. One of the women caught a glimpse of me as she shuffled some paperwork into a pigeonhole. She didn't let me in. A complicated looking keypad by the left of the doorframe had a multitude of names written by each button.

Philip Brown.

Angela Snow.

Anna Göransson.

Freddy Hardcastle.

After I had read name after name, I found the button marked 'reception' and pressed it. Nobody spoke to me until I had a hand resting on the reception desk.

'You are here to see?'

'Anita Fox.'

'Do you have an appointment?'

'Yes. I am here for an interview.'

'Oh. I see. Here, you have to wear one of these

visitor badges.'

The receptionist handed me a huge badge. The large safety pin on the underside would have punched a hole in my jacket pocket and I was reluctant to use it. I opted to hold it in my hand instead. The word 'visitor' was encased by the company's square logo.

'You have to wear it. Company rules.'

The receptionist smiled at me. I looked down at my suit and decided to pin the badge to my tie instead. It was already halfway to ruin anyway. The receptionist's smile faltered as she witnessed my odd positioning of the badge.

'Anita will be here in a moment. Why don't you take a seat over there?'

The receptionist pointed to an area of plush leather armchairs and expensive looking coffee tables. A pile of reading material had been stacked up in the middle of one of the tables. I chose a red seat withgreen cushions and picked up a brochure. It was the company's own in-house magazine featuring a smiling but obvious photoshopped image of the CEO with the headline "Positive Thinking Leads To Results" written above his neat haircut.

'Mark?' asked a voice to my right.

It was the voice of Anita Fox. I looked up and saw a tall middle-aged woman with black hair staring down at me with a half frown.

'Yes. Hello. I'm here for the interview.'

I stood up and shook her dead fish of a hand. It was a sorry excuse for a greeting.

'Follow me.'

Anita led me through the office, passing through department after department. The carpets and wall colours marked where one department ended and another started. I didn't find it strange. It was my first interview ever and I didn't know what to expect. Anita Fox led me to her office, ending our colourful walk, and leading us to take our seats. She had a Salvador Dali painting on her wall and neat organised paperwork on her desk. The air smelt of lavender from a potpourri bowl situated near the rubbish bin. It was the one flower that set off my hay fever and I couldn't help but feel its affect on my nose as I breathed in.

'My name is Anita Fox and I am the manager of the finance department. Now. This interview will take 45 minutes. Let me tell you about this company.'

I nodded with a constant rhythm.

'*The* company was set up in 1932 by George Stanchurch who built it up from his marketing and trading days in London.'

After the first sentence, I started to zone out and ignore what she said. Her droning monotonous voice had started to hypnotise me and send me to sleep until the inevitable happened.

'So, why did you apply for this job?'

Earth to Mark. I turned my head, looked at her, and shook myself out of my lethargic trance.

'I, er, well, read the job section in the local newspaper, saw the job, thought I could do it and applied.'

It was blunt. It was to the point. It was too much to

the point. I didn't know what I was doing. I didn't know what to say, how to act, or what answers she expected. I hadn't researched interview technique as I had done with writing technique for my CV. Anita looked down at her notepad in front of her and started to scribble.

'I see. Do you know anything about *the* company or did you know anything about *the* company before applying?'

I rolled my eyes up to the ceiling in the hope that it would give me an answer fast. It didn't.

'I only know what you have told me so far.'

Anita stabbed her pen down on her notepad and it sounded as if the pen had torn through the page.

'Well, I think you should have known something about us before applying.'

I had taken a dislike to her and only 5 minutes had passed. Her eyes cut through me like Superman's lasers and I could tell she didn't like me. She seemed angry and annoyed that I didn't know anything about the company, and her disappointment created a dull and tumultuous atmosphere that only her sharp words could cut through.

I sneezed.

I sneezed again.

And again.

The lavender had set off my hay fever and made my nose run. As I checked my suit pockets, I remembered that I had left the house without taking any tissues with me. This interview was turning out to be a disaster.

'Here,' said Anita, handing me a box of her scented

tissues.

'Thanks,' I said, pinching a tissue out of the box.

I blew my nose with some force and made a small *parp*. Anita scowled at me and I half expected her to eject me from her office. Instead, she rattled off the remaining questions so that she could move onto the next candidate that didn't have an allergic reaction to lavender.

'What do you expect from us?'

'What is your greatest strength?'

'What would other people say about you?'

'Where do you see yourself in 5 years?'

By the time I got to the last question, I had all but given up on the Junior Trainee Analyst position. I wanted to leave, go out in the rain, and write the whole experience off.

'I can see myself on a sunny island with a beer in one hand, cocktail in the other and being fanned by servants with palm leaves.'

I stared at Anita and watched as her shocked reaction started to paint her face with horror. I felt I had hammered an extra nail into my already airtight coffin. Anita flipped the cover of her notepad over and placed it on her desk. She wasn't going to take any more notes on me that was for certain.

'Mr Gallacchi. I don't think you are here under any serious capacity. I think it is appalling to waste someone's professional time in the way you have wasted mine. We won't be contacting you again. Thank you.'

Anita opened the door to her office and ushered

me out with her pointed finger. I wasn't sure what the "thank you" was for but I assumed it to be part of company protocol and not because she meant it. As we reached the reception, Anita said goodbye and left me to find my way out.

Once out on the street, I could only think about my hay fever as I opened my umbrella to resist the rain. After a while I stopped sneezing, and the mad internal itching sensation in my nose faded. I got on the first bus, and moved the interview to the back of my mind by the time I reached home.

Several days later, I was stunned to receive a phone call from the CEO's assistant calling me in for an interview with the director of the finance department, Freddy Hardcastle. What on Earth could this be about? I thought to myself. There was no way I was a contender for any job at that company after that terrible interview.

'Mr Hardcastle can do either 10 a.m. or 4 p.m. or 2 p.m. tomorrow or 9 a.m. on Wednesday,' said the CEO's assistant.

I was stunned. There was a small silence while I digested the fact that I had a second interview. 9 a.m. and 10 a.m. were out. There was no way I was getting out of bed that early to face an interview that I was convinced was some kind of practical joke.

'2 p.m. is fine,' I replied with a smirk on my face.

'Good. Well, I'll book you in and we'll see you at 2 p.m. tomorrow.'

After I had hung up, I raised my eyebrows to such an

extent that they looked as if they were running away to join the rest of my hair. It was unbelievable. A second interview? I spent the rest of the day shaking my head and laughing to myself while I waited for tomorrow.

The rain had stopped falling on the day of the second interview. I slipped into the same suit I had worn for the first interview and opted not to wear the tie at all. It felt liberating not to have something choking at my neck but to be honest, I wasn't serious about the interview. If the company was thinking about employing me, they must have been mad.

Silver sliding doors again.
Glass lift again.
Same reception.
Same receptionist.
Same comfortable red seat.
Same in-house brochure.
Same visitor's badge.
'Hello. I am Angela Snow, the CEO's assistant. Nice to meet you.'
Angela was in her mid-twenties and beamed a smile from ear to ear. She seemed to give a slight laugh at the same time she spoke which I found odd but charming. She started to guide me through the same colour coded departments until we reached Freddy Hardcastle's office.
'Mark Gallachi to see you, Freddy.'
Freddy was on the phone, sipping down a glass of

water between comments. He raised his finger in the air and struck a '1'. Angela nodded at me and walked off, leaving me in the doorway to his office.

'Yes. Yes. Well, it's great there this time of year. Dangle your plates in the wa'er, sink a line or two and soak up the currant bun. That's me advice. Yeah. Yeah. Same to you, son. Bye.'

Freddy leant back in his chair, picked up his glass of water and gulped it down.

'Come in. Come in. Don't loiter! Put the wood in the 'ole and grab a pew - or should I say put the glass in the 'ole. Ha! Ha!'

He had a thick East End London accent and couldn't help sounding like a working class man to me. He didn't strike me as being a director of finance. He didn't strike me as being a director of anything. He had a head of white disheveled hair and a white-grey beard to match. He looked like Papa Smurf but lacked the blue skin and red hat. His shirt was soaked through with sweat and there was a whiff of perspiration in the air.

'No Peckham, ay? I 'ate wearing them too. Feels as if I'm being strangled. Sit! Sit! Grab a pew!' said Freddy, pointing to the empty chair opposite his desk, 'Nah, you have applied for the trainee analyst job, yeah?'

'That's right.'

'You had a natter with Anita Fox the other day, didn't ya?'

'Right again.' My flippant tone of voice seemed wasted on Freddy.

'"I can see meself on a sunny island wiv a beer in

one 'and, cocktail in the other and being fanned by servants with palm leaves." Did you actually say that?'

I was caught in a precarious situation. Had he brought me here to have a go at me or was this leading somewhere? I couldn't work out what I was doing, sitting opposite the director of finance, having an interview for a job that I had no hope of getting. How could I answer his question? If I said no, he would know I was lying in an instant. If I said yes, maybe he would throw me out of his office and laugh at me for being cocky. Maybe this was revenge for wasting their time. I couldn't work it out.

'Ha! Ha! It's ok, son. You don't 'ave to answer.'

Freddy got up from his desk, walked to his office window and looked out. His suit trousers had more creases in them than a roast chicken wrapped up in foil. His office stank of B.O. but at least it didn't set off my hay fever.

'Do you like rock music?'

Freddy turned around fast and pointed his finger at me. It was another question that took me by surprise. I started to look in the corners of the room for hidden cameras.

'I bet you do by the look of ya'.'

I could understand why he thought I liked rock music. My fringe was made up of a wave of black hair that swept across my forehead as if I was a member of an emo band. I had a beard made up of stubble, which was due to being lazy and not because I wanted a designer beard. I had the odd zit here and there but nothing too troubling. I wore jeans and gig t-shirts when I wasn't wearing an overused suit in desperate need of dry-cleaning. I liked rock music but had no idea where he was going with his question.

'I'm an 'uge fan of 'endrix. He was the bee's knees. In fact, I luv anything from the late '60s. Joplin. Cream. Grateful Dead. Canned 'eat. I'm inta all of 'em. Listen to me. Rabbitin' on as if you know what I'm gasbaggin' about.'

Who was this guy? I remained still in my seat and kept quiet while Freddy continued to talk about music. Was I about to be ejected from his office when he remembered the reason I was there?

'Anyway, back to you, me ol' china. It's lucky I make a point of reading all of Anita's notes. As soon as I cast me mince pies over your honest answers, I knew I 'ad to give you a go. Congratulations and welcome to the team, son.'

Freddy outstretched his hand and shook mine. He continued to look at me with a beaming smile on his face. He was happy. Almost too happy.

'Start in two weeks time. No. Make that one-week. Pah! What do I bleedin' care? Start tomorrow. We'll sort out all the paperwork and digits later. 3 month trial, yeah? You need to get one of these pass card thingies from reception with your mug on it and report to Anita Fox tomorrow. I'll let her know that you are coming so don't worry about that.'

I wasn't worried. I was shocked. I had got a job. It was a job that I didn't think I would get, didn't want and didn't care about. 3 months was enough time to find something else or so I thought. It was the start of *work* work. I was in disbelief. If all job interviews were like this, I wouldn't have any trouble finding other work. Making Miracles Materialise.

'Thanks.' I stood up and put on my jacket.

'No probs, mate. See ya' tomorrow.'

I opened the door to Freddy's office, stepped out, and took care as I closed the glass door behind me. As I looked up, Freddy was standing behind his desk, pretending to take golf swings towards the window with a pretend club in his hands.

3.

'Do you really want all of this information to be in the book?'

Lisa looks up from her laptop and resembles a human question mark. I have been spouting out everything I could think of and everything I can remember. It was what happened to the best of my memory but, perhaps, not the best material to put into a morale-boosting book for employees. It doesn't matter. I feel liberated when the words of my story leave my mouth and form notes on Lisa's laptop. I have had these memories and experiences trapped in my head for years and now is the perfect time to open my can of worms. The meeting is between myself and Lisa and in the strictest confidence. It isn't as if any sensitive information is going to leave the room.

'No. No. Of course not. It's your job to edit all of the information and turn it into a blockbuster for *the* company. I have faith in you.'

Lisa raises her eyebrows, looks down at her laptop and taps some keys.

'Oh!' says Lisa, 'I have just received an email from

the sub-directors. They're not happy, Mr Gallacchi. They say it's essentially important for me to help them right now.'

'They say it is essentially important?'

'Yes.'

'Well. The last time I checked, I was the CEO of this company. Tell them they can contact, let's see, I don't know, erm, Anna. She can help them. She's helped them before. Suggest that.'

'Ok. I'll let them know.'

'Now, where were we?'

I can hear Lisa's enter key snap down and bounce back up again as she hits it hard with her fingers. She looks up and appears to be ready to continue taking notes.

'You were saying something about getting the job and it being your first day.'

'Yes. Yes. That's right.'

The silver sliding entrance doors were a sight I thought I would only see for 90 days or however long I lasted working for the company. I didn't have any ambitions of grandeur. I didn't envisage myself being promoted. I didn't expect to be working for the company full stop. Unbeknown to me, the glass lift, and passing by the reception with comfortable leather armchairs, would become part of my daily routine for years to come.

I hadn't made an effort.

I wore tight ripped jeans that allowed some of my leg hair to poke through, trainers, an Obituary band t-shirt, a pair of sunglasses + baseball cap with an adhesive circular label stuck to the brim.

'Can I help you?'

The smart dressed receptionist looked at me with an upturned nose.

'I'm starting today.' I took off my sunglasses.

'Oh. I see. What department?'

'Finance, I think.'

'Very good. You'll need to wear this.'

The receptionist handed me the same oversized visitor's badge she had handed me before. I took off my baseball cap and attached the badge to it, covering the adhesive circular label. The receptionist looked less than impressed and watched me return the baseball cap to my head.

'Right. Ok. Well. I guess you will need to meet with Anita Fox. Just one moment and I will contact her. Why don't you take a seat over there?'

The receptionist pointed her arm to the same waiting area featuring the comfortable leather seats and corporate literature. I headed towards a coffee machine that had been set up near the waiting area, grabbed a paper cup featuring a coffee bean design and pressed *Wiener Melange*. I had no idea what a *Wiener Melange* was but I was willing to give it a try. A red swirling button complimented the churning noise of the coffee machine as it gurgled and spat the drink into my cup. I emptied the contents of two ecological packets of sugar onto the foam and watched it seep through, leaving a hole behind.

'Mr Gallacchi?'

It was Anita Fox. I could tell it was her without even turning around. Her cold monotonous voice was easy to recognise. I took a swig of my coffee and turned around to face the woman whose professional time I had wasted the day before.

'Hi!' I outstretched a hand out of politeness. Anita looked me up and down.

'Well. Do you think you could unpin and wear your visitor's badge in the proper place?'

'Erm. I don't want to ruin my t-shirt.'

Anita Fox looked at my t-shirt that featured a picture of a rotting corpse laying near a drain. Her face screwed up and contorted.

'Obituary?' quizzed Anita. 'May I remind you that the dress code is quite specific here. We have a smart dress code, Mr Gallacchi. We have people from all over the world who come to visit us and this t-shirt is not only unacceptable, it's offensive.'

'Ok.'

My dejected tone was not going to win Anita over and I wasn't trying to win her over.

'Good. So long as we have got that straight. I would prefer it if you turned your t-shirt inside out but you can do that later. Let me show you to your department and desk first. Walk with me. Walk with me. Time is money.'

She ignored my handshake, turned her back on me, and started walking at a fast steady pace in front of me. I hadn't met anybody who had used the phrases "walk with me" and "time is money" before. I had always regarded them as cliché lines used in movies but Anita Fox seemed to like them. She led me through the same colour coded departments until we reached our end destination – my desk. It was a big desk featuring an array of pens, paper and paper clips. A small layer of dust covered the areas untouched by the computer keyboard and flat screen.

'Here. You will sit here next to Brian.' Anita nodded to the man sitting behind the desk next to us.

'Hello. Nice to meet you,' said Brian. 'Nice t-shirt!' We shook hands as Anita exhaled a deep irritated sigh.

'I'll get I.T. to sort out your necessary passwords, but in the meantime, I want you to read this introduction booklet to *the* company. I would recommend that you go somewhere quiet to read and allow the information to soak in. It's really vital information. It also contains information on dress code. Dress code! I'll leave you to it.'

Anita walked away from my desk without so much as a welcome or relaying any information on what my job entailed. I picked up the introduction booklet off the desk and brushed away the dust that lined the cover. It featured a picture of a smiling woman on a bike with a man on roller skates holding onto the rear mudguard.

'It's a load of ...' Brian shaped his hand into a mouth and snapped it open and shut again. 'What brings you to this hellhole?'

'I just applied.' I shrugged my shoulders.

'Same story for all of us and now we're stuck here,

in this shithole. I'm sorry, I should be saying welcome shouldn't I?'

Brian's sarcastic tone reinforced my main aim of finding another job as fast as possible and before my three month trial expired. I didn't have any enthusiasm to do the job in the first place and if Brian had this attitude all the time, he would succeed in sucking me into the same depression he suffered from. He looked to be in his mid thirties, wore a typical white office shirt, and a typical pair of black trousers with typical black shoes to match. He had a bald spot and indents on his face where bad acne had left its mark.

'How long have you worked here?'

'Oooh! Too long. Feels like an eternity. Coming up to seven years now. Seven years in this dump. Christ! I feel like furniture.'

I flicked through the first few pages of the introduction manual and saw various clip art images scattered throughout. Hours of work. Rules of conduct. Emergency procedures. It all seemed like standard information that any company would have.

'Take my advice. Go and read that over a coffee and take a long time over it. You have to make the most out of wasting company time when you get the chance.' Brian winked.

'Thanks. I'll just go to reception and ...'

'Reception? No. No. No. You see the purple area over there? Go to your left and there is a general break room that hardly anybody uses anymore after they revamped the cafeteria.'

'Oh. Thanks.'

I headed towards the purple zone and looked to the left. I spotted the break room that contained a small sofa and coffee table with corporate brochures placed on it. I grabbed a coffee from the machine outside the room, walked in and shut the glass door. The room became impervious to outside noise, making it feel like a cocoon. The slurp from sipping my coffee almost seemed to bounce and echo off the walls. The corporate magazines on the coffee table were dated from two years previous and featured pictures of the new appointed CEO's inauguration. I started reading the introduction manual:

> *Each employee is only entitled to three cups of coffee or tea a day from the vending machines.*

I was on my second cup, and I wondered if the rule applied to me as I hadn't signed my contract. Bizarre rule. I continued reading:

> *Facial hair must be smart in appearance. Long beards and moustaches are hereby prohibited. Please note: this rule does not apply to managerial staff.*

Another strange rule. I had a shadow of a beard caused by shaving every other day. I wasn't sure if that counted either.

> *The company adopts a smart but casual dress code. For men, a tie is not necessary but a smart work shirt with*

trousers and shoes is mandatory. For women, excessive use of make-up is not permitted and the wearing of jewellery is to be kept at a minimum. Skirts are to be no shorter than knee length. Suits and trousers are also acceptable.

Thank God for that. I didn't have to rush out to buy a tie for every day of the week. I hated ties. I only wore the one I had to weddings, christenings and funerals, and the latter occasion was on behalf of someone who wasn't even going to see me wear it.

Each department bathroom has been equipped with hand towels that match each employees' company employee number. Please make sure to use the correct hand towel that corresponds to your employee number. Anyone caught using somebody else's hand towel will be reprimanded.

What the hell was this? Separate hand towels for each employee? They must employ a specific person to wash the hand towels and replace them with new ones. How could they catch anybody using the wrong hand towel? Dust it for prints?

Top managerial: Please hang your outer garments on the hook that corresponds to your job title. The CEO's coat hook is the furthest to the left and all the others to the right accordingly. Any outer garment found hanging on the wrong hook will be removed and destroyed.

Wow. That's some serious punishment for the wrong

placement of somebody's coat. I might consider going up to the eighth floor just to get rid of some old jackets.

> *Anybody found to be bringing in food and drink from home or outside the premises will be deducted £10 from their wages. We encourage the purchase of food and soft drinks from our refrigerated machines and hot drinks from our hot drink vending machines.*

It became obvious that the company had a deal with the vending machine operator for them to make up a rule forcing employees to eat their food. I guess that's how business is done.

After I had skim read the rest of the introduction book, I placed it on the coffee table and looked around the room. There was nothing special about it and I could see why it had been abandoned as a break room. The sofa had a cushion that was ripped. The small window only let a small amount of light into the room and looked as if rivets had shut it tight. A huge old discoloured monitor with Post-it notes stuck to it lay stricken in the corner, topped with dust. One of the Post-it notes read: "HAZARDOUS WASTE: Dispose of responsibly." As I started to read the other Post-it notes, the rap of somebody's knuckles on the glass door got my attention.

'Have you finished reading the introduction manual?' Anita had opened a gap in the door just enough for a quarter of her face to be visible. 'What are you doing?'

'Oh. I was just stretching my legs. I have just finished

reading it actually.' I hoped that she hadn't detected my time wasting.

'Hmm. Ok. Well, I have your passwords so you can go back to your desk and Brian can train you. Come on! Back to your desk! Time is money. Walk with me.'

Anita turned her back and walked away from me as quick as she had before. She was in a mad rush to return me to my desk, but I wasn't in the mood to hurry. I walked at my own calculated pace and noticed her annoyance when I reached my desk several seconds after her. She looked daggers at me and was tapping her foot on the floor. It was as if she believed a few seconds of wasted company time would eat into profits.

'Come on. Hurry up! I have a managers' meeting to go to. Brian, can you show Gallacchi the system and what to do? I will come back later for a progress report.'

She had called me Gallacchi. Just Gallacchi. She had dropped the "Mr", which offended me. I had a name and it was either Mark or Mr Gallacchi. Not Gallacchi on its own. Anita dashed away from my desk and left me with my new work colleague, Brian, who didn't look too pleased with his new assignment.

'It's like the blind leading the blind in this place. Pfff! We have just had a new CMS installed and I hardly know how to use it myself. Bloody useless. Nobody knows what they are doing in this place,' said Brian as I sat, 'click on that logo that looks like a badly drawn cinnamon bun.'

I clicked on it. A screen with a multitude of windows

popped up with titles and buttons that confused the hell out of me. I had never seen its like before and I didn't know what I was looking at.

'Confusing, eh? Click on import.'

A list of names, addresses and website links started to fall from the top of the screen. The scrolling block to the right shrank in size until it was a minuscule dash. The list wasn't long, it was gigantic.

'These are our competitors. We have to make our way through this list, find information on them, and write everything down in the note section in this window here.'

'Is this what we are analysing?'

'Hmph! Analysing, my arse. We collect data.'

'But I thought I was ...'

'You thought.. Yeah well, it might have said analyst in the newspaper but it's far from it.'

'Oh. Why is the list so long?'

'The company doesn't know how to define itself. It's like us. They can't define our job either. We're kinda like in a void. Forgotten. We're lumped in with finance but that's only because they didn't know where to put us ... or they ran out of department colours. Either one of the two.'

It didn't bother me that I was undefined because it didn't matter what the job was. I wasn't planning on working for the company for years. It was a stopgap. Pure and simple. I had great optimism that another company somewhere else would offer me a better job. A job that I liked.

I double clicked on the first entry and looked at the details with Brian advising me. It seemed like boring painstaking work that would take months. To add to the boredom, the CMS system was unstable and kept crashing at regular intervals, losing all the information that I had entered.

'Ah. Yeah. Well. It does that a lot. It's a piece of shit.'

Brian shook his head, hit the computer's reset button, and I watched the information disappear into the black void of the monitor screen.

'Welcome to the shithole!'

Brian returned to his list that looked equal in length compared to mine. I started to question myself about what I had got into.

4.

'You don't have to leave out any information, you just have to reword it. Make it sound good. Make it sound as if anything is possible. Make it sound like a Winston Churchill speech, packed with patriotism and spark. I have faith in you. You have talent. If there is anyone I trust more than myself - it's you.'

Lisa sits in silence for a while and looks me in the eye. I know the information I have given her isn't the best information I could give her. I am just sounding off, shaking off the shackles of being a busy CEO. Brian's depressed state. Anita's hard arse yuppie attitude. My Obituary t-shirt. The word "shithole". They would all have to be reworded. I know none of these descriptions would ever see the light of day on any bound note in the upcoming book as they stood. It isn't the language *the* company uses and I know it. I am having some fun for the first time in ages and am letting things fly. The stresses and strains of being the CEO of *the* company has made me lose sight of fun. Don't get me wrong. I love this company. I love *the* company. They have been good to me and I work hard

35

and play hard to get my job done. *The* company won't just be *the* company, they will be *the best* company in the world. We "Make Miracles Materialise" not just in what we produce and sell to the public and corporations, but within the workplace as well. Lisa is fantastic in sticking by me and listening to my tale, which disgusts me to some degree. I can't imagine being that version of myself again.

'Oh!'

Lisa's disappointed cry disturbs my train of thought.

'The sub-directors say that it is unacceptable to not have my assistance in their errand and they will be in touch with the chairman about the matter. Should I drop what I am doing here and contact them and say I will help them?'

I suck in a pocket of air between my pursed lips and breathe out, making the sound of trapped air leaving a balloon. The subs never compromise on anything and they have never gone to the chairman before. I'm not scared. The chairman and myself have not locked horns on any matter concerning *the* company. We see eye to eye. There is no need for me to be concerned. The subs can wait.

'No. We'll carry on with what we are doing. I'll deal with the sub-directors later. This is far more important than anything they are doing. Shall we continue?'

Lisa's shocked expression is the look a child exhibits when they meet a fake Santa Claus for the first time. I don't want to get her into trouble but I know that won't happen if every decision is mine. I will take the rap if any rap is to be taken.

'Ok. I'm ready.' Lisa nods her head.

I had worked for the company for a month. It had been enough time for me to get to know Brian well. He may have had his faults, but we had started to like each other, despite his dim outlook of life. The job itself was dull. Dull, dull, dull, dull, DULL! I came to work the same way every day. I greeted the same people with a "hello" every day and I didn't know their names. I sat at the same desk every day. I looked at the same spreadsheet every day. I even looked at the same names on the spreadsheet because it never changed ... every day. I would continue to look at this spreadsheet unless something changed and I hoped that change would be an offer of another job somewhere else. I continued to check the daily paper and the Internet for job vacancies and sent my CV out to every vacancy that sounded halfway decent.

'There's fuck all out there.' Brian was eating a vending machine croissant, spitting small globules at me as he spoke. 'Trust me. I have looked.'

Crumbs from Brian's breakfast fell onto his keyboard and lodged between the keys. The keys were stained brown and black from years of use andmy keyboard hadn't fared any better. I looked in the drawers behind me for something to wipe my keyboard. I found a lemon wipe next to a multitude of old pens and paper clips. I tore it open and started to clean.

'God! There's no point in doing that. The dirt will

only come back again. Ring I.T. for a new keyboard. It's a lot easier.'

I looked up at Brian and placed the crumpled, stained, moth-eaten lemon wipe on my dust-saturated desk. I didn't like waste. I had a functioning keyboard that just needed to be cleaned. What would happen to it if I ordered a new one from I.T.? Would they clean it or just send it to a landfill? I took the decision to clean my keyboard later while Brian was on a break. I couldn't bear the thought of listening to his criticism.

'You had any luck yet with any job? Any bites? Any interviews?'

'No, but I spotted some really good job adverts online. I'm pretty sure that I will hear something back from some of them.' My enthusiasm seemed lost on Brian.

'Pfff! I doubt it. I think internal candidates fill all jobs. Companies have someone lined up for the jobs they advertise. They are just going through the motions to comply with the law.'

'Do you think so?'

'I know so.'

I didn't know how Brian knew so. He had worked for the company for seven years and if what he was saying was true, then he would have been working higher up as a manager, filling one of those internal job vacancies. His pessimism wasn't going to rub off on me and turn me into furniture. My plan to leave the company was going to happen one way or another.

'So why haven't you been promoted?'

Brian's face soured and his scowl confused me. He complained more about the company than I did and it hadn't occurred to me that he even wanted to be promoted.

'Too many cooks. Nobody starting here stands a chance of being promoted.'

'Really?'

'Yes. Really. Why do you think I am still here in this position?'

Brian turned away and scrolled down the list of contacts on his spreadsheet. His bottom lip drooped and extended out, making him look like a sulking toddler. I didn't want to turn out like Brian and work seven years for a company without any promotion in a job I didn't like or want to do. The mere thought caused me to worry about my future.

'Well. I'm optimistic. I'll find something. I won't be here after three months.'

'Hmph! Yes, you will.' Brian swallowed the last chomp of croissant and brushed the remnants on his lap onto the floor.

'You wanna bet?'

'Oh yeah? You want to bet now? How much do you want to bet?'

It was the first time I saw Brian enthusiastic and exert energy.

'How about a beer?'

'One beer? You lightweight! *One* beer! That's what I have for lunch. You'd have to buy me a beer every Friday for a year.'

'A beer every Friday?' I stopped and thought about what I was getting myself into. 'Ok. You're on. You'll buy ME a beer every Friday for a year.'

'I don't think I will. Ha! Ha! You madman!' Brian laughed and shook his head in disbelief.

It was unusual for me to bet on anything. In fact, I hadn't bet on anything in my life. I had never played poker or watched horse racing. The mention of going to the greyhounds had always made me question why people would want to watch dogs run around in circles, chasing a bit of white fluff on a stick. I had got sucked up in the moment; sucked up in Brian's goading; sucked up by my own confidence. Other employees who looked in our direction could hear Brian's loud laughter. When his laughter had died down and stuttered to a stop, he composed himself and spoke again.

'What are we betting on exactly?' asked Brian.

'That I won't be here after three months," I replied.

'Then there have to be some rules. You are not allowed to get fired by punching the boss on the nose or any other type of stupid stunt. That's too easy. You are not allowed to turn down a permanent contract if offered. You have to be simply let go—be made redundant—before your three months is up or you find another job.'

'Ok. That sounds fair enough.'

We shook hands and the bet was official. I couldn't go back on a handshake. I didn't need to go back on it. I was brimming over with confidence that I would find another job, and if I didn't, I could get laid off and find something temporary as I had done when I was studying. I was certain to succeed. The beer was inconsequential. I had to prove Brian wrong and shatter his illusion that leaving the company was impossible.

I had complied with the company rulebook that I had been given on my first day. I had not worn my Obituary t-shirt or any of my baseball caps. I wore a plain white shirt, black trousers and black shoes that I had bought to mark my beginning at the company. I left my hair's fringe to flop over my left eye and I still shaved every other day. I wasn't sporting a full-blown beard and that was allowed according to the rules. I didn't stand out. In fact, I was like a chameleon, blending in with all the other employees who also wore the same as me, albeit with different coloured ties. It was all about to change. I could let my dislike for the job take over; let my suppressed bad attitude out; let my inner hatred of the job rise to the surface. I started to think of all the things I could do so that the company would not extend my contract. I could turn up late; miss essential deadlines; drink more than three cups of coffee from the vending machine; grow a moustache. They were all gimmies and would lead me to being ejected from the building by security.

'Gallacchi. Have you got that report ready that I asked you to do?'

I jumped with fright. Anita Fox had approached my desk without making a sound, despite wearing heels.

'I dunno. Was it for today?'

'It's "I do not know" and yes, it was for today,

Gallacchi.'

'It's Mark.'

Anita glanced down at my desk. The pupils of her eyes shrank in size as she frowned at my newfound bad attitude. I had written the report on time and before the deadline, but I had decided that now was the time to start turning the tables.

'Well, this is unacceptable. We will have to have a meeting about this and I will make sure Freddy gets to hear about it. I will not accept such insolence.'

The loud sound of Anita's heels stomping away from my desk could be heard by everyone as she marched through the blue section and into the green. It made me wonder if she had a volume switch and a pair of speakers attached to the soles that were turned up when she was angry. It was going to be easier than I thought to win the bet. I turned to Brian and raised a smug smile on my face.

'The beers are as good as mine.'

Brian shook his head and continued to work his way through his spreadsheet, pretending to be unaffected by Anita's angry reaction and my upcoming meeting with Freddy Hardcastle.

As the day drew to a close, I was surprised that Anita had not returned to my desk. I hadn't received any emails requesting my presence at a disciplinary meeting. Nothing. It was eerie. I assured myself that I had done enough to start the ball rolling towards my ejection from the company.

'It's odd. I thought I would have heard something

by now.'

Brian looked in my direction with an odd smile on his face accompanied by a half laugh.

'Anita swung by earlier while you were in the toilet. I told her that you had finished the report and that she should take it. You left it in the top drawer, didn't you?'

'You bastard!' I said, shocked by Brian's underhanded tactic. 'It's like that is it? I see.'

Tears ran down the side of Brian's face. His laughter made his head bob up and down in front of his monitor as if it had been the funniest joke he had played on anybody. I tapped my fingers on the desk, grabbed my coat off the back of my chair and got ready to go home.

'Right. I'm outta here. To be continued tomorrow. You just wait and see.'

Brian, unable to speak, waved his hand in the air as if to say goodbye. I walked past reception and out of the door knowing that I had to be extra vigilant the following day.

5.

As I awoke, the following day, I looked at my smart clothes that I had thrown on my bedroom floor. They didn't matter anymore because I wasn't going to wear them. Not today, not tomorrow, and not the days the followed. The Obituary t-shirt was going to be my second skin from this day on and would be a reason for the company to let me go.

As I ventured downstairs, my dad was sipping a cup of tea and watching the news. He worked as an architect and always wore a smart suit regardless of where he was. He had designed the house we lived in, a detached country house where journeys into the city took more time than I liked. My parents liked the peace and tranquility of the open countryside and never spoke about moving nearer the city. My mother worked as a freelance writer and never woke up when my dad did. Any time before midday was too early for her. When I reached the bottom of the stairs, my dad looked me up and down and paused during a sip of tea.

'Aren't you going to work today?'

'Yeah, why?'

'Don't you think you should get dressed?'

'I am dressed.'

'Really? They must be really relaxed about dress code there. I thought you had an office job didn't you? Some trainee job?'

My dad had never taken a real interest in what I was doing and it had led to our disjointed relationship. I had told him about the job I had been given, but he had been too busy working on a sketch to pay full attention.

'Yeah. It is an office job. A boring, dull office job.'

'Hold on. Hold on. Are you saying you don't like the job?'

'It's so bloody boring. I sit at my desk and look at a spreadsheet all day long.'

'Well. You should be thankful you have a job in this day and age. There are people out there who would kill to be in your shoes,' said my dad, looking down at the floor, 'make that trainers. What's going on with you? What on earth is that ghastly t-shirt? Why are you dressed like that? Is it rebellion?'

'I dunno.'

'You'll get fired looking like that and then you won't get another job at all.'

The words resonated and introduced me to a new experience: getting good advice from my dad. He was right. I would get fired and lose the bet.

'I think you should go upstairs and change.'

I followed my dad's advice and changed into the same shirt, trousers and shoes that I had on the day before. Common sense had prevailed and stopped me from walking into work and coming out with my government papers. It had also made me realise that I needed to be subtle if I was to be let go instead of sacked.

I walked back into the living room and grabbed my car keys off the elaborate mantelpiece also designed by my father. My dad twitched his newspaper aside and grumbled.

'Well. That's better, I suppose. Do you know how to use an iron?'

'I don't have time, Dad. I have to go.'

I stepped up my pace and headed for the front door.

'What about breakfast? It's the most important meal of the day!' yelled my dad as I slammed the front door shut.

After I walked through the silver sliding doors and into the glass lift, a group of people rushed towards it and hailed for me to keep the lift doors open. I leant across and pressed the button from the multi-coloured array of circled numbers and noticed something that I had missed before. The lift only went to the seventh floor. There were eight floors in the building and as far as I knew, the CEO worked on the very top floor - the eighth. The group of people, consisting of two men and three women, entered the lift. The men were dressed in expensive looking suits and the women in expensive looking dresses. I was lacking a suit jacket and the clothes I wore had more creases than a pensioner's face. I felt like the odd one out even though my clothes were appropriate according to company rules. I didn't want to talk to the people in the lift with me, but my curiosity nagged me to open my mouth and release it.

'Does anyone know how to get to the eighth floor? There doesn't seem to be a button for it.'

The lift fell silent. The egotistical banter of the men bragging about their weekend spent with a bottle of claret stopped. The women's laughter ceased. I didn't know what I had done. It was if I had asked them all to undress and swap clothes with each other. I could feel them staring at me, not out of anger but in astonishment.

'Did he just ask about the eighth floor?'

One of the women whispered to one of the men. The man nodded his head and looked at me with a direct stare.

'Is he crazy? Who asks about the eighth floor?'

'A crazy person! That's who.'

The lift arrived on the fifth floor and the doors opened. The group of people pressed themselves up against the glass walls of the lift, making sure they gave the maximum room for my exit. It was if I was infected with a contagious disease that they didn't want to catch. I turned around once my feet were resting on the fifth floor's polished tiled surface. The group of people was still looking at me in shock, muttering to each other.

'That guy has some nerve. The eighth floor, I mean, come on.'

I stood and watched the lift doors slam together, cutting out the conversations of the people inside. I was confused. I had only asked them a simple question, and they had reacted in such an odd way towards me. My curiosity still nagged me. How did someone get to the eighth floor if there wasn't a lift? I decided to save that question for Brian as he had worked for the company longer than I had and, therefore, would know more than I did.

Brian was already at his desk when I arrived. The smell of stale cigarette smoke emanated from his clothes. It was his usual morning ritual. A cigarette, followed by a croissant, for breakfast.

'Alright mate. You're a bit late.'

I sat down at my desk and looked at my watch. Brian was right. The time it had taken me to change my clothes, and process what had happened in the lift, had pushed me seven minutes past nine o' clock.

'The strangest thing just happened actually. I noticed that the lift only goes to the seventh floor, so I asked the people that were in the lift with me why that was.'

Brian's face went as white as the plywood tiled ceiling above our heads. He brought his index finger up to his mouth and went 'shhh!'

'Not you as well. What the hell is this? Why can't I mention the eighth floor?' I said.

Brian pushed off from the ground with both feet, making his chair roll towards mine until he stopped as close as he could get. He leant forwards and moved his lips so close to my ear that I thought he was nibbling my earlobe.

'It's an unwritten rule,' whispered Brian. 'Nobody is

allowed to talk about the eighth floor.'

'Why?'

'You just don't. That's all. Just leave it alone.'

'Will I get fired if I talk about it?'

'No but ... I have said too much already.'

Brian propelled his chair back behind his desk with his feet.

'I see you have managed to come to work today,' said a voice.

Anita Fox had crept up on me again and made me jump out of my skin. Spies would have killed for the level of stealth that Anita had. She must have been creeping up on me on purpose.

'You are seven minutes and twenty-six seconds late. Time is money, and when you are late, time is *the* company's money. You can make up the time by forfeiting your break, but we can talk about it after the meeting that starts in precisely twenty minutes. We have a new logo to discuss and I am looking forward to what you have to say, Gallacchi.'

'Mark. My name is Mark. Call me Mark.'

Anita turned her back on me and walked away, leaving me to ponder over the reason why she was looking forward to my input in the meeting. She never seemed to look forward to anything I said or did. It surprised me. I was sure Brian had overheard what she had said, but when I looked across at him, he was transfixed by the names scrolling up and down his screen on his spreadsheet. I wanted to quiz him about the eighth floor again but thought better of it.

My curiosity would have to be satisfied by my own investigation.

It was 9:30 sharp as I stood by the coffee machine and collected a *Wiener Melange*. I planned to enter the meeting at least a couple of minutes late. It was a sure fire way of getting my name onto the black list. As I entered the meeting room at 9:33, I noticed two plates of fruit situated on either end of the long table in the middle of the room where ten co-workers plus Anita were sitting. The room was cold, sterile and lacked any soul. The fluorescent light bounced off the beige walls, making the room feel gloomy and dull. Anita glared at me as I shut the glass door hard, creating a loud thud.

'So nice of you to join us, Gallacchi.'

'Mark. My name is Mark. Mark.'

Anita continued to glare.

A PowerPoint presentation was underway and hadn't moved past the title screen entitled *The Future Of Making Miracles Materialise*. I hadn't missed anything.

'Right. We are here to discuss the new corporate company logo that has been designed by Gamma Design Studios. As we all know, the logo has been under development for six months now and we have seen many changes made to it. This is the final version and *the* company needs your feedback. Of course, Gallacchi hasn't been with us very long, so he is seeing this for the first time and his opinion could be useful,' said Anita.

'Please, call me Mark.'

The other co-workers sitting around the table all came from different departments, and although I knew their faces, I didn't know their names. Anita pressed a key on her laptop and revealed the logo.

'Here it is. The new corporate company logo.'

I couldn't believe my eyes. She had to be kidding. It was a blue oval with a double black lined border with the company's name in the middle. "Making Miracles Materialise" had been written with three big Ms and the rest in small italics. It looked as if a child had drawn it on a piece of blotting paper. I could have designed something better in five minutes and I wasn't even a designer.

'Oh wow! What a fantastic logo. I mean, I am speechless, Anita. The six months that has gone into creating that has been worth the effort and the wait. I love it.'

The comment came from a young woman who wore a cheap beaded necklace and a white blouse with the top three buttons undone. She wasn't wearing glasses, which I assumed she needed if she thought this logo was fantastic. Anita forced her lips upwards, straining a fake shuddering smile as if the muscles in her face had wasted away.

'Thank you. Anybody else?'

Anita's face started to spasm.

'I think the logo represents *the* company moving forward. It feels fresh, modern and contemporary,' said a man wearing a pinstripe suit.

'Yes, I agree,' said another man with slicked back

hair and glasses. 'I like the use of the corporate blue, the solid black curved borders and the Ms delivering our message.'

I couldn't believe what I was hearing. Were they all kidding? Could they see what I saw? The projection screen was old, and someone had made the mistake of trying to use it as a whiteboard, but it was no excuse. I could see the logo and it was the epitome of awful. The eyes in the room turned their attention on me, waiting for my response. It was the perfect time to start operation let go.

'Gallacchi. What are your thoughts?' Anita stared at me; her smile had been dropped.

'I'm Mark by the way,' I said, waving to everyone in the room.

Everybody remained unmoved. They continued to look at me without turning away or flinching or making any kind of movement.

'Erm. Well. To be honest, I think the logo looks terrible.'

My co-workers started to shift in their seats and all looked at Anita for a response.

'Carry on,' said Anita.

'I mean, going from a square to an oval isn't exactly rocket science.'

'Do you think the oval is too curved? Do you think people will think that it is some kind of blue egg?' said Pinstripe. 'Maybe people will mistake it for a blue egg. Maybe it's too egg-like.'

'I'm not sure that the egg is the problem,' said the

woman wearing the cheap beaded necklace. She cleared her throat as if she was about to make a speech. 'I think the corporate blue doesn't look right. I think it's maybe a shade of Pantone out. Other than that, the logo is fantastic. It's the best piece of design I have seen for quite some time. It's wonderful.'

I nicknamed her Brown Nose.

'Ok. Everybody. Please be quiet. Gallacchi was talking,' said Anita.

I didn't bring the issue of not being called by my first name up again. I let Anita have her fun on this occasion. I wasn't going to waste my breath, I needed that to annihilate the awful logo with criticism.

'I mean, if you ask me, a four year old could have designed a better logo than this. Why are those Ms so much larger than the rest of the slogan's letters? Why are the rest of the letters in italics? It just looks awful.'

'It's the three Ms,' said Slick Back. 'Making Miracles Materialise. Don't you know? MMM!'

Everybody hummed 'MMM' except me.

I remained silent as I tried to figure out what was happening. The people in the room seemed to be following a script. The room fell silent and everybody turned their attention to the next words that left my lips.

'The three Ms. Yes. I know that. I saw that slogan when I first walked into the building. I mean, you can't exactly miss it as it is part of the logo stuck to the side of the building, which incidentally is a damn site better looking than that thing up on the screen.'

I had really started to let my cat out of the bag. It felt good to release pent up energy after working with a spreadsheet for a month. Anita seemed to let the comments of others pass over her head like water off a duck's back. Her focused concentration was on me, wincing each time I criticised her precious logo. Anita pulled the projector cable out of her laptop, folded the screen down with force, and gave out a loud choking cough.

'Well, Gallacchi. You've made your opinions very clear. I think this meeting is adjourned. We need to have another meeting tomorrow to discuss the contents of this meeting. If everybody could make themselves available. Thanks.'

A meeting about a meeting? What was this place, and how did it get any work done? Everybody raised themselves from the table, looked at me and shuffled towards the door, clutching notepads and pens. As I reached the door, Anita's hand pushed it shut.

'You and I need to have a little chat, Gallacchi.'

She spat my surname out as if it had become a swearword in her vocabulary. I had got under her skin and started to make her itch with irritation. Anita's reaction to my behaviour was inconsequential. As far as I was concerned, I was going to win the bet with Brian and be supplied with cool frosted beers every Friday for a year.

'Take a seat. Now, first of all, I want to talk about your punctuality. You were late this morning by seven minutes. Was there a reason for that?'

'No.'

I shrugged my shoulders.

'I don't like your attitude, Gallacchi. If you want to continue working here, you need to buck your ideas up.'

I remained still and glared at her in the same way she had done to me. It was a competition where whoever looked away first would lose.

'You can make up the time by forfeiting your break.'

'Isn't that against the law?'

'No. Not when you arrive late to work. It's quite clearly stated in our rule book if you had bothered to read it.'

I had skim read it. I thought that would have sufficed. I was wrong. She had got me.

'Punctuality can be overlooked if your work is of a high standard but, Gallacchi, it isn't. You aren't fast enough in processing the spreadsheet supplied.'

'I'm as fast as Brian.'

'No. Not according to our records.'

Records? Was I being surveyed in secret as I worked? How did they know?

'As for today's meeting, well ... your comments will be passed to Freddy who approved the new logo a week ago. He has endorsed the new logo and will be very interested to hear your derogatory comments. That's it. You can go.'

Anita stood up, wrenched the door open, leant her arm up the side with her index finger outstretched and looked down at the ground. I walked out of the room feeling as if I had done enough to be let go. I was sure

I would be let go after Freddy had been told about my criticism of the logo. Anita wanted me to leave the company as much as I wanted to leave, and the meeting seemed like a trap set by her for me to fall into. I hadn't so much as fallen into the trap, but dived into it. I was glad. I would be collecting my P45, my beers from Brian, and looking for a better company.

6.

'If you don't mind me saying, I think this is getting quite personal.'

Lisa had a point. I have lost sight of the book's original intention of being a morale-boosting book for employees and have turned it into a memoir instead. I don't care. It feels good to reveal my innermost feelings towards the people I had or have grudges against. It is a confession and I look to Lisa to be my priest. I am twiddling a silver pen around in my fingers, and I am thinking about the next sequence of events in my mind. Although I know I should censor my personal thoughts, I know that I can't. Although it's fun, it also highlights how I have changed and become more responsible. It is a good example of not how to act when you work for a company. I was a rebel back then and not the confident successful man I am today, and it's all thanks to *the* company. They have straightened me out and turned me into a professional CEO, working in the hustle and bustle of London, making decisions that matter, making the lives of ordinary people better and providing important services and products. I owe *the* company my life. I love *the* company.

I am thinking about the information I am telling Lisa and feel horrified. I have told her everything for my own personal and therapeutic reasons. *The* company is fantastic and I wouldn't change my work ethics for one minute but, now and again, I need a little release. I am sure I can trust Lisa. Pretty sure.

'Is there a problem, Lisa? I mean ... you're not going to tell anybody about this are you? This is strictly confidential between you and me and the four walls of this room. I trust you implicitly.'

'No. No ... No. Of course not. I wouldn't tell anybody about this, but I think for me to be able to turn this into something that I can work with, I will need to gloss over a majority of the information you have told me. It'll almost be like making the whole book up.'

'Not really. Just take my notes, strip them back to the bare bones, and write about the basics. You know, I started from nothing, and worked my way up the ladder through hard work, determination, and not being afraid to voice my opinion.'

'Well, yes, I guess I can do that but ...'

'No buts or guesses about it Lisa. I have every confidence in you as my ghostwriter to write the best employee morale boosting book this company has ever had.'

It is to be the only morale-boosting book *the* company has ever had because nobody else has written one before. The book is essential, and I need to keep her on my side just as I do with every employee, hence the reason for writing it. I have faith in Lisa and I wouldn't have employed her if I didn't. She is a perfect assistant, the best a CEO could wish for.

'Ok. I'm ready.'

I am about to divulge the next chapter about my rise to the top when my mobile vibrates and moves across my desk. It is the chairman. Is this call about the subs' complaint that I have kept Lisa from them? I don't want to take the risk. I pick my mobile up off my desk, hold down the power button and turn it off.

'They can call me back.' I stuff my mobile in the top drawer of my desk. 'Now, where were we?'

I had not shaved for a couple of days, and an unruly 5 o' clock shadow had formed on my face. It was intentional. Although the company rulebook banned "long beards and moustaches", I couldn't believe that it was a sackable offence. I looked at myself in the bathroom mirror with a razor blade in my hand, still undecided on whether I should leave my stubble where it was or scrape it all away. It wasn't an easy decision. I placed the razor on the bathroom countertop and convinced myself that I had neither a long beard nor a moustache and therefore would escape being fired. Instead, I guessed that I would be reprimanded by Anita Fox and have black marks added to my profile.

The first meeting of the day was about the previous meeting about the logo, which I had blasted for looking childish. I made my way to the meeting room, late again as planned. I wondered if holding meetings about meetings was a common occurrence or happened at other companies. If every company operated in the same way, I wondered how they became successful. The meeting seemed pointless and wasted my time, but it provided me with another chance to disrupt proceedings. The same ten people were deep in conversation when I entered the room. Everybody had a cup of coffee in front of them. The fruit bowls had been replaced with plates of sweets and chocolate bars. I could hear Anita's whining voice through the glass door as I bent down the handle and walked in. I slammed the glass door behind me, making the glass wall wobble backwards and forwards. Several people jumped and held their hands over their hearts as if the bang from the door had been a shot from a gun. A deafening silence greeted me as I sat down. Everybody's eyes were staring straight at me. I didn't pay them any attention. I sat down in my seat in a casual manner and started doodling on my notepad.

'Nice of you to join us, Gallacchi.'

Her loud sarcastic voice grated on my nerves. I kept focused on my doodle and tried my best to ignore her, keeping my head down. Anita exhaled a huge irritated breath, letting the room know that she was dissatisfied with my bad attitude and lack of enthusiasm.

'Right! Welcome back everybody. This meeting is a recap on the meeting we had yesterday. We have to go over what was discussed in order for us to move forward with the new corporate logo, which nearly everybody seemed to like. I would like to start with Anne and your thoughts on yesterday's ...'

Click!

Crack!

Snap!

Ever since an early age, I had the ability to pull and crack the joints in my fingers, making the same sound as snapping twigs. My fellow classmates at school were usually repulsed by the noise I made, and I ended up playing on my own most of the time. On the other hand, this talent came in useful in certain situations and this one was perfect.

Silence.

The room was silent.

I had cut off Anita in mid sentence, and I didn't need to look up to see her sour face staring back at me. I could feel her hatred through the dead air. I stopped cracking my knuckles and continued doodling an evil face with devil horns.

'Is there something you wanted to say, Gallacchi?'

I shrugged my shoulders.

'It seems as if you want to say something. You have our attention. Why don't you start off by telling us what you thought about yesterday's meeting, Gallacchi.'

'Well, I thought it was stupid.'

The people in the room started to look at each other open mouthed. Brown Nose shook her head in disgust; Pinstripe seemed to have a slight smirk on his face; Slick Back didn't move at all or show any reaction.

'Stupid. Right. Ok. Stupid. In what way?' Anita

asked.

'I didn't think it was stupid, Anita,' said Brown Nose, 'I thought the logo was fantastic and the comments, maybe apart from ... sorry what was your first name again?'

'Mark.'

'... apart from Mark's comments, were constructive, professional and well deserved.'

'Why were my comments considered unconstructive? I'm allowed to say what I think and I think the new logo sucks arse!'

'Sucks arse. How eloquently put, Gallacchi. Did you learn that kind of language at university?' Anita frowned and shaped her eyebrows into an elongated arrow above her eyes.

'Well, I don't think the logo deserves that, Anita. Mark is clearly wrong and in the minority.'

Brown Nose faked an almost identical smile to Anita's, as if she were related to her. The other people nodded heads and whispered to each other whilst looking in my direction. I hadn't just delivered a killer right hook to Anita's nerves, I had also irritated everybody else in the room, except for Pinstripe who still had a smirk on his face.

'Well, Gallacchi. I want you to tell Freddy exactly what you have told all of us. I have arranged for you to have a meeting with him precisely after this meeting. In fact, I would like you to leave the room right now as you are disturbing all of us.'

I shrugged my shoulders, grabbed my notepad

featuring a great doodle of Satan, stood up and left the room. I made sure I slammed the door harder than I had done on my arrival. Anita had succeeded in demeaning and embarrassing me in front of everyone, and although I had planned and expected it to happen, there was still a part of me that felt shame. I hated Anita Fox. Hate was a word I didn't use very often, but under these circumstances, it was the right word to express my feelings towards her. I hated her fake smile, hated her condescending attitude towards me and countless other people, hated the sight of her. I imagined the meeting with Freddy Hardcastle to be my last hour, my last few minutes working for the company. I knew he would tell me that my contract would not be renewed and that I should leave right there and then. I would win the bet with Brian but lose my battle with Anita. She would win. I could imagine her raising her fake grin, her smug face cracking upon hearing the news of my departure. It made me feel sick to my stomach.

I walked at a snail's pace towards Freddy's office, through the blue section, through the green section and into the yellow. The longer it took me to walk to his office, the more I started to feel anxious and nervous about the meeting. When I reached Freddy's office, I looked through the glass door and wondered what he was doing. He was standing up, facing the window that overlooked the main street and had opened it as far as it could go. He was holding an expensive looking fishing rod in his hand and was casting out of his office window. I couldn't believe my eyes. I looked around and over my shoulders to check if anybody else was watching him. Nobody. Everybody was working as if this was a normal occurrence. I tentatively knocked on the door, which made Freddy stop, turn around, raise his eyebrows and signal with one hand that I should enter.

'Ah! Gordon. Yes. I have been expectin' ya. Come in. Grab a pew.' Freddy rested his rod on the floor.

'I'm Mark. Mark Gallacchi.'

'Ah. Really? You look like Gordon. Me lad's name is Gordon. Must have got ya both mixed up.'

I remained quiet, walked into Freddy's office and noticed how unorganised it looked. There was paperwork strewn across his desk; old coffee cups lined the rubbish bin; a small plastic trophy of a golden footballer sat on a filing cabinet to my right; multiple piles of dusty books sat on a sideboard to my left. A generic black and white photo of workmen sitting on scaffolding had been hung on the wall above the dusty books.

'Now, then. Yes. And you are 'ere 'cos of Anita. Am I right?'

'I guess so.'

'Yes. That's right. She said somefink about somefink. Nah wat woz it nah? Ah yeah, the bleedin' logo. Blimey! That's it. You didn't like the logo.' Freddy clicked his fingers and pointed at me. 'Listen, before we get onto that, do you like fishin'?'

'Fishing?'

'Yeah, you know, aht in the country, just you and

your rod, peace and quiet, a bit of currant bun.'

'Erm, no, I've never been fishing.'

Fishing had never appealed to me in much the same way as going to the dogs had never appealed to me. Standing around for hours, waiting for something to happen and when it did, you had to throw the fish back. I could never see the point in it.

'Never been? Did me lords 'ear right?'

'Erm, yes. I think.' I wasn't sure what Freddy meant.

'Well, you should join me this weekend. There's this fuckin' lake I go to, wotzit's fuckin' name nah? Ah yeah, Willow Lake. There's a 21.2kg wels catfish swimmin' abaht in it. I'm gonna catch it.'

'Ok. Well, I don't know. I have to check my calendar.'

The meeting I had assumed would be my last had turned into something else. It didn't feel as if Freddy was going to let me go, not if he was inviting me on a fishing expedition on Willow Lake. Freddy closed the window, sat down, and opened a drawer in his desk. He pulled out a small box and opened it in front of me. It looked like a collection of feathers.

'Fritz lures. These are the bizniz. We'll use these to catch ol' Moby, ay? I'll pick you up on Saturday. I have plenty of rods. You can borra' one. I have your address on file 'ere so ...'

As much as I tried, I couldn't get a word in edgeways. I couldn't bust through Freddy's enthusiasm and tell him that I wasn't interested. I didn't have a choice. I was going on the fishing trip whether I liked it or not.

'Nah then. Wot were we going to talk abaht?' Freddy

rolled his eyes up to the ceiling. 'Ah yeah. Logo. Ha! Ha! That was it. I 'eard you didn't like the logo and called it 'childish' or somethink.'

'Well, yes. I said something similar to that. I just don't like the logo. I felt it looked … well … in want of a better word … awful.'

'Really?'

I nodded.

'You know wot?'

I stayed still. I didn't nod or shake my head or give any noise that could have been mistaken for an answer. Freddy was living in his own little world, and I had no idea which way his decision would swing. I still believed that he would side with Anita and give me my marching orders.

'I like ya. You've got spunk in ya.'

'I have?' I said shocked.

'I'll let ya into a secret. I 'ate the logo too. The only reason we gave it to Gamma Design is because the CEO's trouble and strife 'as a friend who works for 'em. Can ya keep a secret?'

'Erm, yeah, sure.'

'Is that a porky?'

'Erm … no?'

'Good. Well, I'm gonna scrap the logo and start again with another design agency, but ya know wot? That's not really why I wanted a natter with ya. You've got balls and I like that. I mean, "sucks arse"? Ha! Ha! I could see ya being a manager, even a director some day. Yeah! You've got that special somefink. Plus ya like fishin''

'Well, I haven't been fish—'

'Details. Details. Listen. I'm gonna cut to the chase 'ere. I'm offering ya a permanent contract, startin' today, extra 2 grand a year, all bennyfits, wadd'ya say?'

My mouth dropped open involuntarily and I started to stutter. It took me a while to realise that Freddy was serious in taking me on, making me a permanent employee of the company.

'I ... I ... well ... I'

'Make it an extra £3000 squid and we 'ave a deal? I want ya on board, son.'

Freddy outstretched his hand towards me and I shook it. He had a strong grip that made my fingers crack and my knuckles feel as if they were being dislocated. I couldn't believe it. I had done everything I could do to get myself laid off, and been brandished a slacker, but it had worked against me. I would now have to buy Brian beers every Friday for a year, but even worse, spend more time with Anita Fox.

'Great. Good to 'ave ya on board, me ol' china. Nah, don't forget about Saturday. Nice and early, yeah?'

'Yep. Sure.' I stood up to leave his office.

'Hold on. Wait just a minute!' yelled Freddy. 'Turn arahnd for a sec'. Is that a strange ya sportin'?'

I turned around.

'A strange?'

'It is. Did ya know that is against the rules?'

I stood like a statue and failed to understand his London slang.

'Well, it's ok. I 'ave a beard you could lose a Reg in. I've always been meanin' to talk about the rules to someone. Get 'em changed. Fanks, Gordon. You've just reminded me to do that. See ya' later, son. Keep up the good work.'

I left Freddy's office in a spin. I didn't know whether I wanted to go back to my desk, go out and get some fresh air, or collapse next to the coffee machine. I headed towards the rest area and thought about what had just happened. The extra £3000 was not to be sniffed at, but my permanent contract meant being lumbered with Anita Fox for months, maybe even years. It was a sobering thought and not one I relished. On the other hand, she hadn't won. She hadn't got one over on me. My appointment would really annoy her. I was starting to get a sick sense of enjoyment out of pushing her many buttons and I planned to keep pushing them to the max. My new contract had not changed my decision to leave the company. My job would still be as boring as it was before, I would still sit next to Brian and Anita would still be my boss.

When I had reached the rest area, I pressed the *Wiener Melange* button on the coffee machine. I sucked the foam away from the edge of the cup and sat down on a comfortable green leather seat. The company had ambushed me and taken me captive. I felt trapped in a job working for a company I didn't like, with people I didn't like, and a building interior that must have been designed by an architect on acid. I wanted to leave.

After I had finished my *Wiener Melange*, I returned

to my cluttered desk, still shell-shocked from the meeting with Freddy. I sat down hard in my seat as if my trousers had been filled with lead weights and legs that couldn't support my frame. My computer was showing the company's screensaver and featured three Ms spinning around independent of each other. Brian stopped clicking his mouse button and looked across.

'What's wrong with you? Don't tell me they let you go?' Brian looked worried.

'Erm. No. Actually.' I paused to build up enough despondency in my voice to announce his victory. 'You won. You won the bet, ok?'

'What?'

'They took me on full time, ok. Happy?'

'After a month? Ha! Ha! You lamer. That's the fastest anybody has been offered a permanent contract, probably in the history of the company. You lamer. Ha! Ha!'

'Yeah, yeah. Alright. Alright. That still doesn't mean that I want to be here, ok?'

'You're stuck here just like the rest of us now. Welcome to shitsville, lamer. Ha! Ha! What a lamer!'

Brian's jibes were getting on my nerves. I knew I would never hear the last of it so long as he was sitting next to me. If the situation were reversed, I wondered if he would have been able to take the insults as much as I was taking them. He seemed to take pleasure out of other people's misfortunes and my bad luck would keep him fed for weeks.

'I remember hearing "I won't be here after three

months" and "WHEN I get another job". You lamer! I'm thinking about the first beer that I will order tomorrow, with the cool condensation dripping down the glass ...'

'Ok. Shut up. I've had enough of you, ok? Just, shut it. I'm still planning on leaving here as soon as possible.'

'How soon will that be? In another month, perhaps you'll be manager! Ha! Ha!'

'Yeah. Yeah. Very funny coming from the man who said nobody gets promoted.'

It was a good line that I threw in Brian's face with gusto. I knew I had to fight fire with fire to silence Brian, and my cutting remark seemed to work.

'I'll find something else, I'm sure.'

'You said that last time, **lamer**.'

Brian spat the word lamer at me like a true insult. Now the conversation was becoming personal.

'Ok. Ok,' I said. 'Let's add another year to the bet.'

'You want to bet again? You're not very good at winning.'

'I'll be out of here within six months.'

'Six months now?'

'I have to take into account the notice.'

'You madman! Six months? I still think you'll be here.'

'Are we on?' I extended my hand, looking for a handshake.

Brian shook my hand and his head at the same time. The anger within me had made me lose all of my common sense and I had made a rash decision to bet again. I rested in my seat, listened to Brian's laughs die away and went back to flicking through my spreadsheet again. The names on the list seemed to scroll forever as if there was a bottomless pit of other companies that I had to research. I couldn't do this for all of eternity and I wondered how Brian had managed to survive all these years. Maybe Brian was on anti-depressants and they had been the key to his survival. If this was the case, not even pills could stop Brian's bleak outlook on life.

'You're still buying me the beers. I still won that original bet.'

'Fine. I'll buy you those beers.'

The abrupt end to my sentence brought the angry conversation to a close. The new bet had calmed Brian's insults and jibes towards me. I felt relieved. Now all I had to do was to carry on sporting my bad attitude in the hope that it would get me a P45 sooner rather than later.

'This is from Freddy. Fill it in. Return it to me quickly. Time is money.'

Anita had vanished before I had the chance to look up and see her sick face looming over me. Where did she go? There was something odd about someone who could approach my desk and not be seen or heard. I hated her. She was the real reason I wanted to leave the company. She took her job as serious as the CEO, if not more so; she had become her job; she was a company robot devoid of empathy and feelings. The only person who seemed to get along with her was Brown Nose and that was only because she wanted a promotion. My job was starting to get to me, and I needed to find a quick way out before I lost all sanity in the same way Freddy Hardcastle had.

Freddy Hardcastle.

The fishing trip.

God!

What could I do about that?

There wasn't any way of backing out of it and Freddy would move heaven and Earth so that I could go. Then it struck me. The catfish. If I could hook the catfish, maybe Freddy would start disliking me to such an extent that he would have no choice but to let me go. I stopped scrolling down my spreadsheet and looked to Brian for some advice.

'Have you ever been fishing?'

'Fishing? Once, a long time ago. Why?'

'Oh. Just wondering. I was thinking of taking it up and need some advice.'

'You? Taking up fishing? I can't see you standing up to your armpits in water, throwing a line into a lake, mate.'

'Yeah, well, I thought I would give it a go. Just an excuse to get out of the city.'

'You could do that by buying a mountain bike or something else. Fishing?'

I turned away from Brian and returned to looking at my glaring monitor. I half expected Brian to hurl insults at the prospect of me taking up fishing, but, instead, he offered some advice.

'You know who would be the person to ask?'

'No?'

An air of expectancy started to build up before Brian answered. It was as if he knew something I didn't. Something that would unlock the world of fishing in ten minutes. Something that would help me catch ol' Moby. The idiot's guide to fishing for whoppers.

'Freddy Hardcastle. Have you seen that guy fish in his office? The bloke's a nut. Apart from him, I don't know of anyone else.'

My heart sank. There had to be other keen anglers who worked for the company apart from Freddy. There wasn't any time to practice for Operation Catfish before Saturday, and it looked as if my plan had hit a snag. The only solution I had was to do some online research and hope that it had some answers.

7.

I felt worried about tomorrow's fishing trip with Freddy Hardcastle as I thought about it, standing by the bar of a pub with fellow workmates after work. It felt surreal to be asked by a director of the company to join him on his quest to catch a monster catfish. I hadn't been asked either. I had been hijacked. I had researched the subject of fishing as much as I could and was still none the wiser. Dead baits. Pellets. Hook links. Reels. I didn't understand any of it. I thought I would have understood the rods but there were various versions of them as well. I was kidding myself if I thought that I was going to be the one to catch the catfish over Freddy Hardcastle. Tomorrow was going to be about surviving a day with a crazy man standing in a lake.

Brian tapped me on the back of my shoulder. 'I'll have a Guinness. Ice cold.'

The pub of choice was a fair walk away from the company's headquarters. It was decorated in old English style with red and orange carpets, dark wooden furniture and beams as far as the eye could see. An old abandoned pool table was taking up space in a room around the back of the bar. It had been damaged in a recent flood, and as a result, it was like trying to play pool on the Titanic. The landlord of the pub, a bald gentleman of advancing years with a handlebar moustache, was one of the reasons the pub was popular. He stood, like a strong man from a circus, behind the bar, pulling pints and having a laugh with all who frequented his establishment.

'Yes, squire. What will it be for you today?' asked the landlord.

'A Guinness and a glass of white wine,' I replied.

'A white wine? He will have the same as me,' said Brian, interrupting my conversation.

'Very good squires. Two Guinnessesseseseses!'

I wanted to pace myself and not suffer a hangover the day after. I was safe with wine but not with Guinness. I had not told Brian about my little expedition with Freddy and I was not about to. I knew I would be branded an arse kisser and frowned upon by my fellow workmates. I didn't want that to happen. I drank down the first pint of Guinness like a fool, followed by another, then another. Brian had insisted on buying rounds, and before I knew where I was, my vision was dizzy, my words slurred.

'You lightweight! You've only drunk two.'

'Fack off! I've had six. Six!'

The landlord looked at us with a hypnotist's glare from behind the bar, wiping down a beer glass with a tea towel. He didn't look happy.

'Shall I call for a carriage to escort you all home,

squires? I believe you've all had one too many for my liking.'

The landlord was not to be argued with. He may have liked having a laugh with patrons but couldn't stand for rowdiness. Brian threw back the remaining gulp of his stout and nodded in his direction. The landlord rang for a taxi to remove us from his pub before a fight broke out and not because he wanted us to get home safely. When I got home, I walked into the living room, collapsed on the sofa and fell asleep as my head hit the pillows.

I awoke to the sensation of somebody poking me on the arm.

'Mark? Mark? Wake up! There's someone at the door for you.'

The light hurt my eyes as I began to open them like a newborn. My head felt heavy and hurt with a pain I hadn't felt since my graduation party. My dad had been awoken by the sound of the doorbell that I had been too concussed to hear. He was wearing his expensive silk pyjamas and a pair of super grip slippers to combat the shiny kitchen floor.

'There's a man at the door. Freddy. He says you wanted to go fishing with him.'

Wanted to go? Now there was a phrase that was new to me. *Coerced into going* would have been the more appropriate phrase. I lifted myself off the sofa, rubbed my face with my hands, and stood up. I felt worse standing up than I did lying down. The blood seemed to rush from my feet to my throbbing head.

'God! Look at you. Where were you last night? I didn't hear you come in.'

'I was out. What time is it?'.

'7:30. You'd better get ready quick. Freddy-I think he said his name was-will wait in the car for you.'

It was a ridiculous time in the morning to be awake, regardless of my hangover. I needed at least another five hours sleep to ease the headache away. I still had the same clothes on from yesterday, and there didn't seem to be enough time to shower and throw on some new, beer scent-free clothes. I decided to go as I was.

'You're not going like that, surely?'

'Yes. I am. I don't have time to get ready.'

'Oh. Well. Have fun then!'

My dad watched me walk out of the house and enter Freddy's executive silver car.

"Otcha, son. 'Owz it 'anging? Jeezuz. You look as if you've 'ad a skinful mate. Were you dahn the nuclear last night?'

'Erm ... Yes? I was? I guess so?'

I put on my seat belt.

'Ha! Ha! You only live once, son. There's nofink like fresh air to cure ya loaf.'

I smiled and played along with Freddy's banter. I only understood half of what he he said and assumed to know the other half. Freddy's car had that new car smell. My fragile head was thrown against the leather headrest of my seat as Freddy pulled away. He liked to drive fast. He also liked to swerve in and out of traffic to get ahead of the car in front. Sweat started to drip from my forehead as Freddy pulled out to overtake a lorry, driving towards oncoming traffic. A double decker bus started to fill the windshield's view and sounded its horn. Freddy jerked the steering wheel with a sharp short action, cut back in ahead of the lorry, and rejoined the right side of the road. I gripped the handle on the inside of my passenger door and held on for dear life. I thought I was going to be sick.

'Bloody traffic's terrible today, and it's early.'

Freddy shook his head in disbelief and continued to drive like a psychopathic formula one driver. I held the handle so tight that I could feel my hand become cold. My hangover was the least of my worries.

'Dahn't worry, son. We'll soon be there. I bet you can't wait, eh?'

I couldn't answer. Freddy turned his head and looked at me. I hoped he would see my pale ghost face and slow down.

'I know what. Hah abaht some music?'

Freddy took one hand off the steering wheel and started pressing several buttons on the control panel in front of him. The car started to veer into the middle of the road. I shut my eyes and braced myself for impact. A song started to play at full blast, penetrating my ears like the sound of a pneumatic drill on a building site.

'Ahhh! This is the shit. Canned 'eat, mate. *Well, I'm so tired of crying, but I'm out on the road again ... I'm on the road again ... dee deedee dee deeeeeee.*'

Freddy's singing was as bad as his driving. He was

tone deaf and had no sense of timing but it didn't seem to stop him. I toyed with the idea of opening my passenger door and hopping out, preferring the thought of hitting the tarmac to Freddy's version of a death race but I thought better of it. Every bone in my body had stiffened through fear as I sat rigid and petrified in my seat. A brown sign that read Willow Lake offered me some comfort in knowing that the journey would soon be at an end, so long as Freddy knew how to use the brakes.

''Ere we are, son. Owt in the country.'

Freddy skidded the car to a halt, turfing up pellets of mud. I unhooked my coiled hand from the handle inside my passenger door, and I started to hyperventilate. I could feel my heart rate racing in the same way a gazelle's heart must feel after escaping a chasing lion.

'Nah son, 'elp me with the gear and we'll be fishin' for Ol' Moby before he knows wots 'ooked 'im!'

Freddy left the car as fast as he had driven to the lake. I stepped out of the car once some feeling had returned to my legs, and I felt I could stand up. Freddy was frantic, pulling all of his fishing equipment out of the boot and laying it all on the damp muddy ground.

''ere! Ya need to wear this clobber.'

Freddy handed me a pair of army green waders. They smelt of musty stagnant water and looked as if they hadn't been used for years. I held them up by the braces and let the weight of the rubber wellingtons unfold the complete outfit to the ground. The pair of waders looked two sizes too small for me, which proved to be right when I tried to squeeze my feet into the wellies. I felt and looked like an idiot. If any of my friends could have seen me, I would have been a laughing stock for sure. I wouldn't have been able to go to any punk gigs in fear of being picked on and being the butt of jokes. The chances of me pulling would be slim if this fishing episode ever got out—unless I wanted to pull a female angler. No thanks. My image would be ruined. This fishing trip was going to remain a secret.

'I think this is too small for me,' I said.

Freddy was wrestling with his fishing gear and I wasn't sure if he had heard me. It was an attempt to spare me the indignity of wearing waders and looking like an idiot. They were too small anyway.

'Too small? Oh! Blimey! I hadn't figured on that. Ya looked like the same size as me son. Now wot? Hmm.'

Freddy reached up and shut the car boot with some force, creating a loud thud as the lock slipped into place. An assortment of different boxes, bait, reels and rods lay on the car park ground as if ten more people were going to be fishing with us.

'I've got it. There's a spot over there where we can go. You can stand on the rock; I can stand in the lake. Sorted. We'll catch Ol' Moby if it's the last thing we do, eh?'

'Yeah, sure. But these waders feel really tight.'

I pleaded to Freddy's common sense to fix my outfit before my blood stopped circulating and my toes needed to be amputated. I wanted to be rid of the fisherman's skin.

'You'll be alright, mate. You'll be alright. We're both keen fishermen so I'm sure we'll catch the bugger fast and be out of 'ere before ya know it.'

My pleas had fallen on deaf ears. I decided to put up with the waders, arching my feet into an uncomfortable position they were not meant to be in.

'I've never been fishing before.'

'What? I thought ya said you'd been? Fuck a duck!'

'I did say that I—'

'No matter. No matter. I'll show ya. It's easy once you get the 'ang of it.'

We picked up all of the equipment off the ground and made our way to a secluded spot of the lake. Mist filled the air, and I could see water boatmen skid and jerk across the surface of the water. The scene was eerie and reminded me of a Hammer horror film.

'Nah put all the gear dahn here. You take this rod and ya see that rock over there? That's ya spot.'

I took the rod from Freddy's hands and made my way to the small rock he had pointed at. It was a lot smaller than I had imagined it to be, but at least I didn't have to wade into the lake and get wet. I stepped up onto my base and looked ahead of me. Just trees and water. A duck. Lily pads. There was nothing out of the ordinary that I could see, but Freddy knew otherwise. He was dead serious about catching the catfish and nobody was going to talk him out of it.

'Nah son. What ya do is think of the rod like a golf club. Do you like a rand of golf?'

'Not really. I'm not very good at it.'

'GOOD GOD! Wots wrong with ya? First ya tell me ya like fishin' and then say ya haven't fished and nah ya don't even like golf. Bleedin' 'eck! I've got a right one 'ere.'

My head hurt. It hurt more when Freddy shouted at my face and into my ears. I couldn't have cared less about where I was or what I was doing. I just wanted the day to pass and end as fast as possible. My lack of enthusiasm seemed to be making Freddy more and more agitated. Perhaps I was falling out of favour. Perhaps I would be let go if I carried on displaying my disinterest in fishing and golf.

'As that band said—wotz their fuckin' name nah? Ya know. '80s band.'

I shrugged my shoulders.

'Yeah, Frankie Goes To Hollywood said—*you gotta relax and do it*—remember it?'

I knew the song Freddy was trying to sing with the wrong words but I didn't let on. I shrugged my shoulders again in a nonchalant way.

'Anyways, wot ya do is 'old the line against the rod, release the bail arm off the reel, and then frow the rod up, cast the line be'ind ya', then cast it forwards in one smooth sweeping mowshun, and let go of the line as the rod comes forward. Nah, you try.'

I hadn't understood a word Freddy said. I was nervous. My head still hurt and the action of casting off would use energy that I didn't have. What if I got it wrong? Freddy would be standing next to me all day whistling and humming tunes in my ears. I raised my rod, threw the line back, then forward and released the reel. It was a perfect cast as I watched my hook plop into the water, attracting the attention of the sole duck that had swum by earlier.

'Bloody hell! Are you sure you 'aven't been fishin' before? Ok. Ok. Reel it back in. I'll attach some bait to ya line.'

Freddy rooted about in one of the boxes by his side and held up a small fish that looked like a sardine.

''ere. Ya won't get anywhere withaht one of these fella's.'

Freddy grabbed my line and attached the fish to my rod. The concept of catching a fish with a fish felt odd to me. I had imagined a bundle of feathers on the end of my line after Freddy had shown me his prize box of baits in the office. I was bewildered.

'Nah, cast off again.'

The fish had added some weight to the end of my line as Freddy let go of it. I breathed out a sigh, composed myself, and cast off again; performing the same motion Freddy had shown me. My bait flew through the air and down into the lake, destined to become fodder for an unsuspecting passing catfish called Ol' Moby.

'Fuck a duck! Ya got some talent son! Ya got *some* talent! Nah, whatever ya do, keep an 'old of ya rod. Don't let go of it. When Ol' Moby bites, he'll try and pull ya into the ten furlongs, he'll try and wrestle ya for all ya got. Whatever you do, just keep 'old of ya rod, yeah?'

'Erm. Ok.'

My nerves had started to tick upon the mention of being pulled into the "ten furlongs", which I assumed meant lake. Freddy hadn't mentioned anything about being dragged into the water or being taken for a death roll once in it. It now sounded as if I was fishing for a crocodile. If Ol' Moby did take a fancy to my bait, and then started fancying me as a potential meal, I didn't have the strength to keep hold of the rod. As far as I was concerned, the catfish was welcome to it.

After a couple of hours of watching a perfect still lake swarming with insects, I sat down on the rock to ease my tired legs and loosened my wellies. The sun started to rise and hit me in the face, making me squint like a mole's eyes being exposed to daylight. It didn't help my fragile head and neither did the fishing trip, which was turning out to be more boring than I had imagined. Freddy was in his element. He had cast, reeled in, cast again, reeled in, cast again so many times that I had lost count. He hadn't caught anything. Not even a tiddler. His whistles and hummed tunes annoyed me. I couldn't have imagined anyone else being so happy wasting their time and coming home with nothing to show for it. I would have been content with catching the stereotypical old boot, made famous by cartoons and bad comedies. At least it would have been something. I had to think of a conversation to break the monotony. The eighth floor. Freddy would know something about the mysterious eighth floor, and since we were getting on well and he seemed to like me, he would be the one to spill the beans.

'Freddy. Do you know why there isn't a button in the lift for the eighth floor?'

The whistles and hums came to an abrupt stop. Freddy froze and became a statue of the lake. The rod in his hand didn't wobble an inch, not even a centimetre. He turned his head towards me and revealed an expression that looked as if Ol' Moby had jumped out of the water and slapped him around the chops with its fins.

'The eighth floor? You want to know about the eighth floor? Did me lords 'ear right?' Freddy was aghast. 'There's nuffink to say abaht the eighth floor son.'

'But you are a director. Surely, you must have meetings on that floor, you know, with the CEO perhaps.'

I was being bold, but my curiosity needed to be satisfied, and Freddy was the one to tell me what I needed to know. After all, he liked me.

'Look. I'm not abaht to give you any details about the eighth floor, but I will say that I chose not to take an office up there. I wanted to be with the people, ya know, the cogs of the company rather than sit with the whistles, and besides, the office I have now has a much bigger window.'

Freddy looked at me and reeled in his line. It had been the first time that I had seen or heard him be serious.

'That's all I can tell ya. Don't ask me about it again.'

I didn't ask about the eighth floor again. Several hours went by. We ate the lunch Freddy had brought. A Scotch egg, a jam sandwich and a flask of tea. It was not substantial and I felt the fish I was trying to catch would be getting a far more substantial meal with my bait if it ever bit. The sun shifted across the sky and removed itself from my eyesight. The afternoon was dragging on and I had had enough. I was hung over, hungry, sunburnt, and without a catch. I wondered when Freddy would call time on this pointless exercise.

'Deee dee dee dede dedededede deee de dede.'

It wasn't going to be soon. Freddy was still *dee deeing* a tune and sounded happy. I looked at the lake and imagined that I had dived in, caught the catfish with my bare hands, wrestled it into submission, and brought it out of the lake, holding it arms aloft in anticipation of a hero's welcome. Camera flashes. Roses thrown at my feet. The catfish had been defeated, the day was over, and I could return home to my bed and sleep.

Ripples.

Splash!

The reel on my rod started to spin fast, and a tremendous force on my line jerked me forward. This wasn't an old boot.

'HELP!'

'Bloody 'ell. 'Old on. Don't let go! Just 'old on!.'

Freddy dropped his rod into the water, fetched a net and started to splash his way to me. I sat down on the rock and held on with all my limited strength. My head thumped and pounded. I wasn't in the right condition for any kind of adrenalin rush and I was relieved when Freddy took over from me.

'Friggin' 'ell. You got an 'eavy bastard 'ere son. Shit!'

Freddy panicked and wrestled with the reel. The veins in his neck seem to pop and his face was turning a shade of scarlet. The resistance of the huge monster on the hook made it hard for him to turn the reel. Freddy struggled for thirty minutes until the catfish was closer to the shoreline and I could see it splash out of the water.

'Shit! It's Ol' Moby! It's bloody Moby! 'ere, take the net and scoop 'im up when he gets close to shore. Go on! 'urry!'

The rampant splashes and sploshes of the catfish's quest for survival didn't encourage me to meet it at the shoreline with a net. It might have had razor sharp teeth as well as tough fins that could slice my arms off. Would I need to go into the water? Right into the water? As in - get wet?

'Wot are you waiting for? Bleedin' Chrimbo? Go on. Get in the wa'er and scoop 'im aht!'

I scrunched my feet back into the tight fitting wellies and, with reluctance, made my way down from the rock and towards the shoreline with a big net in my hand. When I reached the water's edge, I could see the catfish almost leap out and into the lake again as it struggled to keep itself alive. A splash of water hit me in the eye.

"urry son, 'urry, or 'e'll get away!'

I wiped the water away from my eye and waded in.

I didn't have a choice. Freddy was insistent and I felt compelled to help him. If I had listened to my fragile hung over head, I would have turned tails and walked off in the opposite direction. It might have been a sackable offence, but for some reason I couldn't do it to Freddy. As much as I wanted to leave the company, I had some respect for him, and his dream of catching a catfish had come true. As I waded closer to the wriggling mass of aquatic life, I readied my net and lowered it into the water, hoping it would all be over without injury.

'Good! Good! We're ... almost ... there.'

Freddy struggled and strained to reel in his dream catch for another ten minutes, his face turned from scarlet to a deep shade of beetroot. The splashes had turned into plumes and it was difficult to see what I was doing with the net. I held the handles with both hands, extended my arms in the direction of the catfish and raised them. The weight of Ol' Moby almost made me fall over forwards into its jaws before I managed to regain my balance.

'YEAH! YA GOT IT! YA GOT IT! WOO-HOO! BRING IT 'OME SON. BRING IT 'OME!'

Freddy was shouting and jumping up and down like an excited child. I stumbled backwards towards the shoreline with the catfish jumping and writhing around in the net. It was a monster. I had never seen a fish as big as this in my life. Freddy ran into the water and took control of my feeble attempt of "bringing Ol' Moby 'ome". When we got to the shore, I looked at the catfish as it wriggled in the net with tremendous spirit. It's mouth opened and shut at regular intervals. It was an ugly looking fish that looked as if it had swallowed five whole ducks for dinner. Its whiskers looked like giant snail tentacles and it felt just as slimy.

'Blimey! Shit! Wot a beaut'. I mean, look at it son! Wot a whoppa!'

Freddy leant forwards and wrapped his arms around the mid section of the huge catch, muscling its head onto his lap.

'Quick! Take a snap!'

I walked over to the car, fetched my mobile and took several pictures. One of Freddy and the prize. One close-up of the prize. One close-up of the winner. Freddy didn't need to say cheese. He was beaming a smile from ear to ear.

'We need one of us too. 'as that fing got a timer?'

Without any thought, I set up my mobile, placed it on the ground and joined Freddy for the photo. Once the phone had faked a camera click, I got up and retrieved it.

'What do we do now? Do we chop it up and make it into fillets or let it go?' I asked.

Freddy's smile turned upside-down and a look of shock dawned on his bearded face.

'You wot? Fillits? Wot are you rabbiting on abaht son? Ya don't make fillits outha a catfish. It's not a Yul Brynner for no one. God, man! Wot is wrong with ya? Nah! Ol' Moby 'ere is going back in the drink to live another day—besides, catfish taste nasty or so I 'ave 'eard.'

I knew it. We had spent a whole day fishing and for what? Something we could neither keep nor eat. It confirmed my worst fear and suspicions about fishing, and reaffirmed my belief in its absurdity.

'Ya wait until I report this to the rags. They'll be swarmin' all over us. Once you send those photos that is. Wait until they cast their mince pies on this beauty!'

'Us?'

'Yeah. We caught this bugger. Wot a team!'

'Erm ... Well, you were the one that really caught it. I mean, it just happened to bite my line. It could have bitten yours but it was just luck that it bit mine. I mean, you brought it to shore. I had very little to do with it.'

I hadn't thought about the photos being made public. I didn't want to be named in the newspapers. If the photos were seen by any of my friends, I would never be able to live it down. I was into indie/punk rock music, drinking beer, playing pool, and being a townie. If Brian saw the photograph, there wouldn't be any let up in his mocking for weeks. He would call me "arsekisser" or "brown nose" and that was something I was far from being.

'Rubbish, son, rubbish. We're a team. You and me.'

Freddy put his arm across my shoulders and pulled me in close, assuring me that we were now pals for life alongside Ol' Moby. I took a deep breath and promised myself that I would delete the photograph of the three of us when I got home.

The timer didn't work.

The memory card corrupted.
Sorry, Freddy.

8.

'Again. I'm really not sure where or how this fishing trip adventure fits into everything.'

Lisa sounds annoyed. It isn't like her to question me.

'You don't have to go into detail about the fishing trip, but you do have to write something about bonding with your managers. Respect your managers. They will be the ones responsible for your professional guidance. Without them, a company simply can't exist. Good managers. Write something about managers.'

I repeat the word managers as often as I can. Lisa looks as if she understands where I am coming from, and I am satisfied that I have appeased her annoyance.

Lisa checks her phone.

'The chairman says he is on his way here to see you. He has tried to get hold of you constantly and only gets your voice mail each time. Shall we continue on with this tomorrow?'

This is serious. It's rare for the chairman to travel to the headquarters unless it's a special occasion. There are some employees who joke about the chairman's invisible status, claiming that he is like *Dracula* who sleeps in a coffin on a make believe ninth floor, only waking to suck the blood of new employees. It is a childish joke that I once laughed at when I started at *the* company but it has worn thin. The chairman is a man to be respected. He founded *the* company and is responsible for all the fantastic jobs created within it. I have made a note for Lisa to write a chapter based only on the chairman and how his magic hands created *the* company from scratch. It needs to be mentioned.

'What do you want to do?' asks Lisa.

'Hmm? Oh. Yes. Well. Maybe we should go out and get a bite to eat and continue what we are doing in more, let's say, salubrious surroundings,' I reply.

'Do you think that is wise? The chairman is on his way.'

'It'll take him hours to get here and by the time he does, the office will probably be closed or near closing. That will be enough time to get what we want finished and if we don't, we can continue on into the late hours if need be.'

Lisa looks like a statue.

'I'll pay you triple time,' I say, pleading with her.

'Well, I don't know really.'

'We really need to get this done. Come on. We can talk about it more over lunch, which is on me by the way.'

We leave *the* company headquarters and walk across the busy London street. I take Lisa to one of my favourite restaurants called *L'olivia Ripiena*, who specialise in Italian pastas and Parmesan cheeses. The restaurant has succeeded in creating a calm rustic atmosphere accompanied by a strong smell of garlic. Italian artworks hang on the walls and opera can just be heard playing in the background. A waiter takes our orders and brings us a decanter of water.

'Now, should we continue on while we wait for our lunch?' I ask.

'Yes. Ok.' Lisa unfolds her laptop and starts to write.

After the fishing trip, a few weeks went by without anything remarkable happening. I had been acting my usual obstinate and irritating self, but people were starting to warm to me. No matter how many sarcastic comments I made, and no matter howmany times I cracked the joints in my fingers, fellow workmates invited me to after work drinks and parties. My mission in being let go was starting to fall apart, and the prospect of buying Brian beers for two years was close to becoming reality.

After a team meeting, Brian and I returned to our desks to carry on trawling through spreadsheets we had trawled through several times before. I could hear the voice of Freddy behind us as we took our seats. He had been on holiday, and I hadn't seen him since the fishing trip.

'*Dee dede dee deeeee, dededede dee deeeeeeeeee.*'

As Freddy passed my desk, he stopped and tapped me on the arm.

'Oi!'

Freddy stopped, leant backwards and pretended

to reel in a fish. If air guitar existed then this was air fishing. I looked at Brian and shrugged my shoulders in the vain hope that it looked as if I had no idea why Freddy was acting the way he was.

'Ol' Moby stood nah chance, eh? HA! HA!'

Freddy patted me on the back and walked off, *dee deeing* the same tune. Brian stared at me.

'What was all that about? Ol' Moby?'

'Oh. Well. I mentioned to Freddy that my dad is a keen fisherman and that there was a lake where he always goes to catch this big fish that he calls Ol' Moby. I told Freddy about it and I think he must have caught it or something.'

'You told Freddy about it? You arsekisser! Getting chummy with the manager now, eh?'

'I'm not an arsekisser. I'm not. It just came out in conversation, that's all.'

'Yeah. Yeah. Right.'

'Look. I'll be out of here in six months. Why would I want to hob-nob with my superiors?'

Brian nodded his head, raised his eyebrows and focused his gaze over my shoulder. I hadn't noticed that Anita Fox was standing by the side of my desk.

'That's interesting, Gallacchi. Do you consider your development dialogue hob-nobbing with your superiors? Is that why you did not show up in the booked room at the booked time? Time is money, and I have a managers' meeting to go to after the meeting with you, Gallacchi. I can't be late, Gallacchi, because some of us think punctuality is the key to success.

Come on! Walk with me! Time is money! NOW!'

Anita Fox sped away from my desk and left me for dust by the time I found out where I was supposed to be. I had deleted the event from my calendar on purpose so that I would have no chance of remembering my development dialogue.

'It's usually yellow room 765,' said Brian.

'Thanks, Brian. I'll be out of the door after I'm through with this meeting.'

'Yeah. Yeah. Heard it all before mate. You're stuck in Shitsville with all of us now. You're not going to escape that easily. We still have that bet - remember?'

'Yeah? I know, I know.'

I stood up and made my way through the blue zone to the almost fluorescent yellow zone. The garish colours of the fluorescent ceiling lights hurt my eyes as I tried to find the room. The size of yellow room 765 shocked me when I found it. It was small. Tiny. Miniscule. There was just enough room for two chairs and a small coffee table, and Anita had taken up most of the room by sitting on the chair to the right. She had a clipboard balanced on her lap. As I pulled down on the metal handle, she looked up at me with her stony cold face that lacked any trace of humanity.

'Well, Gallacchi. Thank you for joining me. We were already five minutes and twenty-six seconds late and now we are seven minutes and forty-two seconds late. Time is money. Sit down!'

I sat down and tried my best to accommodate my legs by crossing my right leg over my left leg. It felt uncomfortable so I swapped legs and balanced my left leg on my right leg. Nothing seemed to improve my comfort in such a tight cramped space. Anita gave out a sigh of displeasure as she watched me fidget in my seat.

'Now, Gallacchi,'

'My name is Mark.'

'Gallacchi. This is your development dialogue after three months of employment. How do you feel things are going?'

Anita held her pen like a knife and looked down at her clipboard, armed and ready to stab bad remarks onto the paper.

'To be honest,' I had to think of an appropriate answer, 'shit!'

Anita banged the nib of her pen on her page and looked at me in disgust.

'Shit? Really? Is that all you have to say?'

'Yeah. Pretty much. The job is boring.'

'Boring,' Anita paused. 'I see. And what exactly is boring about it?'

'I look through a list of the same companies, the same people, on the same spreadsheet, day in and day out. I must have rung every one of them at least three times.'

'Really. Well. That is most interesting that you feel that way, Gallacchi. You have to remember that you are here to work and complete the tasks given to you by *the* company. If you feel that you can't complete the tasks then perhaps I might have to write down something about your unwillingness to do the job.'

Anita licked the end of her pen and started to write on the clipboard. I wondered what she was writing and I tried to lean forwards and read it, but in such a small space, I was in danger of head butting her. I cretainly couldn't read her handwriting upside down.

'Now then, when it comes to the work you just mentioned, I have to say that it is below average. Your call rate has slipped below the standard that *the* company deems to be worthy. I am therefore writing in your development dialogue that you need to up your call rate and work harder.'

I couldn't believe what I was hearing.

'I have called everybody on my list. I can't up my call rate as there is hardly anybody left to call.'

'Start from the top of the list and start calling.'

'But ...'

'Start from the top of the list and start calling. There is no reason for sloppy idleness on this job.'

Sloppy idleness? Now that was an insult even to someone who wanted to leave the company. As desperate as I was to leave, I didn't want my reputation in tatters. Anita licked the end of her pen again and continued.

'What would you say your strengths and weaknesses are? What would you like to improve?'

'My strengths? Well ...'

'Let's start with the weaknesses first as there are lots of them to discuss. I have had complaints from people about your conduct in and around the office. You have a bad attitude and people say they have been affected by it. You don't take part in meetings and only offer one-word answers. We expect more, Gallacchi.'

Complaints with an 's'? Plural? It seemed I had ruffled the feathers of a few people, and maybe, just maybe, my mission to be let go was starting to work.

'I will write down that you will improve your attitude towards your work, *the* company and your fellow employees.'

'Fine. I guess.'

My despondence couldn't have been more apparent. Anita squinted at me as if she had just tried to drink battery acid. She hated me. There was no doubt in my mind. The feeling was mutual. I had never met anybody who had sold themselves out as much as Anita Fox had. It had got to the point where I couldn't tell if she had any feelings for anything. I wondered if anybody loved her.

'That is the attitude that I want to see removed from your persona, Gallacchi.'

'For fuck's sake! It's Mark. My name is Mark. It rhymes with hark but uses an 'm'.'

Anita dropped her pen on her notepad and took a few silent moments to comprehend my swearwords.

'Ok. Well. It appears that you are even unwilling to take part in your own development dialogue. I will be having a meeting with Freddy Hardcastle later about today to discuss your repugnant behaviour. The company does and will not tolerate insubordination.'

Anita rose from her chair, clipped her pen to her clipboard, opened the door to the small room and squeezed out, and shook her head from side to side. I uncrossed my legs and stretched them across the coffee table, reintroducing blood flow.

I had snapped.

I was frustrated in not being able to answer or respond to any of her questions. She had not taken the answers that I had given her with any seriousness. She kept calling me Gallacchi and it irritated me. The whole development dialogue seemed like a waste of time as Freddy had given me a permanent contract.

I waited for a moment before I opened the door and stepped out. I skulked back to my desk, playing the events of what had just had happened over in my brain. I felt I was going to get the chop, and although this is what I wanted, part of me had started to like working for the company. It wasn't anything I could explain, but there was a whisper of enjoyment in looking at my spreadsheet of company names and contacts. I got some fun out of marking some of them black and writing comments like "never contact them again" and "receptionist is like *Gandalf*". It made me more determined to break through their defences and get the information I wanted. By the time I got back to my desk, I had talked myself into thinking the job was ok until I looked at my spreadsheet again. The difficult contacts were far outnumbered by numbers that didn't work, the numbers I had to call back, and by the numbers who wanted to divulge information but were never there when I called. The job was dull.

'How did it go?' Brian teased out the question with

a smirk on his face.

'Terrible.'

'Oh.' Brian assumed I was being let go.

'I think—I might be getting fired.'

'Oh?' Brian now assumed he had won the bet.

I picked up the phone and started to call a contact when I noticed an email from Anita had dropped into my inbox.

No subject.

Meeting with Freddy Hardcastle.

Now.

I cancelled my phone call and left my desk without saying a word to Brian. Freddy may have taken me fishing and seemed to like me, but there wasn't any excuse in shouting and swearing at Anita Fox. I would not only be fired, my working life would be ruined with bad references. It wasn't the way I wanted to go.

When I reached Freddy's office, I was shaking. My legs had turned to jelly. Sweat had started to moisten my forehead. My hands were numb with chills. Freddy was reading a large book called *How To Bake Bread Country Style* as I looked into his office. I tapped my finger on his door. He rested the book on his desk and waved at me to come in.

'Ah! Gordon. Come on in and rest ya plates. I was just havin' a peep at bread making. Talk abaht using me' loaf, eh? Geddit?'

Freddy displayed an immense happiness; happier than he usually was. I wondered if he slipped something into his tea for him to be this happy. It was either that or he had taken too much acid in his youth.

'I'm Mark, not Gordon.' My voice was shaky but I retained a small amount of composure.

'Mark. Yes. Of course. Mark. You look like me son Gordon. Listen. Do you like bread?'

My nerves calmed as I tried to digest his question. Bread? Why was he asking me that? Was there a bread making competition he wanted to take me to?

'Erm. Yes. Sure. I like bread.'

I could not say anything else. There weren't many people who didn't like bread.

'Ah! Good. Good. I was thinkin' of bakin' this fella' 'ere ...'

Freddy opened the book to a page devoted to a sour dough loaf.

'This bugger takes fuckin' free days to make. Free days!!!! I'm gonna slop this dough togever and slap it in the oven and I want ya to be the first to 'ave a nibble!'

'Erm. Thanks.'

My nerves had started to settle and I felt some warmth returning to my hands.

'Good. Good. Nah. Wot else woz I gonna rabbit to ya abaht? I woz sure it was somefink important.'

The nervous jingles in my arms and legs returned as I sat sweating.

'AH YEAH! Golf.'

'Golf?'

'Yeah. That woz it. I 'ave this set of golf clubs 'ere, in this cabinet 'ere. 'Old on a sec.'

Freddy bolted out of his seat and started to enter a

security code on a panel on the cabinet door. A loud beep sounded each time he entered a number.

'Ah. Nah wot woz the code again? Wot woz the code? Do you know the code?'

'Erm, no. Sorry.'

Freddy lifted his finger in the air and punched in a code that opened the cabinet. He lifted a golf bag out and placed it on the floor, standing it on two support legs that sprang out of the back. Three of the larger clubs had soft toy heads of tigers on them and the rest of the set looked as if they had been used for digging holes rather than playing golf. A divot of old dry dirt was still attached to the 9-iron, and I couldn't see the head of the sand wedge because of all the sand stuck to it.

'If you fancy it, we can play a rand.'

Freddy had forgotten our previous conversation about golf.

'Oh, well, I'm not really a golfer. My dad is but I couldn't get into it.'

'18?'

'I'm sorry?'

'Did you play an 18?'

'Yes. I think so.'

'There's ya fuckin' problem. Ya dad started ya out on a full course. Come and play some 9-hole par-3. That'll get ya birdies flowin'. These are me son's clubs but you can use them. You can 'ave 'em if you want.'

'Maybe your son will want to play.'

'My son? Oh.' Freddy paused and looked down at

the floor. 'My son doesn't play anymore.'

An eerie silence fell in the room as I detected a sadness sweep across Freddy's face, reducing his jovial mood to a somber one. Freddy turned his back and brushed his hand over the driver's tiger head cover, stroking it as if it was a real pet cat. I was certain that something serious had happened to Freddy's son, Gordon, and assumed that he was no longer among the living. I felt guilty and I couldn't take back the words I had just spoken, but then again I didn't know if Freddy's son was deceased.

'Yes. I would love to play a round of 9-hole par-3s.'

Freddy lifted his hand from the driver's tiger head and turned around with a smile on his face.

'Fantastic! 'ow abaht it after Captain Kirk today?'

'Well, I have something on but ...'

'Great! After Captain Kirk it is then! Nah there woz somefink else—ah yeah—your development dialogue with the Fox. So, ya find your Uncle Bob boring, eh? It's a bit of an egg yoke to ya, eh? Well, I can see where ya comin' from. You've highlighted somefink that I've been meanin' to rifle. Yes.'

Freddy sat down, spun around in his seat once, landed his elbows on his desk and clasped his hands together. He had a strange glint in his eye and I wasn't sure what it meant. In fact, I had no idea about what he was talking about at all.

'Yes. You, me son, are goin' places. You need a challenge and ya ain't geddin it where you are. That's why I am gonna put ya in charge of a brand spankin' new department, once it gets goin'.'

I was speechless. Another promotion? After complaints? After a bad development dialogue? After my work had been rated substandard? I couldn't believe it.

"ere. I 'ave this bit of paper for ya to scribble ya monica on.'

Freddy sifted his hands across his messy desk and found my contract, complete with a coffee stain circle, amongst a disorganised pile of paperwork. I lifted it to my eyes and started to read it.

'Ya dahn't 'ave to take a butcher's at it nah. Just sign it. I'm not gonna con ya!'

Freddy handed me a heavy silver pen. I signed.

'Great! Great! I'm gonna move a few people rand. 'ave a bit of a shifty abaht, so to speak. You'll be at the top of the food chain. I'm thinkin'—wots her fuckin' name nah— Anne could be in ya team or somefink. We'll create some job title for her.'

Anne. Anne? Brown Nose Anne? Brown Nose Anne who is close friends with Anita Fox Anne? Oh God!

'Then, I'm thinkin' maybe—God! That fella, you know, the one with the strange bonnet ... Robert ... and ... thingy, you know that guy who always wears a nice whistle ... Alonso. Maybe that Brian could join ya too. Ya seem to get on well with 'im. Keep all you china plates togetha'.'

My worst scenario. I now would be head of a department with a team I didn't like. Pinstripe and Slick

Back? On the plus side, I could handle Brian despite his obvious depression and Anita Fox would no longer bother me.

Anita Fox would no longer bother me.

It felt good to repeat those words to myself.

'Well. I don't know what to say. Erm.'

'Don't say anything, mate. Just a Tom Hanks will do.'

'A Tom Hanks?' I thought of a word that rhymed with Hanks. 'Well, erm, thanks, Freddy.'

'Nah need mate. Ya goin' places. This won't come into effeck until free months time. Sorta arahnd Chrimbo. Just keep stum abaht it, eh?'

I lifted myself from my seat and opened the door to Freddy's office.

'Oi! Gordon! You forgot somefink!'

I walked back into Freddy's office. 'Sorry?'

'Ya forgot ya clubs.'

'Oh yes. I forgot. Can I collect them later? That's if we are still on after work?'

'Nah. I need the space in me cabinet for all the bread I'm gonna bake. Yes. Gonna put up some shelves or somefink.'

I raised my eyebrows and shook my head. I had never come across anybody so detached from their job in my life. It made me wonder if Freddy got any work done at all - ever. I walked into the office, grabbed the golf club bag by the strap and walked towards the door.

The driver with the tiger head cover hit me in the back of my head as I swung the bag over my shoulder.

'Sees ya later.'

Freddy turned to the empty cabinet, shaped his hands like number sevens and started to count. It looked as if he was going to paint a portrait and was framing the best details. I couldn't work out what he was doing and I gave up trying to figure it out.

Fellow employees squinted strange expressions at me as I walked through the office with a set of funny looking golf clubs over my back. I tried to ignore them and concentrated on returning to my desk when I bumped into Anita Fox. She had appeared from out of nowhere and blocked my way. I stopped and put my clubs down. The clump of dried mud attached to the 9-iron crumbled and fell to the floor, creating a patch of brown dust on the hard carpeted surface.

'And,' Anita also squinted at me with a strange glare, 'where do you think you are going with those filthy things, Gallacchi?'

'I'm going to my desk.'

'Well. You haven't got far. Walk fast. Time is money. Why are you carrying a set of filthy golf clubs anyway? May I remind you of the company code. All sports equipment or any other kind of equipment must be left in the equipment room behind reception. The receptionist will give you a number tag.'

'Well. That's where I am going now. To reception, to get that number tag.'

'Gallacchi. If you brought them in this morning, late

as usual, then you should have left them at reception.'

'Well, I didn't bring them in this morning.'

'You didn't?'

'Yes.'

'Then where did they come from? Never mind. You are not supposed to have them full stop. May I also remind you of your development dialogue. The improvement in your attitude. The improvement in your working practice. It seems as if you are not upholding the agreement on your development dialogue. Did Freddy have a meeting with you?'

'Yes, he did.'

'And what did he say?'

There was an expectant confident air surrounding Anita that seemed as if she was sure that I had been reprimanded. I thought I saw a small upturn of her bottom lip. The first sign of a smile. The sign of her first smile since I had known her. Her first authentic smile.

'You would have to ask him. It's confidential.'

Her smile faded into the usual grimace after a split second and the normal Anita Fox returned.

'Oh. I see. Well. I will. Get those clubs behind reception, clean up this mess, and get on with your work. Time is money, Gallacchi.'

I picked up my clubs and swung them over my shoulder. I left the patch of dry mud behind me with no intention of cleaning it up. It would stay there to infuriate Anita after she had talked to Freddy. She could lick it up as far as I was concerned. As I started to walk away, I stopped and turned around to look at Anita entering Freddy's office. Freddy was the first to talk and remained seated. He seemed calm as he started to talk to Anita - probably about our meeting. Anita, on the other hand, started to wave her hands around in semaphores, and I swore I could hear her high-pitched shrieking voice pierce through the glass. Freddy shrugged his shoulders and showed Anita a piece of paper, which I assumed to be my contract. Anita dipped her head, threw the piece of paper at Freddy, and stomped out of his office, halting her march to look at me and then head in the opposite direction. We now had the same status at the company and there wasn't any way she could get at me now. My development dialogue may have stated that my attitude needed to change but I hadn't expected my job to change. Things were starting to take a turn.

When I returned to my desk, I had received an email from Freddy. I felt scared and thought that he had gone back on his promotion promise after speaking with Anita, but to my surprise, he only wanted to cancel golf and save it for another day.

9.

'Thank you for lunch. It's good,' says Lisa.

Lisa is tucking into her panzanella and seems to appreciate the good food as much as I do. It is the least I can do for an employee who is so professional, so willing, able to do her job, and goes that extra mile to get things done. She is a model employee and a role model to others. I make a note to myself to nominate her for *employee of the year*, an award that I started as one of my first initiatives as CEO of *the* company. A holiday will be Lisa's prize. No other employee deserves it more.

'My risotto is fantastic, as always,' I say.

I lift a second fork of risotto to my mouth and take delight in the creamy vodka sauce that hits my taste buds with strong tangy flavours. I wonder how they can cook food as good as this. Lisa has remained unusually quiet throughout her meal, and I wonder if anything is wrong or if there is anything I can do. Maybe she feels guilty because she has been fobbing everybody off who is trying to contact me or her. Maybe she is so overcome with the book that she is planning how to write it. Maybe she is hungry.

'How do you think things are going? Are you ok with everything? Let me know if you need anything, anything at all. Just ask. I will make every resource available to you.'

Lisa is bending over backwards for this project, and I feel it only fair to give something back in return.

'Everything's ok. It's just ...' Lisa pauses to sip some water, ' ...just that I had something on tonight. I appreciate the triple time you offered, but I can't get out of what I have planned.'

I slump in my chair and roll the water around in my glass. I want to get everything down on paper before *the* company's annual meeting. It is the first time Lisa has let me down over something as important and essential as this.

'Quadruple time and a fantastic dinner later. Can you cancel for that? I'm sorry, but I desperately need you on this, Lisa.'

'It's not about the money. I just can't cancel. I'm sorry,' says Lisa.

I decide to back off, and I have to accept that the afternoon is all the time we have unless we start extra early tomorrow. It is something I can suggest later, but for now, I have to let Lisa eat her meal and cool off before I ask how early she can start. We finish our meals and Lisa continues to take notes.

After Freddy had told me about my promotion and new department within the company, I couldn't work out how it had happened. I had made sure that I was late every day. I had made sure that my attitude stank in meetings. I had lost my temper and swore at my manager, which wasn't my intention. I was being promoted when I should have been let go. I should have won the bet with Brian, but instead I was going to be picking up his alcohol tab for the next two years. But the bet didn't matter anymore. It was inconsequential because I had now climbed to the dizzy height of manager in the space of six months. I didn't know how I had done it or if I deserved it. In any case, I was going to be placed in a position of responsibility and authority with a salary that was beyond my expectations. If I had carried on with my telejob, staring blind at the same spreadsheet for years, I would have gone crazy, but now I had something to get my teeth into. I didn't know the first thing about being a manager. The only people I could look to for managing tips were Anita Fox and Freddy Hardcastle, two bizarre people that seemed to be worlds apart and working against each other. It wasn't much to go on.

Brian found out about my promotion when the standard company email went out about internal affairs:

Promotions: *We welcome **Mark Gallacchi** to his new position and wish him all the success.* " Section Transfers: *"We are glad to announce that **Clare Danes** is moving to the cleaning logistics department. She will be an asset to the cleaning staff."* Departures: *"Darren Higgins has decided to leave the company to pursue other ventures. We wish him luck."*

Brian didn't tease me about losing the bet at all

after he had read the email. Instead, a blank expression filtered over his pale face. My promotion to manager had blown apart his theory that nobody ever rose to the upper ranks from starting at the bottom. I had trodden on his toes. In fact, I hadn't just trodden on his toes, I had hacked his feet away with a scythe.

I carried on trudging my way through my ancient spreadsheet filled with the names I had called over and over. Until my promotion took effect, I still had to work as before, beside Brian, and annoying people with phone calls. As time moved on, and I was nearing my final days of working with my spreadsheet, Brian's attitude started to change.

'Mr Gallacchi, can you take a look at this contact here and check if there is anything wrong?' asked Brian.

Mr Gallacchi? What happened to Mark? What happened to lamer? He hadn't called me a lamer for a while. He hadn't called me lightweight for a while either. His sarcastic jokes had fizzled out.

'Brian. I'm Mark, remember? What is wrong with you?'

'Ok. Mark. If it's ok to call you Mark that is. I mean, Mr Gallacchi sounds more respectful.'

'God! You'd better not be like this when we are working in a team.'

'Like what? What am I doing wrong? Tell me, Mark, I mean, Mr Gallacchi. I can improve.'

Brian was pleading with me. Begging. I didn't know what to say. He started to jolt his leg up and down as if he had a trapped nerve.

'Brian ... Brian! Please. Just relax and be yourself. I don't know. Tease me about losing the bet, you like doing that. Call me a lamer or a lightweight or something.'

'Oh no! I couldn't do that, Mark ... Gallacchi ... I, erm.'

Who would be scared of me? I was going to be his boss, but I felt I was still the same person underneath. I was still going to crack sarcastic jokes with him, and have beers at lunch and after work. I wanted us to have the same relationship.

Anita Fox still treated me with the same contempt as when she first interviewed me. She continued to complain about my time keeping, my work and, sometimes, my appearance. She arranged and more more meetings than my calendar could handle in an attempt to unnerve me and throw me off balance. I treated every meeting with the same flippant and frivolous attitude that I usually used where Anita was concerned.

'Now, I don't need to remind you about your development dialogue where we said that you would improve your attitude.'

Anita's hard wrinkled face reminded me of someone who had just sucked a lemon. Bitter. Sour.

'I don't think I need to remind you that I have been promoted to manager of the new social media department,' I said with a degree of smugness.

I took pride in addressing Anita in the same condescending manner as she addressed me. I was now a manager and had the same status as her.

'You are not the manager of the new social media department because that department does not exist. You are an employee of *the* company, working in my department, under my supervision, and that means I get to say what I think.'

Anita was using all the time she had in our remaining working relationship to get under my skin, twist herself into my brain, and make herself feel as uncomfortable as a tumour.

'You still have a problem with punctuality, your work is still not of the standard *the* company requires, and your attitude combined with your shabby appearance tells me that you don't take this job seriously at all. Where do you see yourself in five years time? Because at the moment, it'll be out of the door looking for another job.'

Shabby appearance? I had grown a beard, which was now allowed after Freddy had changed the rulebook. I had dyed my hair black and had a slight quiff. I complied with the smart but casual rule by wearing a shirt and a pair of trousers, but always wore my worn stylish black leather jacket with name badges of my favourite punk bands sown onto it. I wasn't shabby. I was stylish.

'Five years? Well, the way things are going, I will still be here but in a higher position than I am now, and I won't be having these pointless meetings with you,' I said.

I couldn't hold back. Anita wanted to make my

life hard, right up until my last day until I left her department, which I considered nothing short of heinous and vindictive. I didn't care about her and I gave myself permission to say what I wanted.

'Pointless meetings. I see, Gallacchi. I will write down this revelation on your private company profile that the CEO has access to. I'm sure he will find it interesting that you brand meetings as "pointless".' Anita formed speech marks with her fingers. 'He will find it especially interesting because the kick off is next week.'

'I said, meetings with you were pointless. Not every meeting.'

Anita sucked in a breath and breathed out.

'Nevertheless, it will be written down, Gallacchi. I will be keeping a close eye on you at the kick off and gauging your reactions. Anything less than positive will be a black mark against you, Gallacchi.'

'Whatever.'

'I would have liked to have shown you the new corporate logo, but I am told it is still in progress and under wraps,' said the CEO. 'Never mind. Instead, I will move on. In times of economic crisis it is normal to see share prices dip slightly.'

The CEO pointed to a bar graph on a large screen displaying a PowerPoint presentation. The company had booked a modern conference facility to hold their kick off. A large stage had been set up with huge beam spotlights, a podium, and a large projector screen.

I was disappointed that Freddy had chosen not to present anything. It would have been the most uplifting presentation about fishing and golf and bread, and nothing about work. It was the first kick off I had been to and the first where I had seen the CEO in the flesh. The CEO was a thin man with hair that looked as if it had been moulded out of clay. He wore an ill-fitting suit and large shoes that made him look like a human golf club. He seemed to be able to present and give a good presentation, gaining the attention of all the hundreds of employees in the room. I tried to ignore him by playing *Tetris* on my mobile phone, but despite this, the words of his speech still penetrated my ears.

'*The* company is not afraid of difficult times because *the* company has confronted this situation before and not only survived but flourished into the success it is today. Because of our broad range of products and services, *the* company is able to fend off any economic crises, and I want to reassure those who have contacted me about the possibility of redundancies by saying that *the* company will not make anybody redundant. I also want to reassure those who have shares in *the* company by saying that the stock market has no effect on the company's profits. In the first quarter, we were up. In the second quarter, we were up but not as much as we would have liked. And in the third quarter we are on target to meet our goals.'

I looked up from my mobile and tutted. It sounded like a subtle way of saying that the company wasn't doing well and that there was nothing the CEO or anybody else could do about it. The share figures had inspired panic within the subs, panic in investors and, most of all, panic in employees. Anita Fox, who sat in a row in front of me and to the right, turned around and glanced at me. She must have had the hearing of a bat to have heard my tut. I had got used to her stare and ignored it, and turned my attention to my mobile and carried on playing *Tetris*.

'Many of our investors have heard about the current value of the company on the stock exchange. I have reassured them in much the same way I have reassured you all gathered here today.'

I tutted again. The CEO considered himself a superhero if he thought he had "reassured" everybody in the packed conference hall. Even though I had been promoted to manager, the thought of leaving the company entered my head again. The company seemed to be going down the drain, and instead of waiting for the inevitable trip down the plughole, it occurred to me that I should keep my eyes peeled on the job market.

'I, therefore, appeal to all of you here today to do your best and work hard for *the* company as you are the ones that make the company successful. Each and every one of you is highly valued and we wouldn't be here if it wasn't for your hard work. Together we can make miracles materialise!'

A large "mmm" emanated within the hall. The gathered mass of suits and casual but smart frocks clapped and gave themselves a pat on the back. I kept my hands clasped on my mobile, keeping an eye on the next zigzag block falling from the top of the screen. I could feel Anita Fox's anger transmitting through the air without looking in her direction. I had acquired a sixth sense when it came to Anita and her reaction was nothing short of predictable. I didn't care. She wasn't going to be my manager for much longer.

'We want to help you achieve your goals within *the* company. That is why, today, in this unique setting, I want to announce—Operation Gambit.'

The CEO flicked a button, which revealed the next slide on the PowerPoint presentation. It featured an awful animation of a cloud that rained letters down towards the bottom of the screen. My mouth opened in shock to its crudeness in design, and the fact that somebody had missed the ways in which a rain cloud could be misunderstood, especially in times of, as the CEO put it, "economic crisis".

Everybody clapped; everybody, it seemed, except me. Why were people clapping? They had no idea what "Operation Gambit" was. I had no idea what it was, and judging by the puerile graphics, I didn't want to know. If the imagery was anything to go by, it must have involved being soaked by rain clouds or being out in torrid weather. I glanced at Anita who signalled with her hands and dipped eyebrows that I should clap. I didn't and, instead, turned away, unpaused my game of *Tetris* and laid down a straight long block that gave me 4000 points for a tetris.

'We have arranged for everybody to take part in a personality and work analysis, structured and engineered by successful psychologists, White & Heinsteiger. When you return to your desks, you will find a questionnaire that we want you to fill in. Once you have, two cinema tickets will be given to you so that you can see whatever type of film you wish to see—except horror, of course.'

Everybody laughed. I started to look around for a person who was holding up a cue-board with the word "laugh" written on it. Had the CEO told a joke or had I missed something? Everybody seemed to laugh in unison. Except horror? Why was that funny? The person next to me gave me a nudge. The force of their elbow jogged my hand and made me drop a block in the wrong place. My new high score was ruined and a new game of *Tetris* would have to be started. It irritated me.

The person whispered: 'Anita wants you.'

I looked across and saw Anita's shaky finger pointing at me. She then mimicked a laugh and pointed at the CEO. She then pointed at me again, then at her laugh, and then at the CEO. She wanted *me* to laugh at the CEO. She wanted *me* to laugh at the invisible joke. I kept my mouth shut and did nothing. Anita turned away and shook her head from side to side in disbelief at my disobedience.

I took a break from *Tetris* and looked at the CEO standing in front of the inadequate PowerPoint presentation. What was Operation Gambit all about? It felt as if company employees were going to be profiled and the information logged away to be used either for or against them. Why did I have to fill in a questionnaire based on who I was when I knew who I was? It seemed like another pointless exercise and a huge waste of company money; a company that could ill afford to waste it.

'Once you have filled in the questionnaire, a meeting will be booked with White and Heinsteiger who will discuss the results with you. We hope that you will find the results interesting and that they will provide an insight into what you need to do to achieve your goals. With that said, this concludes my presentation, which leaves us with one thing left to do.'

Everybody stood up and stretched their arms out in front of them, almost linking everybody together. I didn't know what was going on, but I slipped my phone in my pocket and followed everybody else by raising my arms in front of me. The CEO started to wiggle his hands from side to side whilst lowering and raising his hands to the floor. Everybody followed his lead. He lowered and raised his hands at a faster and faster rate. On each ascension, he raised the height of each wave until his arms pointed up towards the ceiling.

'Wooooo ... ahhhhh! Wooooo ... ahhhhh! WOOOOO ... AHHHH! WOOOOO ... AHHHH!'

I looked from side to side and noticed that everybody was copying the CEO. I lowered my hands and didn't raise them again. Instead, I looked on, shocked by the hundreds of employees before me, going through the motions of some kind of corporate chant. As the CEO raised his hands one last time, he shouted "YEAAAAAAAHHHHH!" as if he had just orgasmed. The large hall was filled with the cheer of the company's employees as they clapped the CEO off the stage. I blinked and shut my eyes longer than they needed to be, hoping that the whole scene had been a dream. When I opened them again, I was still in the large conference hall, the crowd employees were recovering from their corporate orgasm, and the CEO's PowerPoint was on its last slide, which displayed the words "Making Miracles Materialise". I was dumbfounded.

As the employees filed out of the hall, I kept an eye on Anita Fox's movements and opted to walk in the opposite direction and into the nearest W.C. to compose myself. I was still shocked by what I had witnessed. Grown adult people acting automatically as if the company had hijacked their minds. I didn't want to become one of them. As I walked into the W.C., I noticed Brian was at the urinal relieving himself.

'Brian. Mate! What on Earth did you make of that?'

Brian cut off his urination in midstream, zipped up his trousers, and turned around. A wet patch started to appear through his trousers close to his groin. I tried my best to ignore it.

'What was that Mexican wave thing all about? Did you do it?'

'Erm. Yes. Sure. I did it, Mr Gallacchi. Why wouldn't I do it?'

Brian's shaky nervous voice echoed around the W.C.. He avoided eye contact as he walked to the washbasins.

'What is wrong with you? I'm Mark.'

'Yes. I know but you are also my manager now or will be,' said Brian with a shaky voice.

'Oh come on, Brian. I'm not going to report you or fire you or anything like that. I'm your workmate and friend, or at least I thought I was, and I still owe you those beers, remember.'

'Ah. That was just a little joke. Nothing I took seriously. You don't owe me anything.'

'But a bet is a bet. Shall we grab a beer tonight?' I asked.

'Erm, no, I am, erm, busy tonight. I, er, have things to do.'

'Seriously?'

Brian nodded. I didn't believe him. I didn't even believe that Brian had done the wave either. I couldn't imagine him doing a Mexican wave at a sporting event. I couldn't imagine him even dancing. Not even once. He was too straight. Too rigid. Brian brushed his hands down his trousers, looked at me, and left the W.C. as fast as he could. It seemed he did not want to talk to me at all, now that I was going to be his manager.

I looked at myself in the mirror, and tried to comprehend the bizarre events I had just witnessed. I had to find another job, and the sooner I did, the better everything would be.

10.

1. When conflict arises with a work comrade, do you:

A. Have a frank discussion to solve the problem.
B. Just comply with your work comrade although you disagree.
C. Force your point of view across strongly to dominate your work comrade.
☑ **D. Stay quiet and try to suppress your inner rage.**

2. A work comrade asks you to do something, do you:

A. Jump at the chance to help.
B. Say that you will help but not at that precise moment.
C. Ask them to ask somebody else as your time does not allow it.
☑ **D. Bluntly refuse to help them at all.**

3. You think of an idea that you believe will benefit

the company but you are unsure if the idea is good. Do you:

A. Convince yourself that it is a bad idea and scrap it.
B. Tell the nearest work colleague about your idea and gauge their reaction.
C. Keep the idea to yourself and try to use it without discussing it with anyone.

☑ **D. Bounce the idea off as many work colleagues as possible for their opinion.**

I ticked d for every box without even looking at the question or the answer. I didn't care for the questionnaire that was going to evaluate my personality and tell me who I was. I knew I was a person who wanted to escape from the crazy corporation that felt as if it had kidnapped me and was holding me captive. The prospect of handing in my notice became a notion. I started to toy with the idea, but the job market wasn't buoyant, and the fact that I had not had a whiff of an interview worried me. Was I destined to be stuck at this company forever? I hoped not. My common sense told me to stick it out and handle the job with more sincerity, but my nature told me to keep being nonchalant and obstinate. I got a kick out of playing the rebel and if I became a suit, I would lose some of my identity if not all of it.

After I had finished ticking the boxes, which should have taken an hour instead of ten minutes, I posted the envelope into an "Operation Gambit" postbox by reception. After a few days, everybody got their results back along with a group number and a time to visit White & Heinsteiger. I didn't know who the other group members were but I hoped that I hadn't drawn the name of Anita Fox.

The White & Heinsteiger office building was situated in West London and took an hour to reach. It was a Tudor style building featuring black beams and white walls. The smell of old must and sawdust wafted up my nostrils as I walked through the imposing black wooden door.

'You must be Mark Gallacchi. Please, take a seat.'

The cheap and cheerful receptionist, who pointed to a waiting area, took me aback. How did she know who I was? Other employees were sitting and waiting to be processed by the psychologists, who I assumed had cost the company a king's ransom. Brown Nose was sitting on a seat, sipping a cup of tea and nibbling on a biscuit. I jogged my head upwards with a slight movement to acknowledge a hello without saying a word. Brown Nose looked at me with cold eyes and a drooping smile. A man dressed in a fetching tailor made suit walked out of a conference room, clutching a large packed binder under his right arm.

'Yesssssssss. Hello and welcome to White & Heinsssssssssteiger. Pleasssssssse sssssssstep into our conferencccccccce room where you will find refreshmentssssss and drinkssssss.'

The man spoke with a speech impediment that

made him sound like a snake. I walked into the room with Brown Nose and two other employees who I recognised but couldn't name. The conference room was white and shiny and I could see my reflection bounce up off the large glass table in front of me. The walls were bare and devoid of pictures or decorations, and it felt as if I had walked into John Lennon's living room minus a piano, John and Yoko.

'I bet you are all eager to find out the resultsssss of our psssssychological analysisssss! If I may, I would like to sssssstart with Anne. Where is Anne? Ah! There you are!' The man looked at the raised arm of Brown Nose. 'I'm sssssorry, I didn't introducccce mysssself or what we are about to do. It'sssss been one of those dayssss! My name isssss Roger and I am the head psssssychologissssst here at White & Heinssssssteiger. We have developed a tesssssst to help businesssssessssss maximisssse their employee'sssss potential. We like to think that we help people work together in a more harmonioussss way.'

I was glad I was sitting some distance away from Roger as I would have been on the receiving end of an unwanted phlegm shower.

'I would like to sssssstart by going through the four profilesssss we have drawn up to bessssssst identify the traitsssss and qualitiessssss in every individual.'

Roger pressed a button and a screen that split up into quarters appeared on the wall behind him.

'We have the foxxxxxx who is analytical and methodical. The lion who issss quick and getsssss thingsssss done. The cat who isssss generally eassssssy to work with and isssss laid back. And we have the dog who hassssss a creative ssssstreak, but hasssss a habit of chassssssing itsssss own tail. Depending on how you have ansssssswered the questionnaire determinesssss which of thesssssse creaturesssss you become! Excccccciting!'

I reached across the glass table and poured myself a glass of water from the supplied decanter. My fellow workmates looked at me as I took a loud sip on purpose.

'Are you ok there?' asked Roger.

'Oh yes. Quite. Thanks,' I replied.

'Good.' Roger raised an eyebrow. 'Now, Anne. When we look at your profile, we can sssssee that your triangle pinpoint liesssss sssssquarely and firmly in the foxxxxx sssssquare.'

A blue triangle appeared in the fox square, making me choke on my water. The company didn't need to pay a bunch of top psychologists to tell me that Brown Nose belonged to the fox profile.

'We can sssssee, from your ansssssswersssss, that you like to think about ssssituationsssss before you act on them; are methodical when it comesssss to your work; you like order and probably arrange your dessssssk neatly and tidily. Are we right?'

'Wow! I can't believe how accurate your test is. You have got me down to a tee. I am astonished! I am beside myself in awe of your professionalism and expertise.'

'Thanksssss. There isssss more information in thisssss folder I am about to give you and it containsssss your complete profile, your sssssssstrengthssssssss, weaknesssssssssessssss and your persssssssssonality idiosssssyncracccccciessssss.'

'Gosh! Wow! You are certainly thorough. Thanks once again!'

They were telling people things about their personalities that they already knew. Brown Nose jumped at the chance to lap up the attention she was getting from the so-called expertise of White & Heinsteiger. She sported a false beaming smile, which made me sick to my stomach.

'Now. We come to Mark. Where issss Mark?'

I raised my empty glass and banged it back down on the table.

'Yesssssssss. Mark. Before I go through your ressssultsssss, can I assssk you a question?'

'You just have but you can ask another if you want. I'll let you'

I gave Roger a smug smile. He didn't seem to appreciate my sarcasm.

'Right. Ok. Did you take thissssss tesssssssst sssserioussssly?'

'Yes. Of course. Is there a problem?'

'Ok. I jusssst wanted to make sure.'

Roger pressed a button and a multi-coloured triangle fell right in the middle of the screen, highlighting that I was either a bit of everything or nothing at all, or so I assumed.

'You are actually off the chart.'

'Oh right. And what does that mean?'

'Well. According to our ressssssultsssss, you are an eassssssy going perssssson prone to violencccccce, a helpful perssssson who doesssssssn't help, and a persssssson who makesssss friendsssss eassssssily but issssss lonely.'

'I think there could be something wrong with your test.'

'I don't think there isssss. You ticked box d for every ansssssswer, which isssss highly unusual and I'm not sure if you really did take thisssss tesssssst sssssseriosssssssly.'

'I ticked the box with the most appropriate answer and that just happened to be d every time.'

'Our tessssst is formulated sssssso that isssss very unlikely to happen.'

'So, your test is rigged?'

Everybody in the room fell mute and gawped at my audacity. I had really let my cat, maybe lion, dog and fox, out of the bag, and it felt good to throw a spanner in the works of something I considered to be superfluous. White & Heinsteiger's psychological profile had been the last straw. I had not been through anything so pointless as this before, and I could sense that it wasn't going to be the only organised event the company would throw at me. I could work in a kitchen, as a cleaner, or even deliver newspapers rather than work one more day for this company.

'Show some respect,' said Brown Nose.

Brown Nose focused her anger in my direction with squinted eyes and clenched facial muscles. I shrugged my shoulders and ignored her comment. I thought I had been respectful enough. They were the ones with the rigged test.

'No. The tesssst isssssn't rigged. It isssss formulated to create an accurate profile. If you are ssssssaying that the ansssssswersssss you gave are genuine, then I would ssssssuggesssssst you book yourssssself in here at thisssss clinic and undergo a thorough pssssssychoanalysssssissss.'

Roger pressed a button and moved onto the next slide fast, a tactic to avoid any further comments or questions from me. I picked up a beige plastic coffee cup, pressed down on the thermos flask on the table, and squirted out a cup of brown liquid posing as drinkable coffee. To pass the time, I started to doodle on the notepad in front of me with a shortened White & Heinsteiger branded pencil I could just about hold. After the meeting had finished, Brown Nose frowned at me as we walked into the reception area. She didn't say anything but I knew she would be straight on the phone to Anita Fox to tell her what I had done and what I had said. It didn't matter. It didn't matter because I had made the decision to hand in my notice.

The following day started the same way as every other day with my journey to the office, only today I had an envelope to give Freddy. It was my intention to see him first thing before Anita could pull me to one side and dress me down for my behaviour at White & Heinsteiger. When I reached his office, I could see that he was in a meeting with a woman. Freddy looked over her shoulder and saw me hesitating between knocking on his door and walking away to try later. He waved his hand at me to enter his office.

'Ah! Gordon. Nice to see ya'. How's it hangin'?' Freddy was cheerful as usual. 'Things went a bit chicken oriental yesterday with that bloomin' test fing, eh?' Freddy looked at the woman. 'We had this fing yesterday. Took all day. Anyway—Gordon! I would like you to meet Janey. She's gonna be startin' in your department so I want ya to take good care of her.'

'I'm Mark. Pleased to meet you.'

'Mark, yes, of course, yes. Sorry, son. Mark.'

The woman turned her head and shook my hand. I heard: *Haaaallelujah, hallelujah-hallelujah, Haaaallelujah, hallelujah-hallelujah* being played in my head as my eyes fell on the most beautiful girl I had ever seen. There wasn't any room for any butterflies because my stomach had melted. A tingling sensation caused the hair on the back of my neck to stand up. Every nerve in my body was on edge. There hadn't been a girl that had caused this type of reaction in me for a long time and I knew, by my instinct, that I was smitten.

'Janey joins us from, wotzits fuckin' name nah, you know, the site that all the sprogs use.'

'Facebook?'

'Thatzit. Yeah. Cheers, mate. Me loaf ain't wot it used to be.'

I smiled at Janey and she smiled back. She was gorgeous. She had short jet-black hair, the darkest brown eyes I had seen, a smile that knocked me sideways, and a tattoo on her left arm that I could just see through her blouse. It looked like a logo of one of my favourite bands but I couldn't be sure.

'... anyways, anyways. Wot can I do for ya, Gordon?"

Janey smirked as Freddy called me Gordon again.

'Well ... I ... Erm.'

The envelope containing my notice was now staying in my backpack after seeing Janey. I could endure anything the company could or was going to throw at me, and even the prospect of being bollocked by Anita Fox if it meant I could stay and get to know Janey.

'I really just wanted to pop in and say hello actually. I was going to ask how you saw yesterday's meeting with White & Heinsteiger but this is, perhaps, not the best time to have a chat when you have company.'

'Nah. Best not to.'

'Well, nice to meet you and, maybe, you know, we'll see each other again today or tomorrow or next week, or something.'

My nerves had taken me over and turned my speech into hesitant rambles and stutters. Janey had floored me. I smiled at Janey and had to force my eyes to look away to be able to leave Freddy's office.

''Ere, Gordon. I almost forgot. You know that bread, I was rabbitin' on about before— that sah dough fella'? 'Ere it is. Give it a go and see wot ya think.'

Freddy punched in the code to the cabinet that had contained my golf clubs, took a loaf from one of the many shelves and gave it to me. It had a rough bobbled appearance and didn't look fit for human consumption.

A sprinkling of flour across the bread's surface didn't disguise the burnt black edges.

Freddy turned to Janey. 'That took free days to make. Free days!!!!'

'Oh. Thanks. I'll, erm, eat this, perhaps,' I said as I tucked the brick under my arm.

I looked at Janey. She smiled and gave out a slight laugh, which attracted me to her even more.

'Of course you'll eat it! Wot else were ya gonna do? Build an 'ouse? Oh yes, and we'll get that rand of golf in soon, eh?'

I concentrated my gaze on Janey's beautiful smile. I was captivated and reluctant to leave Freddy's office.

'Did ya forget somefink?'

'No, I ... erm. That was all.'

'That's it then. Nofink else to talk abaht.'

It was a cue to leave Freddy's office. As I closed the door shut, I couldn't help but look over my shoulder at the girl that had just turned my world upside down.

I placed the burnt loaf in my backpack and took out the envelope containing my notice. I walked across the red zone and into the fluorescent yellow zone where I had seen a shredder. I placed the envelope in the slot and pressed the button. Woomph! It was gone. I had condemned myself to working for the company for a little bit longer and all in the name of love.

11.

'What I am trying to say here is that everything that *the* company does should and must be taken seriously. Employees shouldn't make the same mistakes I did when I first joined,' I say.

'Sure. Ok. I'll make a note of that,' says Lisa.

I notice that Lisa's coffee cup is empty and it is paramount that it is topped up. The caffeine will keep her focused.

'Would you like a coffee or another drink?'

'Erm. No thanks.'

I felt Lisa should have said yes. We have been sitting in the restaurant for over an hour and I always feel odd when I don't have something on the table in front of me to drink and nibble on. I call the waiter over and order another coffee and a slice of carrot cake. I plan to do an extra hour in the gym to work it off later.

'Shall we press on?' I ask.

'Yes. I'm just worried that people have been trying to reach us.'

'You don't have to worry. You are with me. I am giving you permission to be here to do this. I'll take the rap if any rap is to be taken. Don't worry about anything.'

I take a sip of coffee and plunge my fork into the carrot cake. Lisa impresses me. She is always willing to help others, and her concern that people cannot reach her is testament to her positive mental attitude. There are many, including myself, that just want to be left alone now and then, but Lisa? She keeps herself reachable around the clock. It's admirable, commendable and impressive to have someone so dedicated to their job. I am glad that she will be the *employee of the year*. She is the only one that deserves it. Lisa is looking at me and is ready to continue.

The day after the White & Heinsteiger meeting was my last day as a regular employee of the company. My managerial role as boss of the social media department would start on Monday after the weekend but for now, I was still looking at my spreadsheet, working with a paranoid Brian who agreed with everything I said, and I still had the intolerable Anita Fox as my boss. So long as she still outranked me, she would make my life at the company a misery. But it was something I could now deal with as my focus had been turned towards Janey, the girl I had fallen for. I now had the impetus to follow some of the company rules to keep my place at the company just for her sake. I had made it to work on time for the first time in four months, and I had made up my mind to make it to Anita's meeting on time as well. When I opened the door to Anita's office, she was shocked. I had timed my entry to perfection and it was bang on 9:25.

'Ah! Gallacchi. I'm sure I don't have to tell you why you are here,' said Anita.

She hadn't complimented me on my time keeping but then again, I didn't expect her to.

'You have wasted company time and company money by filling in your White & Heinsteiger questionnaire in a trivial manner. May I remind you that *the* company invests money into your development and this includes occasions such as White & Heinsteiger. You have some kind of problem don't you, Gallacchi? You think everything is a joke; that everything is below you; that you think of yourself as some kind of rebel genius, well, Gallacchi, I'm here to tell you that your days are numbered.'

'I have apologised to White & Heinsteiger and I have agreed to fill in the questionnaire again. It's the least I can do.'

It pained me to say the words, and it felt as if I was sucking up to her.

'Really? Well, I ...'

Anita's jaw dropped and her eyes widened. She had never envisaged the day when I complied with the company's ethics on behaviour. Her surprised expression melted and her eyes turned into slits.

'Well. That's something, but you should have filled it in properly to begin with. You are still wasting company time and money by acting as if nothing matters to you. We made an agreement in your development dialogue that you would improve and I still have seen no evidence of it.'

'I was on time to work today and to this meeting. I want to apologise for my previous behaviour and want to say that it won't happen again. Now that I will start my managerial job next week, I will take things more seriously.'

As the words left my mouth, I felt sick to my stomach. I was selling myself out by telling the one person I hated more than anybody else what she wanted to hear. Anita pressed her eyes together tighter, glanced at me, and placed her pen down on the pad in front of her. She didn't look as if she believed a word I was saying.

'That's commendable, Gallacchi. Better late than never, I guess. Will miracles ever cease?'

'Time is money!' I said.

Anita snorted, picked up a glass of water from her tidy desk, and took a swig. I hadn't intended to sound as if I was mocking her.

'Good. Well, you can go, Gallacchi.'

I stood up, opened the door to her office and had half a leg over the threshold when Anita called me back.

'Wait, Gallacchi. I forgot to tell you, we have a manager's meeting next Friday and I will send you an invitation for your participation.'

'A manager's meeting? Ok. Sure. I'll be sure to add it to my calendar,' I said.

'Good. As manager of the managers, I expect you

to be there.'

'Manager of the managers? You are the manager of managers?' I asked.

'Yes. Didn't you know?' Anita replied.

Anita raised a sick smug smile. A manager that managed the managers? I had heard it all now. The company had some dubious titles for people such as Upper Senior Executive Managing Director and Supervising Deputy Assistant, but I hadn't heard of Managing Manager. This had to be some kind of sick joke. I wouldn't be rid of Anita after all. In fact, she would be on my case for months, or years.

'Yes, *the* company appreciated my hard work and saw fit to promote me to this position. It's a reminder that hard work pays off, Gallacchi. You could learn something by my example.'

I ground my teeth together and ran my tongue across my two front teeth. Anita knew she had hit me where it hurt, judging by her smugness and lack of humility. She still had control of what I did and what I was going to do. I could have just continued looking at my overworked spreadsheet with Brian by my side. If I had let the negative thoughts take over, I might have printed out my notice again but for the thought of Janey. She was the reason for my stay at the company, and I was willing to suffer for her, despite not knowing if she was single. I turned my back on Anita and left her office without shutting her door or saying goodbye.

When Monday rolled around, I was nervous for my

first day as manager for a number of reasons. I would manage a team of five people, one of whom I didn't like (Brown Nose Anne); one who I thought was a friend but now mistrusted me (Brian); one who I had fallen for (Janey); the other two, who I didn't really know but had met before (Pinstripe Robert and Slick Back Alonso). I was nervous in case my voice turned to jitters when I saw Janey again. I was nervous in case I had to tell Brian to knock off his inferiority complex. I was nervous because I had never managed or been a manager in my life. Freddy had briefed me on my duties, but nothing he said had made any sense owing to his numerous distractions:

'Nah, it's easy, this managing lark. I might be the gaffer 'ere in this neck of the corporate woods, but I just treat everyone like manhole covers and blisters. It's easy mate. Nah, I dunno much about this social media malarkey but just say to everyone to use it to promote *the* company. Ya know, making miracles materialise and all that shite. Nah, Gordon, onto better things. Howzabout that rand of golf on Monday, after your first day as da' boss? I need to get aht there and give some balls a walloping.'

It was all the guidance I got from Freddy. He gave me nothing that I could use and he kept calling me Gordon. It was pointless trying to tell him that my name was Mark and I wondered what had happened to the real Gordon. There was a picture of, who I assumed to be, Mrs Hardcastle on his desk and a picture of, perhaps, his daughter, but I couldn't see any of Gordon. I assumed the worst and convinced myself that Gordon must have died. I felt a sadness sweep through me, mixed with sympathy and respect every time he called me Gordon, so I allowed him to keep calling me it, even though it annoyed me.

I had arrived early to set up the conference room with a projector and refreshments. I wanted to get off to a good start and impress Janey. It was going to be hard for me to keep myself focused when she was in the room, looking at me and taking in my every word. I had just run through my presentation when Brian walked in the room, carrying a cup of coffee.

'Hello.' Brian spoke so soft that I struggled to hear him.

'Hi Brian. How's it going?'

'Good. Good.' Brian continued to whisper.

Brian took a seat and placed his coffee in front of him, taking sips in quick succession as if he was in a competition to find out how fast a boiling hot cup of coffee could be drunk. He tapped his foot fast under the table and kept his gaze averted from mine.

'How are things? We should go out for a beer, you know, like we used to every Friday.'

'I, er, can't drink beer. I'm on tablets.'

'Oh! I didn't know. Nothing serious I hope.'

Brian shook his head and said nothing. I had tried my best to break the ice. As much as he used to annoy me, I would have given anything for him to relax and call me a lamer again. Just once. Just to prove that the old Brian was still in there.

Brown Nose was the next person to enter the room, clutching a note pad with a salad for the health conscious balanced on top of it. She was wearing a power suit and sported a fair number of expensive looking rings on her fingers. It made a change from her rain jacket and huge handbag that she usually carted around with her. I wasn't sure if it was an effort to get into my good books or mark her territory within the team.

'Good morning,' I said.

'Morning.' Brown Nose spoke without looking at me.

Pinstripe and Slick Back entered the room next, chatting to each other as if they had travelled into work together. I overheard them exchange their profiles from the White & Heinsteiger questionnaire.

'What are you? I am a fox,' said Pinstripe.

Pinstripe raised his hands up like paws and stuck out his front teeth. I couldn't remember beaver being one of the White & Heinsteiger profiles.

'I am a dog. Woof! Woof!' replied Slick Back.

Slick Back rolled out his tongue and started to pant like a dog. It was amazing to me how the White and Heinsteiger profiling had turned people into animal mime artists. The fox and the hound sat down on opposite sides of the table, facing each other. I greeted them the same away as Brown Nose and Brian.

'Good morning,' I said

'Good morning,' they replied in unison.

Then, through the door, waltzed Janey. Nervous

tingles started to flutter around in my stomach, and I couldn't help but keep my focus fixed in her direction.

'G ... g ... good morning, Janey. How are you?'

I spluttered out the words in an attempt to untangle my nervous tongue.

'I'm great, thanks.'

Janey smiled in my direction. The others in the room had stopped talking and were looking at me, waiting for my first presentation as manager, but all I could do was linger my attention on Janey. I managed to snap out of my amorous trance and pressed a button on my Mac, revealing the first slide of my presentation.

'Well, first I would like to welcome you all here to the first meeting of the social media department. Our job is a simple one. We need to market *the* company on social media channels in the most effective way.'

I had placed the current logo of the company with the slogan *Making Miracles Materialise* on the next slide. It was really all I had and all I could show my team. Freddy had not given me any serious help on what I was supposed to talk about and, as way of getting out of the situation, I had decided the team could tell me their own ideas.

'What is the best way of getting our message across?' I asked.

I looked at Janey as much as possible.

'Blogs?' said Pinstripe.

'Well, I believe Google is the way forward, obviously,' said Brown Nose, trying to sound superior.

'Good. Good. Anyone else? Brian? You know a bit

about search engines don't you?' I asked.

'Erm. Yes. I do. Yes,' said Brian.

'Do you think that needs time devoted to it?'

'Erm. Yes. It does. Yes.'

Brian was still tapping his foot under the table but faster than before. I would have to have a word with him after the meeting.

'Facebook!'

Janey shouted her ex-employer's name with enthusiasm.

'Ha! Ha! I knew you would say that! Mmm! I should say here that Janey joins us from Facebook so if there is anybody that knows anything about social media, it's Janey!'

I swept my hand out in front of me until it pointed in a favourable way at Janey. Brown Nose turned to Janey and gave her a tiny uncomfortable smile. Pinstripe and Slick Back remained quiet. It was time to rattle their cages.

'Robert? Alonso? Any ideas?'

Pinstripe and Slick Back looked at each other across the table with neither of them wanting to be the first to speak.

'Erm. YouTube?' said Slick Back.

'You Tube? You mean, we should make a promotional video?' I asked.

'Yeah. Yeah. That's right!' said Pinstripe. 'A music video with our own company song, maybe even an anthem.'

The first image that popped into my head was of a

punk band singing a classic one-two punk song about the company, but I knew it was my own personal fantasy. If any type of song would be recorded for the company, it was going to be a sick overproduced commercial pop song with meaningless text. I was opposed to the suggestion.

'Yes, well, that could work, but it would involve a lot of man hours to pull it off and besides, I don't know if we have any songwriters working here.'

I had deflected Pinstripe's and Slick Back's suggestion. There wasn't going to be a promotional song on my watch. I would make sure of it. I shut down my Mac, panned the room, and looked at each member of my team until I got to Janey. She was smiling at me, which made me feel as if everybody in the room had stopped moving and had become cardboard cutouts. I was in love.

'Well. Thank you all for this meeting. What I want from you all is a developed plan of action of what we have talked about here, and we'll all meet up again and, probably, focus on what we believe the best idea is,' I said.

Everybody stood up and started shuffling towards the door.

'Oh, erm, Janey. If you could stay. I'd like five minutes.'

Brown Nose glanced back at me as she stepped out of the room and it made me wonder if she knew what was going on. I was under no illusion that if Brown Nose had even a hint of my favourtism towards Janey, she would report it to Anita Fox, but I didn't care. Janey was the reason for my shredded notice being recycled and turned back into blank paper again.

'As a new employee to the company, I just wanted to say welcome really. It's going to be good having an expert on my team.'

'Oh! Thanks.' Janey smiled.

'I have something to admit actually. I'm quite new here myself and becoming a manager is not something I'm used to so if you have any problems, just say them out loud and I'll help.'

'Ok!'

I noticed the outline of a tattoo on her left arm. I had spotted it before when she was being interviewed by Freddy. It was the emblem of one of my favourite bands. I couldn't believe it.

'Is that—I'm sorry, but isn't that a Dead Kennedy's logo on your arm?'

Janey looked down and raised the sleeve of her white top further up her arm, revealing the logo in all its entirety.

'Yep. It is. Well spotted. Are you into them?' she asked.

'God! Yeah! I love that band. I like Jello's solo stuff too, but not as much as the DKs!'

'Yeah. Same here. Do you like The Gun Club?'

That was it. As soon as the name of another of my favourite bands left Janey's lips, I was beside myself, open mouthed and stunned.

'Wow! Absolutely. You are probably the first, well,

are the first girl that I have ever met that knows who The Gun Club are let like them. This is amazing! Hold on, I have to show you this.'

I turned around and unravelled my shirt from my trousers, and pulled it up towards my shoulder blades, to reveal a large tattoo of Black Flag's *My War* album cover on my back.

'Cool! I like it. I'm not a huge fan of Rollins, but some of Black Flag's stuff is great.'

As Janey complimented me on my tattoo, Anita Fox walked past the meeting room and stopped dead in her tracks to look at what was going on. I rolled my shirt down as fast as I could but it was too late. She had judged me, made notes, and sent me to execution without a fair hearing.

'Are you ok?' Janey jumped backwards into her seat.

'No. No. I, er.' I turned around and brought my lips close to Janey's ear. 'You have to watch out for Anita Fox. She is one of the managers here. She used to be my manager and still is my manager to some extent. She just walked past—I'm gonna be in trouble.'

I tucked my shirt back into my trousers, adjusted myself, and started to scan my mind for a reason to ask Janey out.

'Listen. Did you know The Jealous Sound are playing here tomorrow? They're more indie rock but I like them.'

'Hmmm. Not sure I've heard of them.'

'They're good. Maybe we can check 'em out?'

'Yeah, sure.'

Fantastic! My first kinda date with Janey, and there was not even a mention of a boyfriend. The company that I had hated right from the start had now thrown me the best reason in the world to stay. I had been promoted to manager after five months, and so long as Freddy stayed at the helm, I was on the way up.

12.

'I saw Gallacchi fraternising with another member of staff, in plain sight of the yellow department, in the early hours of this morning, and I think this type of behaviour is abominable. Where will *the* company be if everybody started acting on their impulses? It would be nothing short of, excuse my language—an orgy!'

Anita, as per usual, was not holding back in her exaggeration of the tattoo incident in the meeting room. She was trying every trick in the book to undermine and tarnish my image. She waved her hands around and pointed at me when mentioning my deplorable behaviour within the company, hammering home the point that I should have been let go instead of promoted. Freddy rested his hands behind his head. He had not made eye contact with either of us during Anita's rant, and he seemed content to look at the flickering fluorescent light above his desk.

'Well? Don't you agree with me, Freddy?' asked Anita.

'Oh? Wot? Sorry. I was miles away there. I was finkin' that that bulb needs fixin' before I 'ave one of those eppy fits.'

Anita's mouth closed. She had wasted her breath ranting about how bad I was affecting the company's morale, and how every employee was going to get off with each other. I, however, had not said a word. I had not shaken Anita's hand. I had not said hello to her. I had not glanced in her direction. I had not even interrupted her. Instead, I had let her say whatever she wanted to say and be done with it, predicting Freddy would do nothing.

'Nah. Wot did you say? Somefink about an orgy? When did that 'appen and why wasn't I invited? Ha! Ha!'

I smiled as Freddy raised his eyebrows towards me, wiped his face clean of an expression and turned back to Anita again.

'Freddy. Please. Be serious. I caught Gallacchi fraternising. Fraternising.'

'Is that true? 'Ave ya' been fra'er-nizing?'

'No. That is not true at all,' I replied.

Anita let out a noise like a bicycle tyre being deflated with a nail.

'Anita. Let 'im explain. Go on, son.'

I breathed in, kept the breath in my lungs for a short moment, and then breathed out.

'I got into a conversation with Janey about her tattoo, and I was just showing her the one I have on my back.'

'You 'ave a tattoo? When did you get that done? You never told me abaht it.'

'I'm sorry?' I asked.

'I thought I 'ad always advised you not to get somefink like that done, Gordon. You're like ya old man. Impulsive, eh?'

My eyes widened. I gave out an uncomfortable cough and collected myself before speaking.

'I'm Mark Gallacchi, Freddy. Mark Gallacchi. I am not Gordon.'

'You're not ... Gordon? But ... you look like him ... Mark Gallacchi? Are you sure?'

Freddy seemed as lost as a tourist on the tube without a map. Anita looked as if she had been stunned into silence; her train of thought disrupted; her psyche disturbed by the fact that Freddy thought I was his dead son. Anita shook her head and continued.

'Yes. Freddy. This is Gallacchi, the person most responsible for bringing this company down, the person most responsible for wasting company time, the person most responsible ...'

'Yes. Yes. Awight! Awight! That's 'nuff. Mark Gallacchi. Ok. Well. Tattoos and all that. Yes. Well, it doesn't sound as if he was fra'er-nizing. You were just 'aving a giraffe with a fellow employee, eh? That's all it woz, eh? Nuffink Pete Tong in that, Foxy.'

'Anita please, Freddy. Call me Anita.' Anita's face seemed to lose its muscle strength and collapsed, making her mouth droop.

'Awight! Awight! Don't get all twitchy on me, Anita. I don't see wotz wrong to be 'onest. Isn't it natural to fra'er-nize with other employees? Was it a twist?'

'Erm? A twist?'

I had no idea what a twist was.

'Yeah, ya know—a twist—a member of the opposite persuasion like?' asked Freddy.

'Oh. Yes, it was,' I replied.

'Ha! Ha! Good man!'

'Now, Freddy. Please, can you at least see some sense here? Some reason?' said Anita, spitting out the words.

'I 'ave plenty of eighteen pence, Anita. Gordon 'ere, 'as been really proactive in shaping up this company. Not the other way rand. He brought it to my attention that the fish 'ook needed to be updated and it's great that you've brought up fra'er-nizing because that's one fing that needs to be rifled.'

'But ... but ... Freddy,' Anita started to sob.

''e also pointed aht that we 'ave too many centrals so I 'ave sent aht an email abaht that.'

Anita caught her head in her hands as it fell towards her lap. She understood what Freddy was talking about. Perhaps she had been working at the company for such a long time that she had learnt slang from the way he spoke. She had probably taken notes, studied them every night, and learnt them like a student.

'You've got to be kidding,' said Anita.

'Nah. Nah rum and coke, Anita. 'e also brought that new company logo to me attention too. Howz that going by the way?'

Anita shifted and fidgeted in her seat, coughed towards the floor, picked up her pen and put it down again. She hesitated as she started to answer Freddy's justified question.

'Well, er, well, you have to take into consideration that we had to start the project from scratch, draft in another design team, hold many meetings to discuss the direction ...'

'Yeah. Yeah. Yeah. But surely you must 'ave somefink. I see you 'ave your pooter there. Can't you show me somefink?'

I noticed Anita's hand start to tremble. It had been the first time that I had seen her flustered in any shape or form, and I would have felt sorry for her if she had been somebody else other than Anita Fox. I smiled and enjoyed watching her fumble open her laptop and skate her fingers over the keyboard.

'W ... well ... as I s ... s ... said, we haven't got very far because of time restraints and the new employees and the new designers and the idea meetings and—'

'Just show me, Anita. Just show me. Gissa butchers!'

Anita got up, placed her laptop on Freddy's desk, sat back down in her seat, and awaited his judgement. She started to move her mouth as if she was chewing an imaginary piece of chewing gum, squeezing her lips together and out again with gym exercise movements. Even her stress and panic seemed to be controlled and organised.

'Hmmm. Yes. Well. Hmmmm. You know wot, Anita? This ain't 'alf bad. Ain't 'alf bad at all.'

Anita stopped chewing and rose to attention, switching off the nerves like she could switch off a light.

'Yes. We have been working hard on this and this is the fruit of our labour, Freddy. We are pleased with it. We think it is contemporary, modern, and represents *the* company in all that it does. It will move us forward in the market and carry us forward to a new tomorrow.'

''ave the sub-directors had a butchers at this?'

Freddy rubbed his beard pensively.

'Yes they have.'

'Wot did they fink?'

'They liked it. Almost endorsed it straight away.'

'Ah!'

Freddy sat bolt upright and displayed a certain style of body language that suggested he knew more than she did.

'The sub-directors said that did they? Hmm.'

'They said they loved it.'

'They say a lot of fings. Maybe they do love it or endorse it, I dunno. All I know is that it ain't 'alf bad, Foxy, ain't 'alf bad.'

'Anita please. My name is Anita.'

I glanced across at Anita and saw a smug content face that didn't show any signs of the nerves that had affected her earlier. She was secure, confident, and full of herself.

'But we don't 'ave to wait for them,' said Freddy.

'We don't?' Anita's smug content face had vanished.

'Nah! Wadd'ya make of this logo?' asked Freddy, turning to me.

'I don't think we have to ask Gallacchi what he thinks. He has no jurisdiction when it comes to the new corporate logo. He hasn't been involved in the process of shaping it into what it has become. I don't think it is fair to ask him.'

Anita's nerves had returned to make her shift like a jumping bean in her seat. I was ecstatic. It was a chance to throw a spanner, maybe even a jackhammer, into her works and screw it up once and for all. Freddy spun her laptop round and revealed the logo. It was different to the last poor effort. The name of the company had been written in a thin, old style font with spacing in between the letters. The slogan *Making Miracles Materialise* had been encased in a rectangular box with triangular pointed ends with rivets. It was, as much as I hated to admit, as Freddy had remarked, "'alf bad". I now had a choice. I could either go against my hatred for Anita and be kind towards her, or be vindictive and take her down.

'Well?'

I looked up at Freddy and then across at Anita. She was squinting at me in the same way she usually did when she was displeased with my behaviour. The memories of all of our awful meetings started to flash by where every snide comment she had made had stuck in my brain and bruised my ego. She had tried to make me redundant every chance she got, and had never complimented me on any of my positive work for the company.

'I'm not so sure, Freddy,' I said.

'Oh?'

'The corporate blue is missing. I'm not really sure

about the font. It looks too old for my liking.'

'For your liking, Gallacchi. My team chose that font after much deliberation and we feel it reflects *the* company. I think you are outvoted when it comes to giving any kind of criticism on the choice of font,' said Anita.

'Woah! Woah! Woah! Let 'im 'ave 'is say, Anita. All opinion ma"ers,' said Freddy, cutting Anita's rant short.

'Yes. Well. I think the font doesn't look modern enough. The slogan underneath looks as if it is in prison in some way. I'm not sure about the box with the pointed ends. In fact, I'm not sure about the whole logo if I'm quite honest. Is it really a logo? It looks as if someone has just typed the name of the company to me.'

Freddy swung Anita's laptop back in his direction and started to rub his beard again.

'Hmmm. You 'ave a point, Gordon. Maybe this does need some more work.'

'Freddy. Just a minute ago, you said that it was good.' Anita was desperate and clutching at straws to save her logo.

'I said it ain't 'alf bad. That means it ain't 'alf good as well. Get your team to design a few logos and see 'ow that goes. I need to show the CEO soon and I can tell ya that 'e ain't too 'appy.'

Anita shut the screen on her laptop, picked it up off Freddy's desk, turned around, and stared at me longer than she had to. I wasn't sure but I thought I saw a tear welling up in her left eye. If it was a tear, it was the reason for the guilt I felt for ripping into her logo project, not once but twice, on purpose. I shouldn't have had any feelings other than hatred towards her, but right now, I felt sorry for Anita.

'I fink this central is finished nah unless eiver of ya 'ave somefink else to natter abaht.'

I shook my head and ignored Anita's response. I remained seated until Anita had got up and walked out of the room. I didn't want to have any uncomfortable contact with her, or feel even worse about what I had just done to her. As I stood up to leave, Freddy called me back.

'Gordon! Are we still on for golf this evening, after Captain Kirk?' asked Freddy.

I had forgotten about the round of golf, but I couldn't renege on my promise to go. I felt awkward about playing golf with a man who mistook me for his dead son, but a promise was a promise. I would have to go and make it the last outing I ever went on with Freddy Hardcastle.

'Yep. Sure. Fiveish?' I replied.

'Yeah. Yeah. That sands great, me ol' china. Meet me in the Noah's Ark dahnstairs and we'll drive aht to Droughton. Just the nine hole par frees, then we'll 'ave a couple of sniftahs in the club'ouse.'

I went back to my office, closed the door, and worried about the upcoming car ride with Freddy for the rest of the afternoon.

BEEP! BEEP!

The rush hour traffic had filled up the motorway and turned it into the longest stretched car park in London. Freddy slammed his fist on the horn every minute, hoping that the noise would remove the cars in front. We were stuck in traffic for thirty minutes, choking on exhaust fumes. When we arrived at the golf course, we only had an hour to get round the nine-hole par three course, which annoyed Freddy to the core.

'Bleedin' traffic. Nah we 'ave to rush and I don't like rushin'.'

I grabbed Gordon's clubs from the boot of Freddy's silver executive car, slung them over my shoulder, bought our green fees from the clubhouse, and walked towards hole one. I looked at my scorecard whilst Freddy picked out a club, tee and ball, and prepared himself for his first shot.

'This is the shit, me ol' china. It's almost as good as fishin' but not really.' Freddy licked his finger and held it aloft. 'Bit bloody windy today. Jesus!'

I realised that I didn't have a pencil or pen to mark down my score, and a frisk of my trousers and jacket revealed that I was pen and pencil free.

'Can I borrow your pencil?' I asked.

''Ave a butcher's in the bag. I'm sure there should be one in there,' replied Freddy.

I unzipped the pocket on my golf club's bag and found a stash of pencils, some old range balls and numerous old score cards. As I grabbed a pencil, a scorecard fell out of the bag and blew towards Freddy who stopped a practice swing, and trapped the card under his foot. He knelt down and started to read it.

'Ah yeah! Remember this, Gordon? You were on fire this day. Ya went rand in thirty-four. Thirty-four! You've never beaten it since.'

I felt really uncomfortable being a permanent Gordon. It was time to set the record straight once and for all before it all got out of hand.

'I'm Mark Gallacchi, Freddy. Mark Gallacchi. I am not your son Gordon Hardcastle. I am Mark Gallacchi. You have met my dad the architect. He is my dad. You are not my dad. I am not Gordon. I am Mark Gallacchi.'

'Oh.'

Freddy turned away to look at the scorecard he held in his hand.

'You're not Gordon? But it says Gordon on the card ... 'ere, in Gordon's 'andwriting.'

'That's an old scorecard, Freddy. I'm not Gordon. I'm Mark.'

'Mark?' asked Freddy confused.

Freddy turned away, clasping the scorecard in his hand as if it was the only memento he had of Gordon. He started to stroke the edges and caress the card Gordon's handwriting had blessed as the wind blew fierce over the first tee. I walked away from Gordon's clubs and approached Freddy who seemed lost.

'I'm sorry for your loss, Freddy, I truly am, but I am not your son Gordon.'

'Loss?' asked Freddy.

'Yes. I mean, I am sorry about Gordon, but I'm not him.'

'Loss? Gordon's not brown bread, mate. Nah!'

Brown bread? I knew what that meant. The shock of Freddy's son still being alive had not been something I had even considered. I had convinced myself that he was dead. If he was alive, why on Earth did Freddy keep mistaking me for him?

'He fuckin' divorced us and fucked off abroad somewhere. Dubai, I fink. Somefink abaht sand. 'aven't 'eard from 'im in donkey's. Fuckin' bastard.'

Freddy grabbed his 3 iron off the ground, lined the club head up with the ball, and lashed at it with some venom. Freddy's swing sliced the ball off to the left of the fairway, where it hit a tree and ricocheted into a patch of rough grass. I stood and watched Freddy in shock. How and why did Gordon divorce his parents? I didn't even know that it was possible to do so. It was something that shouldn't have been allowed to happen regardless of how someone felt about their parents. Gordon must have been an ungrateful unappreciative selfish idiot to cut his nearest and dearest out of his life forever. It was beyond my understanding.

'Fuckin' buggery shitfucks!' The sound of Freddy's swearwords seemed to bounce off the trees.

Freddy stamped his foot on the tee and shoved his club into his bag with force. I didn't know what to say. I felt as if I had put my foot in it, and Freddy was going to see me as just another employee of the company from now on, an employee that could be sacked, fired, laid off, let go by his own fair hand. I was no longer Gordon but Mark Gallacchi. After selecting a 9 iron,

Freddy picked up his bag and turned to me.

'Well, that was a bleedin' bad start. Did you see where that fuckin' fing landed?' asked Freddy.

'It hit that tree over there and bounced into the long grass beside it. To the right,' I replied.

'Shit! Well, ok. Go on take your shot. I'll 'ave to dig mine aht with this niner or a wedgy.'

Freddy seemed to be angrier over his first shot landing in part of the forest than anything else. I was scared to ask any further questions about Gordon, and I decided to be mute for the rest of the golf round. I shuffled the driver and woods with their soft toy lion head covers to one side and drew out a 7 iron out of my bag. The hole was close to 200 yards and I knew that the ball wouldn't reach the green no matter how accurate I hit it. The 7 iron was the club I felt most comfortable using. My dad had taught me it was the best to practice with.

'Ya don't wanna use that son. Use a 3 iron. That'll get ya there.'

I smiled at Freddy, walked over to the tee, and took a practice swing to warm up. I stuck with the 7 iron regardless and ignored Freddy's advice. When I was ready, I lined myself up with my ball and swung a perfect swing, which connected with the ball, sending it right down the middle of the fairway. The ball landed and rolled forwards, coming to a standstill approximately 80 yards from the hole.

'Nice shot. Nice shot. Ya still should 'ave used a free iron. You'd be on the green nah! Maybe even could have got an 'ole in one! Cam' on! Let's go and dig me ball aht!'

Freddy's mood had improved since he took his first disastrous shot. It was as if nothing had happened, as if Gordon had not even been mentioned in conversation. I felt relieved that Freddy still wanted to play the remaining holes. It gave me a sense of security that he was still on my side. Freddy combed the rough grass with his 9 iron and found his ball stuck solid in a damp patch of mud.

'Ah fuck's sake! I need a trowel not a club. Look at that. Just look at that. Jeeeee-suss!'

Freddy replaced his 9 iron with a sand wedge and lined up to whack his ball back onto the fairway.

THWACK!

A large chunk of mud the size of a carton of butter flew onto the fairway with sprinkles of muddy water and Freddy's ball.

'Well. That's the best I could have done.'

Freddy fetched the chunk of mud and banged it back into the corresponding hole left by his wedge's plough mark. The rest of the round went without the mention of Gordon, but it also went without the mention of my name as well. Instead, Freddy had given up on names and called me son instead, which he had done before but more infrequently. Throughout the round, and up until the final putt on the ninth hole, I wondered and thought about Gordon, who he was, where he was, what he looked like and what he had done. Freddy was detached from the real world, but he wasn't a bad person; not bad enough to divorce by any stretch of the imagination. As I sunk my putt to score a respectable score of forty-two, Freddy plopped the flag back in the hole and looked at me.

'Well played, Gordon. Forty-two. Ya' almost beat your record!' said Freddy.

I couldn't believe it.

13.

'Phew! It's really warm in here,' says Lisa. She leaves the table to fetch two glasses of water.

Lisa hands me my glass of water and I drink almost half of it by the time she sits down in her seat again. Lisa checks her mobile and starts to read some messages.

'Oh. It seems the sub-directors will also book a conference meeting with you and the chairman for tomorrow. The chairman has been held up in traffic and won't make it into the city at a reasonable hour.'

The subs? What did they want? Why did they want a conference meeting with the chairman and myself? What has happened? I have been so engulfed in my book that I have lost track of the general running of *the* company. If they want a meeting, I am sure that it is due to their usual over-exaggerated panic over the dipping share prices. I still have concerns over the chairman's appearance at *the* company's headquarters. His visits are a rare occurrence and I know it has to be more serious than just a chat about the share prices.

'What time do you want to meet with them?' asks Lisa.

'Oh. Erm. Maybe the afternoon. That way, we'll have the morning to keep working on this. Make it one o'clock, no, scratch that, three o'clock,' I reply.

'Ok. I'll write back and suggest three.'

Lisa wipes and swipes her mobile screen. I am glad that the bad traffic delayed the chairman's meeting. It is essential to crack on with the book and get it finished. Time is of the essence.

The day after the round of golf with Freddy came my date with Janey to see The Jealous Sound at The Dublin Castle. They had been on stage for close to two hours and had played every song they had ever recorded. When they came back for an encore to play songs they had already played, we decided to hunt the venue's grounds for an unhealthy late night snack.

'That was amazing.' Janey squirted tomato ketchup on her chips. 'I'm not usually into that sorta music but they've got something.'

'Told you you would like it. Trust me! I'm a manager!'

I smiled and Janey beamed a smile back that, to me, signified the start of something special. The biggest compliment that I could pay any girl was stuck in the back of my mind. What if I had misunderstood all the looks that she had given me or she had misunderstood all of the looks I had given her? What if everything was just a big misunderstanding? I gulped and decided to say it.

'I, erm ...' I said, stuttering.

Janey put her plastic fork, which had a large chip

speared on the end of it, down in the polystyrene tray and listened.

'I thought I had seen every beautiful girl in this city until I saw you.'

There. I had said it. Janey gulped, turned her head to the side and back again, not knowing where to look until she made eye contact again. I thought I had put my foot in it, doomed to be rejected by the one girl I knew was *the* one.

'That's, uh hmm,' Janey seemed to almost choke on her words, 'that's the single most nicest thing anybody has ever said to me.'

Janey moved in closer, still holding her tray of chips in one hand, and gave me a kiss on the lips that tasted of a combination of tomato ketchup and chip fat. But the taste didn't bother me in the slightest. Invisible waves shivered up my back, causing a sensation that I can only describe as electric. Janey had plugged me into the national grid and it was a feeling that I had not felt before. She was *the* one.

After we had tossed our empty polystyrene meal trays into a bin, random kisses and embraces hampered our journey home to Janey's flat. Each contact was as electric as the first kiss. When we reached Janey's flat, which was situated on a side street in the city centre, we couldn't keep our hands off each other as Janey fumbled around in her pocket for her keys. If the first kiss had been electric, the night's passion intensified the currents of electricity between us until our fuses blew and caused a short circuit.

When I awoke the following morning, I lifted Janey's arm from my chest and went to the toilet. Her flat, that I hadn't paid any attention to when I entered, was how I expected it to look. Gig posters of punk bands adorned the walls. An immense collection of vinyl records had been stacked into a square bookcase, creating a pattern of colourful vertical lines. Plastic figures of various cartoon characters, some of which I didn't recognise, stood on almost every window sill, posing in different action positions. I walked towards the toilet. Cult movie posters, most of which were horror, had been pinned or blu-tacked up in the hallway. When I returned to the bedroom, Janey threw back the covers and invited me back to bed.

'Come on. We don't have to go to work yet, surely? What time is it?' asked Janey.

'8:15 according to your clock,' I replied.

'Shit! But we can turn up whenever we want, yeah? You're the boss after all. Come on! Come back to bed.'

'Yeah, well, I might be the manager but I'm still watched. All of us are watched— including me.'

Janey bit her bottom lip and breathed out a dejected sigh. I wanted to stay in bed with Janey, but my mind was nagging me to go to work. Now that I was a manager, I felt more responsible, more appreciated, and more important to *the* company. Janey had been the reason I had decided to stay at *the* company, but now we had got together, I realised that *the* company needed me. I was a manager and I had to start managing.

'We're going to have to keep—you know—us

under wraps for now. I think *the* company frowns on relationships between employees.'

'Oh! We're an "us" now are we? What makes you think I'll stay with you, eh?' said Janey.

'Well, I just figured after, you know—everything that happened, you know, erm ... Well ...'

I squirmed and shifted my feet. Janey raised her head from the pillow, rubbed her forehead, groaned, got out of bed, and crawled into the bathroom without saying anything. She didn't need to say anything. Her bright smile said it all. It said we were an "us". After Janey had finished in the bathroom, I took a quick shower, combed my quiff flat, left my beard the way it was, and we left for work hand in hand.

As we approached *the* company building, our hands separated just in case we happened to bump into other employees making their way into work. If we were seen together, our relationship would be turned into a Chinese whisper; a vicious rumour that would keep shape shifting and morph into something far worse than it was. I imagined all the possible scenarios: Janey sleeps with the boss to get herself promoted; Mark is sleeping with Janey. What a sleazy creep!; Mark has slept with Janey and Anne and now has eyes for Helen. There were rumours in circulation about every single boss or manager and none of them seemed to have any evidence supporting them.

The morning was cold and my frosty breath bellowed out of my mouth, forming a smoky cloud.

I gripped Janey's hand tight, and we couldn't stop talking about punk bands and the previous evening's gig. As we continued our journey towards the company headquarters, out of the corner of my eye, I noticed a figure dressed in a smart suit walking down a side street.

'That was the CEO.'

I couldn't control my surprise and sounding as if I had been star struck.

'Where?' asked Janey.

'He just went down that side street. Come on! Let's see where he went.'

'I don't think that is a good ...'

I rushed ahead of Janey and out of earshot of the end of her sentence, trying to hang onto the slipstream left behind by the CEO's dash down the alleyway. As I peeked around the corner, the CEO was standing by a large silver door, looking into a panel fixed to the frame.

'What are you doing, Mark?' asked Janey.

Janey was out of breath from the mad dash and pulled my arm in an attempt to stop me from advancing any further.

'It's the CEO. Look. He's standing by another lift. It must go to the eighth floor. I'm sure of it.'

'And?' said Janey.

'Whenever I have asked anybody at the company about the eighth floor, nobody seems to want to talk about it.'

'And?'

'And? Aren't you a little curious about knowing what is on the eighth floor?'

'Erm. No.'

'No? Well, I am. Have you ever wondered why the lift we use doesn't have a button for the eighth floor?'

'No. I haven't. I think we should just get into the building the usual way,' said Janey, and pulled my arm.

I freed my arm from Janey's pulls. Not even Janey was going to dampen my curiosity.

'Aren't you even curious? Not even the slightest bit? Come on, he's gone in now. We've got five minutes. Let's check it out.'

I dashed down the alleyway. Janey followed at half my speed and reached the door after me. A digital keypad with a video screen had been the device the CEO had looked into to open the door.

'What are we doing here, Mark? We should just go ...'

'This must be some kind of face recognition system thing.'

I pressed my face onto the screen and hoped it would open the door. As I continued to look into the screen, the lift whirred into action and started to head towards us at a fair velocity.

'Quick! Stand here. We'll go in when the person leaves.'

'MARK! This is not a good idea ...'

I grabbed Janey's arm and pulled her to the side of the lift door into a small alcove.

'Don't worry. Just stick with me here.'

The lift door opened and the CEO dashed out, neither looking to the left or the right but dead ahead, unaware that we were there. As the lift doors began to shut, I tugged at Janey's arm and dragged her into the lift, just before the doors shut. I felt like a movie hero that had just dived under a shutting barrier to avoid being trapped. Janey, on the other hand, looked as if a madman who liked confined spaces had kidnapped her.

The interior of the lift had been decorated with mirrors on every wall, the floor, and the ceiling. I couldn't escape looking at a reflection of myself and Janey regardless of where I cast my eyes. Four spotlights had been fitted in the corners of the lift that changed colour at random, from red to blue to green to yellow. If this had been a disco, it would have won an award for being the worst lit. There weren't any buttons to press. As far as I could see, there weren't any buttons at all. Not even a small button marked with an eight.

'Can you see a button?'

'No. Nope. I can't.'

We continued to look for a way to escape from the clutches of the lift, or find a way to the eighth floor, when a loud robotic monotonous voice started to drone. The coloured lamps ceased to shine and were replaced by blinding white lights that illuminated our guilty faces.

'Attention employee 79503 and employee 97835. You have gained access to a prohibited area of *the* company. You do not have permission to travel to the eighth floor of *the* company.'

'What the hell is this?' asked Janey.

'Hell is not a word used by *the* company and is against *the* company rules to do so. Any further use of this expletive will be subject to disciplinary action. This episode has been duly noted and will be logged for further investigation.'

The voice came to an abrupt halt. The lights went out. The doors opened. We were free. We left the lift as fast as we could and without saying a word to each other. We heard the lift doors shut behind us as we ran towards the main street and towards the main entrance. We entered the company building through the proper doors, stood by the normal lifts, and caught our breath.

'What just ...' Janey gasped, '... happened?'

'I ... have no ... no idea,' I replied, catching my breath.

'Disciplinary action? Was ... it serious?'

'I dunno ... I dunno. Let's not ... talk about it.'

The lift doors opened and we hesitated by looking at each other before we climbed aboard, wondering if we were about to be swallowed by technology again. As we boarded the lift, and the doors shut, I noticed Janey was not smiling.

'What did I say? I told you it was a bad idea. Now I'm facing disciplinary action.'

'It was a lift. It can't discipline. It was just trying to scare us,' I said.

'Trying?'

We were arguing like a married couple, and we had only been together for less than twenty-four hours. Janey turned her face away, not able to look at me or speak to me. The lift doors opened for our floor.

'Janey. I'm sorry. I ...'

Janey walked off in the direction of her desk and had left me for dust before I could apologise. It was the worst possible start to a day when I compared it to best possible night I had had. I never intended to get Janey into trouble.

14.

After a week had gone by, Janey and I had patched things up. We hadn't heard anything about the lift incident. We assumed the robot's threats had just been smoke and mirrors. I was spending so much time in her apartment that I had moved in. We had managed to keep our relationship a secret to those we worked with, but rumours were beginning to circulate about us. When anybody asked me direct about being together, I denied it, hoping that I could deflect the suspicion. But the rumours of our relationship didn't scare me as much as some other happenings within *the* company. The thing that I feared the most had reared its ugly head and ambushed me as I stood in the social media department meeting follow-up.

'We've been busy actually,' said Pinstripe, pointing at Slick Back. 'We took the initiative and wrote a song for the company that we'd like to play now and see what you think.'

There was nothing I could do. I couldn't think up an excuse for them not to play it. Janey's eyes bulged out of their sockets as she looked in my direction, dreading the sonic diarrhea that was about to forced into our ears.

'We play a little bit, you see, and we have friend who owns a studio, so we thought - Hey! Come on! Why not use these resources?' said Slick Back.

When the first few bars started to play, I knew the rest of the song. The fake beat of the drum machine, the horrible squeal of the happy synths, the soulless but brilliant polished guitar solo, the "yeahs" of the teen idol vocals, and over enthusiastic backing vocals, were all going to add up to make a song I was going to hate.

Verse 1
You're in control, you hold the keys
To your boat of life sailing successful seas
Climb aboard and on the waves you ride
Towards your goals with us as your guide

Pinstripe sang along to the song and played air guitar to the tacky guitar licks after each line. Slick Back was tapping his foot on the floor and using two pens to play drums on a couple of upturned plastic coffee cups. Janey sat motionless and embarrassed, not knowing where to look. Brown Nose clapped in time to the music, seeming as if she loved every line, every note, and every beat the speakers hurled at her ears. Brian showed no emotion at all and sat like a statue in his seat. I didn't know whether he liked what he heard or not. Just when I thought the song couldn't have got any worse - it did.

Chorus
Open your eyes!
We Make Miracles Materialise!
Open your eyes!
We Make Miracles Materialise!

I sat down in my seat at the end of the table and locked my hands together, forming a place to rest my chin.

Verse 2
You can live the life of your wildest fantasy
Everything is possible with The Company
You want to win and you want success
The Company grants your wishes - YES!... YES!... YES!

I started to see a vision of the tacky video that would accompany the song. There were beautiful smiling people with perfect teeth superimposed over the top of clouds with fifty-pound notes dropping from the sky. Exotic locations featuring people sleeping on hammocks with cocktails in their hands. A man driving a sports car. A woman standing outside a large house. Children running through meadows and playing sports. It all made my stomach turn.

Chorus
Open your eyes!

We Make Miracles Materialise!
Open your eyes!
We Make Miracles Materialise!

Bridge
You'll never see a future so bright
So join The Company and hang on tight - YEAH!

By the time it got to the bridge, I had switched off, and I let the dirge of the song filter through one ear and out of the other. The song faded out after five plus minutes. Brown Nose clapped straight away and stood up from her seat as if she had seen the song played live on stage and wanted an encore. Brian, with reluctance, gave a soft clap as if he was unsure of what to do or who to agree with. Janey breathed out a sigh of relief and swallowed down some water to aid her recovery.

'Well done. Well done. I think it's brilliant. It says everything about the company, what we do, what we do for our customers. Everything. Well done,' said Brown Nose, and clapped with exaggerated enthusiasm.

Pinstripe and Slick Back bowed and sucked in the praise, making the most of their work colleague's admiration before they turned their attention to me. If I had been honest, I would have said the song was the biggest heap of shit known to man. But I was now the manager of a department and, therefore, diplomacy was needed.

'It's nice guys, and I applaud your initiative, but I think we really need to see or hear other ideas before we venture down the road of creating a company anthem,' I said.

Pinstripe and Slick Back nodded towards me, unoffended by my polite way of dashing their efforts.

'We'll get back to the song later but first, I want to hear from all of you what ideas you have or what you have been doing. Brian. You were going to look into the corporate and intranet website plus search engine optimisation.'

Brian turned his head in my direction, but kept his eyes static and focused on the wall in front of him, as if they had been made out of glass and superglued in place. When his eyes did connect with mine, I was met with a faraway gaze that made me wonder if he had heard my question or was capable of answering it.

'Yes. I have looked into the website, intranet, and SEO, and everything is going well,' said Brian.

'What have you been doing? Can you elaborate?' I asked.

'I have compiled a list of companies that build websites, intranets, and provide SEO,' replied Brian.

'So, you don't have anything to show us?' I asked.

Brian fidgeted in his seat, sliding his buttocks left and right as if he had soiled his underpants. If he had done some research, I was fine with it. What I didn't like was his nervous and timid attitude towards me.

'We can talk about it after the meeting,' I said to Brian, 'Ok. Anne?'

I made the amount of words I exchanged with Anne as short as possible. I couldn't help but treat her with the same disdain as Anita.

'I have set up Google alerts and Google analytics to gain information and insight into *the* company's performance in the market. I am monitoring all modes of communication for any positive and negative feedback on *the* company's products and services, and will provide a weekly report on my findings. To change the subject, I must say that I can't get that brilliant song out of my head: "*Open your eyes! We Make Miracles Materialise! Open your eyes! We Make Miracles Materialise!*"'

Janey glanced with contempt in Brown Nose's direction. I coughed and moved the focus of the meeting to Janey.

'And Janey. I know you have been busy building up various different profiles on social media sites but mostly focusing on Facebook.'

'Yes. I have created a page for the company, which is moderated to edit out any negative comments, and sent out invitations to every person who has "liked" us about events - where they can come into contact with the company's products and services. The page will be updated every day so we can keep our reach levels high.'

'Great.' I took a slight pause before turning away from Janey's pretty face. 'It sounds as if things are moving along nicely on this front. Maybe we should have a team evening out somewhere. Bowling or go-karting or something similar as we are all doing so well.'

'That sounds nice but not everyone likes bowling or go-karting. Maybe a nice dinner would suffice more than ... **B**owling or ... **G**o-karting.'

Brown Nose spat my suggestions back as if bowling or go-karting were beneath her.

'Well, I guess we can all come up with suggestions and I'll arrange something. The next meeting will be in a week's time,' I said.

'What about our song? Should we work on that?' asked Pinstripe.

'I would leave that for the minute and concentrate on, maybe, making short films to upload to YouTube.'

I tried to suppress the song as much as possible otherwise I knew I would hear it twenty times a day if it became official. At meetings. At conferences. At work. Maybe in the toilet. It would drive me insane.

'It's just that we sent the song to Freddy, and he was more than pleased with it,' said Slick Back.

'He was?' I asked.

I was in shock. They had already started to leak the song and now it would start to spread like a virus.

'Yes. He said we should develop it and see where it goes,' said Slick Back.

'Ah-ha! Ok. Well. I ...'

I looked at Janey for support, but there was nothing she could say or do. If Freddy liked the song, I would have to change his mind in the same way I had done with the logo. The song would have to be sent to the permanent recycle bin, and the sooner, the better.

'Well. I ... guess, that's great, then. So long as Freddy is onboard. Are you sure he was onboard with it?'

'He did say that it had been the best thing he had heard since—since—what did he say, Alonso?' asked

Pinstripe.

'I think he said Crammed Seat or something. I'm not sure what he said.'

'Well, anyway, he did say it was the best thing he had heard for ages.'

The best thing Freddy had heard since Canned Heat? They must have played a different song for Freddy to say something against his favourite band. A song so different that it sounded like prog rock and lasted fifty minutes instead of five.

'Oh! Ok. Well. I'll have a word with Freddy and see what he wants to do with it. That's it for this meeting!'

Slick Back and Pinstripe stood up, unhooked their computer from the sound system, and walked towards the door with bounces in their steps, singing the chorus of their awful song. Brown Nose also joined in with them, adding a disjointed harmony that was going to offend any ear in the vicinity. Janey looked over her shoulder at me and raised her eyebrows. She walked out of the room with slow strides to create some distance between her and the psycho choir.

'Oh. Brian. Can you stay behind? I need to have a word with you.'

I smiled at Janey as she disappeared from sight. Brian remained in his seat with the same fixed gaze he had when he first walked into the room. I pulled up a seat next to him and sat down. He didn't budge an inch and refused to look me in the eye.

'Brian. I just wanted to ask you about your attitude towards me.'

'My attitude?' asked Brian.

'Yes. Your attitude. I'm not going to bite you if you want to say what you want to say. You used to say whatever you wanted to me in the past. You even insulted me, and you know what? I didn't care. Sure, I was irritated sometimes, but you are who you are. You are Brian. Could you bring some of you to the next meeting? Is that possible? As I said, I won't bite you.'

Brian wiped away the sweat from his forehead with his shaky arm and hand. He tilted his head towards the floor and squirmed. To my surprise, he raised himself from his chair, pushed it to one side, got down on his knees in front of me, and started to kneel, worshipping the hard carpet floor tiles my feet were on. Tears started to flood out of his eyes like a man condemned to death who was begging for mercy. I looked over the top of his balding head and checked if anybody outside was watching his performance only to find nobody was. I had not seen anything like it. I had not seen anyone react in this way before, and I didn't know what to do. I needed somebody to open the door, walk in, pull Brian away, and send him to White & Heinsteiger. Where was the passing Anita Fox when I needed her?

'PPPPPP ... lease don't lay me off. Pleeaaaaaase. I can't afford to lose my job. I can't. My partner has just been laid off. We'll lose everything if I lose my job too. Pleeeasse. Ppppp ... lease don't make me redundant.'

Brian started to sob and attached his hands to my trouser legs. I didn't know where to look. I hadn't done anything to cause this reaction in him.

'Yyy..ou know all those things I said about the company in the past? I just meant that as a joke. I didn't mean any of it. I like working here ... Ppppp ... lease don't lay me off.'

'I've said it before. I am not going to lay you off. Do you understand? I am NOT going to lay you off. I just want you to be you. You have the right to have an opinion. You don't have to agree with me all the time. Just be Brian. I'm making that an order.'

Brian let go of my trouser legs, balanced on one knee, and pushed himself up off the floor. He tried to conceal his red raw eyes by looking down at the floor whilst collecting his jacket off the back of his chair. He left the room without saying a word and moved fast through the door, which attracted the attention of the employees he passed. I picked up my pad from the table, walked through the door, and shut it behind me. I ignored the accusing glances of the employees who I presumed were spreading rumours about what they thought had just unfolded.

When I returned to my office, I could see a bright neutral white light shining, lighting up the whole of my team's desks like a football pitch under floodlights. I held my hand over my left eye and squeezed my right eye shut as I approached the maintenance man on a stepladder who was installing the overpowering fluorescent tubes in the ceiling. He was wearing a pair of heavy-duty shaded visors.

'What are you doing?' I asked.

I looked at the hazy outline of the man through the gaps in my fingers.

'I'm, erm, installing lights,' replied the maintenance man.

'I can see that. They are a bit bright. Whose idea was this? And why are you doing it?'

'I just got told to do it. It's a company rule that every department must have a colour and seen as your department is new, this is your colour.'

I glanced up at the ceiling and got the same punishment I got when I looked into the sun for the first time. I winced, shook my head, looked down at the floor, and watched fuzzy white dots spin and dance their way across the dark carpet. I shut my eyes to relieve my temporary blindness, but I could still see dots as I moved my eyes around in their sockets. The maintenance man continued to twist his screwdriver.

'This is not a colour. This is just a really bright light.'

I shut my eyes to protect them. It worked better than squinting through the gaps in my fingers.

'Nope. This is white,' said the man.

'White? Are you kidding?' I said, raising my voice.

'Nope. All the other colours have been taken by other departments. You are the white department.'

'You have got to be fuckin' kidding me.'

My anger was getting the better of me, and I couldn't hold back from swearing. *The* company must have been playing a very cruel joke on me to expect my department to work under stupid-watt bulbs that were this bright. We would have to wear the same goggles the maintenance man was wearing every day to be able to work. We'd get suntans or, even worse, cancer.

'Ah! Gallacchi. I'm glad I caught you. Do you like the lights? I picked them myself.'

Anita Fox. Even temporary blindness couldn't make me mistake that horrible putrid voice. Now I understood. The floodlights were her idea. Of course they were. Who else could have been evil enough to punish a department like this? Who else hated me as much as she did?

'I thought seen as your department was the latest addition to the company's family, and the most modern department handling the new phenomenon of social media, I thought a bright white would suit you. The department that's leading us into a brighter future. I can see that you agree with me.'

I couldn't see at all. I opened my eyes and tried to look at Anita, but the fading fuzzy dots were obscuring my view of her. When the sunspots had faded enough for me to see Anita's face, I could only make out her fake pretentious smile.

'That's decent of you but I think they are a touch too bright,' I said, in a calm manner.

The corners of Anita's mouth loosened and slipped down the sides of her face towards her neck. She expected me to put up a fight, lose my temper, and spit my teeth at her, but I wasn't going to give her the satisfaction.

'The lights are fine. They are representative of your department. You should be thanking me rather than criticising,' said Anita. She sounded frustrated.

I was never going to thank Anita for anything. I squinted at the maintenance man who had stopped screwing the light into the ceiling to eavesdrop. He shrugged his shoulders and continued on with his work as if the decision to install the lights was not going to be overturned. I turned my face away from the lights, rubbed the bridge of my nose, and looked at the ground, catching sight of Anita's tapping impatient foot, waiting for a thank you.

'Well, they'll take some getting used to,' I said.

I wasn't going to suck up to Anita. No chance. Anita stopped tapping her foot, sucked her teeth, and walked away without saying a word. The maintenance man stopped fiddling with the light, looked down at me from his stepladder, and spoke.

'I feel sorry for you,' said the maintenance man with a nod.

If my department were to avoid bad headaches and migraines, the lights would have to be replaced.

15.

'I'm really going to have to go home,' says Lisa, after checking her watch.

I am disappointed that Lisa has to leave. I have more to tell her about my ladder climb to the top of *the* company, and about the marvelous company that changes peoples lives in a user-friendly and ethical way. I need to convince Lisa to stay, but she is packing her laptop into her bag.

'When can you start tomorrow? There's more to tell you. It shouldn't take us too long to get it finished.'

Lisa looks at me and shrugs her shoulders.

'9?'

9? That is too late for my liking. I won't be able to fit in everything before my mysterious meeting with the subs and chairman. There is more to tell, and I need as much time as I can get.

'Can you make it at 7?'

Raised eyebrows. A lack of speech. A frozen body. Wide eyes. Was 7 really that unreasonable? I get up at 5 to be in the office by 6. *The* company doesn't run itself and without me to do the job, it wouldn't run at all. The public, the subs, the employees, in fact, everyone would suffer if *the* company was ever to lose the keen managerial staff that sacrificed their time. Lisa's eyebrows have returned to their original place, and she looks ready to leave the table.

'8 would be the earliest. I can do 8.'

I would lose an hour of valuable time, but I could tell it was going to be pointless arguing with her. Would she still get *employee of the year?* Probably. I sighed. Despite her unwillingness to meet me at 7, she is still worthy of receiving the award. Lisa lifts her bag onto her shoulder and stands up.

'Shall we talk about Operation Gambit tomorrow?' asks Lisa.

'Operation Gambit? Yes. Yes. I was coming to that anyway.'

Lisa leaves the restaurant and I settle the bill. The time is 9 p.m., a late finish to my working day. I leave for home and can't wait to recharge my batteries for another full working day.

The alarm goes off. It is half past six. I awake with a jolt and fumble my mobile silent. I am worried that Janey has been awoken by the ringtone, but I am thankful that she is fast asleep and, in fact, snoring. I drag the duvet to the side and get up. I perform my usual ritual of fifty sit-ups, fifty push-ups, and a thirty-minute run on the treadmill. I take a quick shower afterwards. I choose a double-breasted suit, blue shirt, and a grey tie with red stripes from my wardrobe. I walk into the kitchen and prepare my standard breakfast of muesli, a boiled egg, and healthy smoothie made out of spinach, broccoli, chickpeas, and live yoghurt. I once thought that this concoction tasted foul, but I have started to like it, and besides, it does me the world of good. It's 7:36. I kiss Janey goodbye on the cheek and leave to meet Lisa. I sit behind the wheel of my gold car and press the button to open the iron gates at the bottom of the driveway. I watch the driveway gates close in my rear-view mirror as I drive towards the city.

Lisa has been waiting for five minutes when I arrive. Her laptop is open at the page where she had last written notes, and she is waiting to tap down more information. She is the example that every employee working for *the* company must follow. Lisa tucks into her breakfast of a croissant, a baguette, a glass of orange juice, and a cup of tea. It isn't the healthiest of breakfasts, but I offer to pay for it regardless.

'Good morning. I have scheduled the meeting with the sub-directors and the chairman for three o' clock. They have confirmed the time,' says Lisa.

Lisa *had* to remind me of the meeting with the subs and chairman. I had almost forgotten about it because of the fun I was having, relaying my story of becoming the CEO of such a fabulous company. *The* company that has given me, and Janey, so much. I reflected on what I had told Lisa. Most of it had been about my bad attitude, the things I had done, and what I had said. I feel ashamed of myself for acting in that awful way and am glad *the* company has turned me around. Without their guidance and belief in me, I wouldn't be the successful person sitting in front of my attractive assistant Lisa. She wouldn't divulge any of the information to anybody else. I was still sure of that. She wouldn't betray me. She was going to be *employee of the year* and employees of the year don't snitch - they remain neutral and keep everything confidential.

I am safe with Lisa.

However, I don't feel at all safe with the chairman and the subs. What do they want to talk about? Maybe it wasn't as serious as it sounded.

The shares.

It had to be the shares.

The slight dip in the shares.

The slightest of dips.

Nothing serious.

I nod to Lisa and we continue working on the book. After the White & Heinsteiger psychological analysis, the CEO, at yet another corporate meeting hosted in a conference facility, revealed the game plan for Operation Gambit.

'We would like everybody who is a dog - woof! woof!'

Everybody laughed except me.

'... to work with a cat - meow!, a lion - growl! And a fox—whatever noise they make. Does anybody know what noise a fox makes?'

The gathering of three hundred employees started to laugh except me. I didn't know whether the CEO was making a reference to a comedic song or not but, in any case, it wasn't funny.

'Ok. Nobody knows what noise a fox makes, but anyway, your groups will be decided by your respective managers for our upcoming team-building event called Operation Gambit.'

I had received some information from other managers about what Operation Gambit entailed and I didn't like it. It involved spending a day at a boot camp, completing mental and physical challenges within a team of seven other employees. As a manager, I couldn't pick any of my own team to be with for Operation Gambit, which included Janey. When I was assigned a team to be in, I was horrified. The name Anita Fox seemed to glare out from the emailed list as if it had been written in a bold font.

'Operation Gambit will bind us all together to form one solid efficient team where nothing can stop us achieving our goals. You are the cogs that keep *the* company moving forward. After Operation Gambit, *the* company will be able to throw these cogs into full speed and thrust us further into the success we all deserve. Wouldn't everybody like that?'

A loud, deafening "YES" bounced off the sound enhancing tiles and finished with some people laughing. I remained quiet.

'With the meeting over, there is only one thing left to do.'

The CEO started to wave his hands up towards the ceiling and down again. A strange tingling sensation made my fingers twitch. The tingles felt as if they travelled up my arm, towards my shoulders, and activated my arms to sway. I couldn't control myself and it seemed the more I tried to resist, the more my arms moved. At first, my arms only raised themselves halfway to the ceiling, but after a couple of swings, I was taking part in the corporate company wave involuntary. There was nothing I could do to stop the motion once it had taken over my body. In the end, I went with the flow. It was futile to resist and, if I am honest, I got some enjoyment out of it.

'YYYYEEEEEAAAAAAAAHHHHH!' said the CEO with gusto.

'YYYYEEEEEAAAAAAAAHHHHH!' I said back with even more gusto.

As I my hands lowered themselves to the ground, I didn't know what had just happened. I shifted my eyes from side to side without moving my head to check if anybody had seen me do *the* company wave. Janey was a few seats away from me and wasn't looking in my direction. Brian, on the other hand, was looking straight at me and our eyes met. A look of sheer shock washed over his face. He had been caught in the act of watching me do *the* company wave when he wasn't taking part himself. He turned his head away with a sharp fast twist and raised his hands in the air, pretending he had been taking part and had just finished. I would have to have words with Freddy about the situation.

Operation Gambit's team-building day arrived and

employees of *the* company were all shipped off to various destinations around London's suburbs. I pulled a piece of paper out of my binder and read the plan of the day's events. My group's mission was to build a tower out of thin wooden straws that could support an ostrich egg. The tower had to use all the parts provided and it had to stand three metres tall. A surprise would await all the teams.

'Well, Gallacchi. As I am manager of the managers, I feel it is my natural place to be the leader in this group. We'll soon have this task finished,' said Anita, and made her way to the back of the bus to be with Brown Nose.

My group consisted of other managers who I knew but hadn't worked with to a large extent. I didn't know what to expect of them, but I knew Anita would take great pleasure in trying to be the supreme commander of all of us. Once we had disembarked from the bus, we gathered outside a large building, situated on a hill. A steep winding path with hundreds of steps, with neat trimmed hedges on either side, led up to a mansion.

'Quite an impressive building,' said Geoff, a logistics manager, and raised his hand to his forehead and squinted his eyes in the direction of the mansion in the distance.

'It's a little superfluous to requirement,' said Anita. 'It's not anywhere that I could see myself living. I don't understand anybody who would want to live here. I think it's ghastly to be quite honest.'

A brief uncomfortable silence fell over my team. I was glad to find out that I wasn't the only one that

Anita bent and twisted the wrong way. She did it to everyone. I didn't say anything. I concentrated on the figure that was running down the steps towards us carrying a box under each arm.

'Hello,' said a woman, gasping for breath as she placed the boxes on the ground. 'My name is Yvonne and I am here to give you your materials for your task. Now, it mentions a surprise on the flyers you were given. I can now tell you what that surprise is.'

The foreheads of some of the other managers creased and rippled. They seemed worried about the surprise. Anita's face remained untouched by any flinch of human emotion.

'Your mission, as you all know by now, is to build a three metre tall tower to support an egg. The surprise, or snag as I like to call it, is that you have to build the tower—there!'

Yvonne pointed to a section of lawn that sloped upwards towards the mansion. The position for the building of the tower couldn't have been more precarious. There were rocks in the way, and the slope would have to be taken into account. The materials in the boxes consisted of normal drinking straws, string and Stanley knives. It was a joke.

'Geeezuz,' said Geoff.

'Child's play! This is one of the easiest tasks that I have ever been given. No. *The* easiest task I have ever been given. We just build four walls out of the straws, lean them towards each other, and make a section that hangs down between them at the top to hold the egg.

A child could do this,' said Anita, flexing her managerial powers.

The other managers shrugged their shoulders and folded to Anita's forceful point of view. She would be the one to draw up the plans for the tower and take all the credit for building it. As much as I hated Anita, I decided to go along with her scheme for an easier life. If we could get the tower built and finished fast, the less time I spent with Anita.

The plastic straws were hard to work with and I spent most of my time cutting holes into them with a Stanley knife. I had only joined a few straws together with the string when I heard:

'Gallacchi? Gallacchi? I want a progress report.'

After ten minutes of joining straws together to form the bottom of the wall, I heard:

'Gallacchi? You need to get a move on.'

And after half an hour:

'Gallacchi? That wall doesn't look as secure as the others, Gallacchi.'

And after an hour:

'Gallacchi? You are letting us down badly.'

'Gallacchi? Do you know the meaning of the word "team"?'

'Gallacchi? We never asked for a handicap for our task, Gallacchi.'

Gallacchi. Gallacchi. Gallacchi. Gallacchi. That's all I heard for the four hours it took us to build our walls and form our tower. I had had as much as I could take from Anita. She had taken every opportunity to blast me in front of the other managers who said nothing and concentrated on the task in hand. I had been called useless, superfluous, awful, ghastly, egotistical, and not a team a player.

I looked up at our tower. I was impressed. It stood over three metres from the ground, and we had taken into account the upward lie of the land. It represented a quick finish to a day I had become tired of. I just wanted to go to the Operation Gambit dinner, slip away, go home to Janey, put our feet up on the sofa and watch a movie. All that was left was the placement of the ostrich egg, which I had plucked from its large padded cardboard box and held in my hands.

'Not you, Gallacchi. You'll probably fall over before you reach the top of the tower and smash the egg. Ha! Ha! Give me the egg,' said Anita.

'Fine. Take the egg.'

My abrupt angry statement as I handed the egg over to Anita fell on deaf ears. I placed the egg in Anita's hands when all I wanted to do was smash it in her face. Anita climbed up the steps to the mansion, walked across a small path created by gardening staff to the top of the tower, leant across and plopped the egg in the chamber we had created. As the egg hit the straw basket, the tower wobbled and looked as if it wasn't going to support the weight. A gust of wind howled across our faces, which made the tower sway and buckle over, sending the egg crashing to the ground. I heard a crack as the eggshell split and puked out its contents over the mansion's lawn. The other managers cried out

"NO!" whereas Anita just stood motionless at the top of her tower's ghost, hoping that she would get another chance with a phantom egg. Maybe fate hated Anita Fox too. I raised my hand to my mouth to conceal my laughter and turned away so that the other managers couldn't see or hear me. I coughed to conceal my joy over the sight of the fallen tower and the premature hatching of the egg, and turned around to face Anita.

'Damn! Maybe it was the way you placed the egg in the basket,' I said.

I took great joy in shouting at Anita and pointing out her deficient shoddy workmanship.

'Whose wall was that that buckled?' asked Geoff.

'I believe it was Anita's wall. Correct me if I am wrong,' I said with smugness.

Anita's face stayed frozen in horror as she looked down at the fragments of eggshell and broken yoke. The other managers tried to console her while I turned my back and walked away.

No amount of "it doesn't matter" and "these things happen" and "it could have happened to anyone" could raise a smile on Anita's lips when we were seated for Operation Gambit's dinner. The result of our failure had meant that there wasn't enough time to build another tower before the mansion closed. We, therefore, received a big cross on our score sheet, symbolising that the managers had had the hardest task of working together. We had lost. We had failed. It wasn't my fault and I didn't care that it was Anita's fault.

16.

That was how Operation Gambit unfolded. Back then I thought the whole exercise was a waste of time but now I realise that it was all about team building. If *the* company works as a team and unites, it will succeed and become the biggest and best company in the world. I tell Lisa to focus on the aspect of team building for the book.

'Ok. I think I have everything. What do you want to talk about next? What happened after Operation Gambit?' asks Lisa.

It is a good question, and I rack my brains to think of the next story. The lift. Yes. Of course. The lift incident. I wasn't sure if it was worth mentioning for the book but I need to get the information out just in case.

'I want to talk about the lift incident. Maybe mention that rules are in place for a very specific reason and that reason is the well being of employees,' I say.

'Ok. I'm ready.'

'Several weeks had past after myself and Janey had been threatened by the eighth floor lift without reprimand. We thought we were in the clear, but as it turned out, we weren't.'

Lisa taps on the keys as she takes notes.

The day had started in the worst way possible. An email, sent by Freddy, informed me that he wanted to see both myself and Janey to discuss the lift incident.

'I told you it was wrong to go in the lift, didn't I? Now I might be sacked because of that, because of you, because of that stupid fucking lift,' said Janey, seething.

I gulped and my shoulders slumped towards the floor. I hung my head in shame and had to admit that I had been wrong in involving her in satisfying my curiosity.

'I'm sorry,' I said with a whisper.

'Sorry won't protect me against losing my job. Grrrr!'

Janey stomped to the front door, opened it, and walked out without me.

When I arrived at work, I made my way to Freddy's office where Janey and Freddy were waiting for me. They weren't talking to each other. Just waiting. Janey was waggling her foot. Freddy was leaning back in his seat and looking at the ceiling, twiddling his thumbs. I felt nervous as I stepped towards the office.

'Ah! There you are. Grab a pew, Mark,' said Freddy.

He called me Mark. For the first time since I could remember, he called me Mark. What did that mean?

'Nah, ya know why yous are 'ere, eh? Gimme ya

reasons for 'itching a ride in the eighth floor lift.'

Janey looked at me with a face like thunder. It jolted and jabbed me into speaking first.

'I ... I ... would like to apologise. It ... it ... it was my idea, Freddy. I don't know what came over me and it won't happen again. I'm sorry. Janey was an innocent bystander who I dragged along with me. She didn't have a choice. I'm sorry,' I said.

Janey looked away and stopped waggling her foot.

'Is this true, Janey? Should I Adam 'n' Eve it?' asked Freddy.

Janey nodded, not saying a word or a murmur. She was still angry with me.

'Ah ha! Ok. Well, in that case, you can leave, Janey. Mark, you can stay.'

Janey stood up from her seat, gave a wry smile towards Freddy, which she let droop for my benefit, and left the room with a semi half stomp. The situation made me feel as nervous as I had felt on my driving test. Was I now going to be let go? Was I about to realise the bet that I had had with Brian after there was nothing left to win? It couldn't happen. I had got used to receiving a wage every month, used to the lifestyle, and used to working and living with Janey who I loved like no other. It couldn't end. It couldn't. Freddy stood up from his seat and walked to the window and opened it. A faint smell from a bakery filtered through and started to make my stomach squeal with hunger.

'Wot is this fing called life all abaht?' asked Freddy

Confusion smacked me like an unexpected football

in the face. I had expected to be reprimanded by Freddy, now that he realised that I was Mark Gallacchi.

'I can't figure it aht even if I use me loaf.' Freddy turned around. 'I'm sorry for calling ya Gordon. It's just ... that you're a dead spit of him.'

Freddy's voice cracked and wavered at the end of his sentence, displaying the sadness that I had seen sweep over him on the golf course. I wanted to know what had happened to Gordon but was afraid to ask.

'I nah 'e's aht there somewhere—living—'aving a right ol' knee's us withaht us in Dubai,' said Freddy.

Freddy glanced straight into my eyes, took a deep breath and exhaled.

''e said, Gordon this is, ged this! 'e said the way I speak stunted 'is growth. Stunted 'is growth. Can you Adam 'n' Eve that? The blessed cheek of the git. 'e said, in court, that 'e never stood a chance to get a good education or pass exams coz I didn't speak proppa like wot other dads do. 'e said wot I spoke 'ad rubbed off on 'im and made 'im sand stoopid. Said I deserved choky. Can you Eve it, I mean, can ya?'

I decided to keep my thoughts to myself and agree with Freddy.

'No, Freddy. It sounds wrong to me,'

'Court didn't fink so. They found in 'is favour. 'ad to pay the little two-bob damages. Bleedin' cheek. FUCKIN' FUCKWIT!'

Freddy shouted out of the window and I was worried that he was going to be arrested by the police for breach of peace. I had not seen Freddy as angry as this before and his ranting had attracted the attention of employees outside his office to stop what they were doing and look. I had entered the office expecting to be disciplined over the lift incident, but it felt like a psychiatric session instead. As Freddy panted and puffed his anger out of his office window, I noticed a row of coloured Post-it notes that lined the left side of his laptop. I had not seen Freddy use them before and leant in for a closer inspection. I read the first red square. Through the paper, I saw Anita's heavy handwriting that had indented the paper. Even in reverse, I could make out what she had written: ihccallaG kraM. My name. Just my name. A reminder to Freddy that I was who I was. I flicked my eyes upwards fast and noticed Freddy was still leaning out of the window. I whipped my hand outwards, like a chameleon's tongue catching its prey, and snatched the red square between my thumb and forefinger, crumpled it up and buried it in my pocket. Freddy brought himself back into the office to investigate the small noise of paper being scrunched. I leant back in my seat, unable to read or detach the other Post-it notes. Freddy pulled his head in from the window, walked to his chair, sat down, picked up a silver pen and started to jab it into his desk like a dagger.

'Wot is life all abaht, son?' asked Freddy.

'Erm ... well, I don't know to be honest.'

'Me neitha, son. Me neitha. All I fuckin' know is that we 'ave to 'ave a bit of malarky while we are 'ere, eh?'

'I guess.'

'Life is too short, me ol' china, too short, and it's

got me finkin'.'

'Ok.'

I wasn't sure of where the conversation was going.

'I'm geddin' on a bit and ain't long for brown bread. So that's why I plan to retire at the end of the year. I'm too cream crackered mate. 'ad enough.'

'Oh.'

I couldn't say anything else. I was taken aback by Freddy's retirement plans.

'But while I'm still 'ere, I can fix your little problem with the eighth floor.'

'You can? Well. I don't expect anything, Freddy.'

'Nah. Nah. It's ok. I can fix it like that pedo bloke, nah wots 'is fuckin' name nah?'

Freddy fingered his beard, and pondered the answer to his own question, failing to produce any answer.

'Fuck it. Don't madder. Anyways, my seat will be empty when I go and I can't fink of a bedder person than you to fill it.'

'I'm ... I'm sorry? You mean ...'

'Yes, son. I'm gonna recommend ya to take me place, and wot I say as influence.'

'Oh well, I don't know if I'm really the man, or the candidate, or the person to take your place, Freddy. I ...'

'Rubbish! You've had an impact ever since ya got 'ere, mate. I mean, who else would come up with a ditty like: *open your eyes, we make miracles materialise, deee deee dee de deee dee?* The CEO is also impressed.'

Freddy's usual lack of tone and rhythm made the awful corporate song sound a lot better than the original.

'Well, I didn't come up with ...'

'Nah. Ya did. You are the guv. It's your kiddy. Well done.'

I smiled and accepted the praise.

'But anyways, anyways, back to the eighth floor. When you take over, you will have access. You can make Janey your assistant. That way, you'll avoid any disciplinary barney. If I make ya my assistant today, or somefink—bah! I'll fix it all for ya. Ya don't 'ave to worry or lift a pinky, mate.'

'Er. Well. Ok. Thanks.'

I just accepted what Freddy said. It seemed pointless to say anything against him, and besides, I couldn't get a word in.

'Personally, I dunno why ya want to see the eighth floor. It's just full of whistles.'

I didn't know what that meant but I smiled.

'So we can forget abaht this lift bizniz.'

Freddy started to read the remaining Post-it notes.

'Ah yeah. You and Janey are togever, yeah?'

'Erm, well ... we are really good friends,' I said with a shaky voice.

'Yeah, yeah. Don't tell me porkies. I know, I know, son. Look, that won't be a problem after I rewrite the company rule on relationships within *the* company. It'll all be ok once the new rule book is aht—and it will be aht tomorrow.'

Freddy snatched the Post-it note away from his laptop screen, threw it in the rubbish, and read the next one.

'Ah yeah. Also, I saw that white plastic tiles 'ad been taken from the store room and fixed under the lights of your department.'

'Yeah. Well. The lights were too bright. My staff complained of headaches. It was like working under floodlights,' I said.

'Gotcha! Gotcha! Sounds reasonable to me. I'll fix those lights too. Install dimmers or somefink. I'll fix it.'

Freddy started to read through the other Post-it notes and became more agitated after each one he read.

'Bah! All rubbish. I can't be arsed with this horse shit!'

Freddy peeled all of the Post-it notes away from his monitor and threw them in the bin. I smiled. Anita still hadn't managed to get through to Freddy in the same way that I could. She had convinced him that I was Mark Gallacchi but it hadn't made any difference to Freddy. He still seemed to view me as someone he respected, liked, and maybe even loved like his own son. I wasn't going to lose my job, far from it. I was going to be promoted again to Freddy's spot, leap-frogging Anita Fox. I would be above her. I would be able to shit on her, which felt amazing, uplifting and powerful. Making up with Janey would be easier to do once I told her the news. We would be good again. Whole. As for my department, I thought of Brian and my need to discuss him with Freddy.

'I wondered if there was something else you could fix,' I said.

'Yes, son. Anyfink. Wot can I do ya for?'

'Brian. He's been acting oddly towards me and I wondered if you could ...'

'Fire 'im?'

'No. I, er ...'

''e's gone, mate. Consider it done.'

'No. I didn't want to fire him. Just talk to him, that's all.'

'Nah, nah, son. If someone's making ya life misery, it's best they go a find somefink else.'

I didn't want to get rid of Brian. It was the last thing I wanted. I didn't want Brian to be out of a job, destitute and broke. Now I would look like the bad man; the manager who people would fear to talk to; the manager who throws employees under the steamroller, makes them into pancakes, chews on them and spits them out. But there was no talking to Freddy. I couldn't reverse his decision. He had spoken, put his foot down, and made a decision carved out of stone on my behalf. A bad decision.

17.

'So Brian really got fired for nothing,' said Lisa, almost in an accusing manner.

'Not really, Lisa. No,' I say, 'at the time, I thought Brian just needed guidance, but as I sit here today, I realise that he didn't have the positive mental attitude required to work for *the* company.'

'Do you want me to write that down?'

'Phrase it something like this: some people are suited to work for us, some are not. Those who are not suited might be suited to work for other companies. *The* company is all about selecting the right employees to maximise potential.'

'I see. Ok.'

'Don't mention Brian's name in the book.' I sip my cup of coffee and bite into an apple. 'Shall we continue?'

A week before my step up the corporate ladder was announced, and before the new media department knew about my promotion, Anita paid my office (that was now lit with a subdued bulb) a special visit.

'Gallachi. I'm assuming you have a minute, probably more minutes than most, considering the fact that you don't seem to do much.'

Anita barged her way into my office, picked up some papers off the chair on the opposite side of my desk and threw them on the floor and sat down. She seemed more than eager to speak. I concentrated on my computer screen, failed to make eye contact, and refused to acknowledge her presence.

'Have you heard the rumour?' asked Anita.

'No.'

I didn't know what rumour she was referring to but I didn't care. I kept my answers short and snappy to save my energy for something useful.

'Freddy is retiring.'

My ears pricked up. I wasn't sure where she had picked up this snippet of information. She couldn't have heard it from Freddy as he would have spilt the beans about me taking his place. I was puzzled.

'You know what that means don't you, Gallachi?' asked Anita as if she had the answer figured out.

I moved my eyes off my computer screen and made eye contact.

'No. What?'

'Seen as I am manager of the managers, and have been here longer than any of you, including you - Gallachi, it would only be fair to assume that I will become director - and you know what that means don't you, Gallachi?'

'Fancy lunches and a new car?'

My contempt for Anita Fox knew no bounds.

'No. Gallachi. Well, yes, actually, it does mean that, but also it will mean that I will be your superior, Gallachi. Things will be run differently in the new media department, Gallachi. I will be making some changes once I am director.'

'Well, I guess, as director, it's your prerogative to make changes.'

I remained calm and threw out logical comments. I could tell that it annoyed her every time I did it. Her eyebrows folded inwards towards her flared nose. Her pupils dilated. If smoke could have escaped through her ears, I'm sure I would have seen that too.

'You should watch your step, Gallachi. Pull your socks up. Start putting in the hours that you are expected to do as manager. Yes, Gallachi. Things will change. Things will change. Do you want to know what I will do first, Gallachi?'

'Start calling me Mark?'

I smirked on the inside but blocked the emotion that made me physically smile and show my teeth.

'No. Gallachi. No. The rulebook.'

'The rulebook?' I asked.

'Yes. The new rulebook that Freddy has released. It's made everyone relax too much. Made us, *the* company, weaker. Turned people into perverts who see their work colleagues as possible boyfriend or girlfriend. Disgusting, Gallachi. Disgusting. I know about you and Janey, Gallachi. Don't think it hasn't escaped my attention. I have my spies.'

I remained quiet and continued to listen to her never-ending rant, safe in the knowledge that I was going to be promoted. I was amused.

'Do we understand each other, Gallachi?'

'I understand you completely, Fox. Do you understand me?' I said.

The question bounced off her ears as if they had been filled in with cement. I had called her Fox. I expected a reaction but it didn't happen. Instead, Anita raised herself from the seat, opened my office door, and disappeared without answering my question.

My promotion was announced at a managerial-cum-directorial-cum-top brass meeting held in one of the larger conference rooms. The top officials of all departments had gathered and filled the room like a small art house cinema. I clocked the back of Anita's head as I walked in. She was sitting on the right side of the room close to the front. I chose the front row and to the left to create distance between us. All of the company announcements about who was being promoted, leaving, let go, or going on some kind of leave, were officially announced at the same time.

'And there are some announcements to be made,' said the CEO, looking at his PowerPoint presentation. 'The first announcement is that Freddy Hardcastle, who has been working for *the* company for twenty-two years, is to retire at the end of the year. Although Freddy is not here today, I would like to extend my gratitude towards one of the key people here at *the* company and say that he will be surely missed.'

A large "oh" circulated around the room.

'His replacement—and it gives me great pleasure to announce this, because this person has been vital to our operation for some time and has excelled ...'

I looked to my right and noticed Anita Fox beaming a smile towards the CEO. She believed, with all her heart, that her name would be the next phrase spoken out of the CEO's lips.

'... I cannot think of any other person who deserves this more than anybody else. I am, of course, without further ado, referring to the manager of the new media department - MARK GALLACHI!'

"Oh!" cried the audience.

The audience's "oh" soon turned to hundreds of whispers, making the room sound as if it was full of snakes. I stood up and bowed, waved in front of me and towards the sad, dejected face of Anita Fox, whose smile had fallen towards the floor. She turned her head and spoke to the people sitting behind her. I translated her animated hand gestures and imagined her saying: Gallachi? *Gallachi?* Is this for real? Is this true? How can this be possible? Gallachi? But, I thought, I would ...

I turned around towards the stage and concentrated my gaze on the CEO. He was clapping, applauding, and congratulating me on my promotion. The CEO himself! I felt an emotion of sheer happiness sweep over me.

'There's only one thing left to do,' said the CEO.

I started waving my hands up and down

before the CEO had even started. I shouted 'YEAAAAAAAHHHHH!' at the top of my lungs and released my positive mental attitude in the CEO's direction.

'YOU'VE GOT TO BE KIDDING. SERIOUSLY! GALLACHI IS THE NEW DIRECTOR? ARE YOU OUT OF YOUR MIND?'

The corporate ritual had been interrupted. People stopped taking part in the wave and focused their attention on Anita Fox whose face had turned red from shouting.

'EVERYBODY KNOWS WHO AND WHAT HE IS. HE'S A LAZY BUM. A LAYABOUT. HE HASN'T DONE A HONEST DAY'S WORK IN HIS LIFE. SERIOUSLY! GALLACHI. I MEAN, GALLACHI? ARE YOU SERIOUS? ARE YOU FUCKING SERIOUS?'

I gulped when I heard the swearword. I had never heard her use any swearwords before. I had never seen her glow red like a hot plate either. I had never seen her lose control. This was a meltdown to beat all meltdowns. If Anita Fox was Chernobyl, her brain was Pripyat.

'Security. Please get security to remove her. Thanks,' said the CEO.

The CEO pressed a red button on the wall to the side of him, pointed to Anita Fox, and nodded towards security, who entered the room to take her away.

'GET YOUR HANDS OFF ME! YOU'RE MAKING A BIG MISTAKE. A MISTAAAAAKE.

GALLLLAAAACCCCCCHHHHHHI!'

Two large security men dragged Anita across the conference room floor, through the doors, kicking and screaming. The end of my name faded away and became silent as the doors slammed behind them. I had not seen anything like it. Even drunk people on Friday evenings behaved better than Anita Fox.

After the announcement of my promotion, things started to change. The reaction to my new job title seemed to shock every employee and mute them. It was as if Obama had won the Nobel Peace Prize all over again.

"No way!"

"You've got to be kidding, right?"

"Mark Gallachi? What does he do anyway?"

Brown Nose's snide attitude towards me did a complete U-turn.

'Is there anything I can do?'

'Can I help in any way?'

'Well, if you thought of it then it has to be wonderful.'

'I think that is a fantastic idea. It's good for *the* company, it's good for us as a department, and, well, just generally good. I think we should all go bowling or go-karting to celebrate.'

The new media team had started to warm to me in ways I hadn't expected ...

... and then Brian's official firing was announced.

The email read:

Brian Watkins has decided to leave the company to pursue other activities and opportunities. We, the company, wish him well in all his endeavours.

I had no way of stopping the axe from falling and once it had, everybody that remembered the ugly scene in the meeting room assumed I had been the executioner. They had taken onboard that I was to be Freddy's replacement after Christmas. They had put two and two together and come up with the wrong number. Employees started to move away from me when I sat down to eat lunch in the cafeteria, tied up their tongues, if they happened to be talking about work and I entered their space, and remained tight lipped when it came to development dialogues. The only person who could see through the haze of rumours and misplaced judgements was Janey. She had become my crutch to lean on and my reason to stay at *the* company. I had often tried to imagine what might have happened if Janey had not started working for *the* company when she did. Maybe I would have been unemployed. Maybe I would have been standing in a queue at the job centre. Maybe I would have been homeless and begging for small change.

And so it was. I was to be become Freddy's replacement.

A director. A director of *the* company. When I told Janey, she exploded with excitement and, it has to be said, some shock. I had been working for *the* company for less than a year, and my barrage of promotions were unprecedented. I promised Janey a role as my assistant, and I stated that the whole eighth floor lift incident had been forgotten. Wiped out. I was going to move to the eighth floor and into my own executive office, despite Freddy's warnings about doing so. Although Janey seemed happy with my promotion, there seemed to be something troubling her.

'I don't know what to say, Mark. I mean, it's great about your promotion and all that but won't it be seen as favourtism? I mean, I think everybody knows about us.'

'Everybody?' I asked.

'Everybody.'

'Even the sub-directors?'

'Probably.'

'How did they find out?'

'I dunno. Anyway, that doesn't matter. I think I'll be seen as an arse kisser, and you'll be seen as, well, maybe, kinda, sleazy.'

'Sleazy?'

After I had thought about the situation, I shook away "sleazy" and replaced it with "boss". I could do what I liked. I was going to be the one calling the shots. The one making all the decisions. Janey's promotion was going to be one of them. I grabbed Janey by her arms and reassured her.

'Look. This has worked out well for us. We'll be able to afford to buy a larger place and fill it with all the things that we have dreamt of owning. I don't give a shit what the others think. I can't take the promotion if you can't be there with me. Just think about it. It'll be you and me, running the show.'

Janey gave me a hug and broke off the embrace in an abrupt manner. She walked into the kitchen and put the kettle on, which I guessed was for some breathing space more than to quench her thirst with a cup of tea. I was adamant that she would come around to my way of thinking because she had to - for us. I started to envisage the future in our lavish apartment, maybe big house with all the mod-cons including swimming pool, home cinema, Ferrari parked in the driveway, maybe even a couple of kids running around, bouncing up and down on a trampoline in a large garden-cum-meadow. I could picture it, but Janey would need more time to get used to the idea.

But my dream had to wait. I wasn't going to be promoted until after the Christmas party and that was three months away.

18.

'It's coming up to 9:30. Should we go to the office and continue?' asks Lisa, glancing at her laptop screen.

The chairman and the subs would want to have their meeting earlier than planned if they knew I was in the building. Lisa still has a coffee and pain au chocolat to finish. We are staying in the café for the time being.

'No. I think we should press on. I'm sure we can get it finished by lunchtime if we crack on with it.'

Lisa takes a sip of coffee and she seems to be ignoring the rest of her breakfast. I always start every day with my muesli and my healthy smoothie. It keeps me focused and channels my energy in the right way to benefit *the* company. I look at Lisa's breakfast remnants and can't refrain from speaking.

'Breakfast is the most important meal of the day.'

'I'm sorry?' asks Lisa.

'You appear to be leaving your breakfast, although in a way, that's good because it is very unhealthy.'

The coffee with sugar. The jam. The chocolate. It is a breakfast designed to clog up her insides and make her teeth fall out. The only healthy item is the orange juice, and I am certain it isn't fresh squeezed.

'I'm not hungry. If we are going to stay here, I might eat it later.'

A waitress approaches our table with a glass jug filled with coffee; coffee that was made several hours ago and left standing on a hot plate. Lisa nods and the waitress fills her cup up.

'Shall we continue?' Lisa asks.

I hold my tongue and don't say anything about the negative effects skipping breakfast has on the human body. I want to crack on with the book.

'Why d'ya fink I'm 'ere? I'm not waiting for bleedin' Santy Claus to burst frew the door and shawwer me with Chrimbo presents!' said Freddy, slurring his words.

Freddy pointed to his shot of whisky and took a sip. It was difficult to hear what he said over the distorted tuneless music played by a tired band. They looked as if they had played one Christmas party too many. The only person in the band that played well was the drummer and he wasn't going to make the music memorable by himself. I wondered where *the* company had found them and why they had booked them.

The Christmas party's venue was the function room of a hotel. A large empty void filled with large tables and chairs for *the* company dinner had been arranged. Christmas crackers had been lined up with the cutlery and people had already pulled them before the dinner had been served. Silly multi-coloured hats made out of tracing paper were being worn. Streamers were being blown. Mimed clues were being guessed. Awful jokes were being told:

> *What do you call a canonised burglar who steals Christmas presents?*
> *St. Nick.*

I had been seated opposite Freddy with Janey to my left and Brown Nose to my right. I looked down at my dinner plate and shuffled the limp grey slices of cold turkey around with my fork. I pronged a slice and took a bite. It was like trying to force down a thick piece of chew proof cardboard. I picked up the gravy bowl and saturated the turkey slices with a light brown watery substance. It made no difference. The turkey was impenetrable to liquid.

'This band is delightful. The company really knows how to throw a good bash,' said Brown Nose, beaming from ear to ear.

I didn't know who Brown Nose was trying to impress. Anita had been sacked. Freddy was on his way out. Her comments were not going to impress me. Freddy stared at her as he rested his whisky glass on the table.

'Are you fuckin' kiddin' me? Thisz band don't know the 'alf the art of jammin'. They'd be great if it weren't—if it weren't for the bum notes, lack of timing, and if the zhinger weren't a bit moby. Ain't that right, Gordon, ain't that right, eh, eh?' said Freddy, winking at me.

He had called me Gordon again after everything we had spoken about. He had called me Gordon. Brown Nose spun her head to her left and smirked at me.

'Gordon? His name isn't Gordon, it's Mark.'

Freddy stared at me for longer than it felt comfortable, raised his glass to his lips, sucked up a swig of whisky and shuddered as it hit his tongue.

'Yeah. Yeah. I know. I know. Mark. Of corz. I'd forget me loaf if it weren't screwed on!'

As the band finished their final song, and thanked everyone for the unenthusiastic claps, the hotel staff cleared up the leftover slop from the unfinished dinners and prepared the floor for the disco. A guy, wearing a white t-shirt with an unlit cigarette balanced in a precarious way from his lips, started to set up his DJ gear. I wasn't filled with the confidence that the entertainment was about to get better. The CEO took to the stage.

'Yes! Thanks to The Chips for their performance. This is some Christmas party. Phew!'

Brown Nose jumped up and down in her seat, clapping as loud as she could, attracting the attention of people seated ten places away from her.

'While DJ David sets up his equipment, I would like to say a special goodbye to someone who has been with *the* company almost since its inception. As a token of our appreciation, I would like to invite Freddy Hardcastle up on the stage to collect his retirement gift. Give a BIG round of applause for Freddy.'

I clapped. Janey clapped. Brown Nose half clapped.

The room gave Freddy Hardcastle more of a reception than they had done with the band. Freddy fell up the steps to the stage and had to be helped up. People pushed him onto the stage and towards the CEO who looked shocked. Freddy batted the CEO's handshake away and grabbed the microphone, ignoring his retirement gift.

'I would like to zay a few wordz.'

I wasn't sure if Freddy meant that in a literal sense.

'Wordz. Hmm. Wordz. Ah! Bugger! I can't fink of anyfink to zay. Letz juzt get shitfaced! Ha! Ha! Ha!'

DJ Dave continued to set up his equipment, letting ash fall from his lit cigarette, which burnt a hole in his curry stained white t-shirt.

'Erm. Yes. Freddy Hardcastle everybody. Freddy. This is yours. Thanks for everything,' said the CEO.

The CEO gave the retirement gift to Freddy who didn't to know what to do with it. The people that had helped him up onto the stage, now helped him down and returned him to his seat. He picked up his whiskly glass fast and threw the contents down the back of his throat.

'Cawwy on the way you meanz to go on,' said Freddy, spitting whisky into my face.

Brown Nose gave a loud tut, stood up, and walked away in the direction of the hotel foyer.

'Stuck up bitch,' said Freddy.

There would have been a time that I would have smiled at Freddy's working class London dialect, even go along with his odd behaviour, but this wasn't one of those times. He had drunk way too much, which made his retirement so much more undignified.

I whispered to Janey: 'I think we should call him a taxi and send him home.'

'I was thinking the same thing. I'll call one,' replied Janey.

As Janey called for a taxi, I walked around to Freddy's seat and grabbed his arm.

'Come on, Freddy. I think you need some fresh air. What do you say?'

'Yeah, zun. Yeah. Zounds great, Gordon. Lead on Mcbezth! Or some shit like that.'

Freddy raised himself to his feet whilst leaning all of his weight on my right shoulder. After Janey had rung for a taxi, she supported Freddy's left side as we struggled to walk him to the hotel's entrance, collecting his coat on the way.

'It'll be five minutes.' Janey had tried her best to whisper but Freddy had overheard her.

'Wotz five minutes? Iz it 'ow long it takes to catch ol' Moby? Remember that, zun, eh, eh? Remember that, Gordon?'

'Yes. Freddy. I remember that,' I answered.

Freddy started to cry.

'I remember it, Gordon. Like it woz yezzerday. I'll mizz Captain Kirk. I'll mizz you, Gordon. And you ...'

Freddy looked at Janey, raised his arm and clicked his fingers.

'... wotsit.'

Freddy stumbled and collapsed on the ground

whilst still clutching his retirement gift in his whisky hand. He looked at it through his tears, became angry, and threw it into the bushes in a fit of rage.

'I dunno wot that woz. Itz friggin' cold aht 'ere.'

I bent down and wrapped a scarf that I found in his jacket pocket around his neck. I buttoned up Freddy's coat as he wept in the cold December air.

'You're too good for me, Gordon. Too good. I don't deserve you. You're the bezt, Gordon. I'll mizz you.'

Janey fetched Freddy's damaged retirement gift from the bushes and held onto it until the taxi arrived.

'Youz stay in touch yeah? We'll 'ave a ruby or somefink, yeah?'

'Sure, Freddy. We'll have a ruby.'

The taxi arrived and Janey placed the battered award in the passenger seat first, and then attended to Freddy. I felt sad about Freddy's retirement even though half of me thought he was a lunatic. Freddy stared out through the taxi's window, frosting up the glass with his breath. I stared back at one of the saddest faces I had seen for a long time. Tears were dropping from his eyes; his usual smile had been tarnished and reversed; his dignity has been lost. The taxi pulled away, confining Freddy Hardcastle to *the* company's history.

19.

Freddy's office was empty. The doors to his cabinet had been left ajar, so I nudged them open and found several open packets of flour. I smiled, shut the doors, and sat down. An outline of a rectangle in the dust marked the place where his laptop had been. He had remembered to take his family photos with him. I looked around the room and looked at the paperwork sticking out of a bookshelf, the crooked poster of men sitting on scaffolding in the 1920s, and a shriveled up pot plant that was too late to be saved by a drop of water. It had been two weeks since the Christmas party where Freddy had embarrassed himself. He hadn't been heard from since. I relaxed in Freddy's chair and started to think.

It was the New Year.

New job.

New responsibilities.

Janey and I were in the process of moving to a bigger house. Marriage was being whistled in the wind. Life would be good even without Freddy backing me up and mistaking me for his estranged son. I convinced myself of it. I put my hands behind my head and leant back in Freddy's executive chair. I looked down at the desk, opened a drawer out of curiosity, and found a photograph of a young man in an expensive looking golden frame. I blew the dust away, picked it up and examined it.

Was it?

It must have been.

I was convinced it was.

It was Gordon.

He looked eerily like me or so I thought.

He looked like my stunt double.

My dopplegänger.

My heart palpitated with a half beat before resting back into its normal rhythm. Freddy had not been exaggerating. Gordon did look like me. It wasn't an excuse for him mistaking me for his son, but I now had some understanding of the reason why.

'Are you coming to lunch or what? I've been waiting for you. What are you doing in here anyway?' asked Janey, poking her head around the door.

'Oh. You know. I just thought I'd check out Freddy's office. Make sure he hadn't forgot anything. You won't believe this but take a look at this.'

I handed Janey the photograph of Gordon.

'Hmph. And?'

'And ... don't you think he reminds you of someone?'

Janey looked again, holding the photograph closer to her eyes and squinted.

'No. Who is it?'

'Gordon. It's Gordon.'

'Gordon? Freddy's Gordon?'

'Yep. Gordon Gordon.'

'Ok. Well, he doesn't look like you. Now, are we getting some lunch or what? I'm so hungry I could throw up dust.'

Janey plonked the photograph down on the desk with a force that clunked.

'Hey! Be careful with that. That's Freddy's photo.'

'What is it with you? Freddy's gone. The photo is chock full of dust. If it was important, he would have taken it with him, wouldn't he?'

'I guess, yes, but ... seriously? You don't think he looks like me?'

'No. Just drop it and let's have lunch.'

I couldn't get the photograph out of my mind during lunch. I could see the mysterious and mean Gordon. Who on earth would divorce their own parents? Who could be that vindictive? I thought about Freddy's sadness and heartbreak when I claimed to be Mark Gallachi and not his son. Every time I told him that I wasn't Gordon, the more I drove the stake into his heart.

'Are you going to eat that?' asked Janey.

Janey pointed to my half-finished bento box, which only had the chicken skewers covered in an odd tasting peanut butter sauce and rice left to eat.

'Oh. Sorry. Yes. I was miles away there.'

'You're not thinking of Gordon are you?'

I tried my best to conceal the fact that Gordon was on my mind with a slow, hesitant shake of my head.

'For God's sake! He's not *your* son. Just forget about it will you.'

I maneuvered some rice onto my chopsticks and lost half of it by the time it reached my mouth. I could never understand how the Asian world used these things. I didn't understand why I just didn't use cutlery.

'So. What about the eighth floor then? You were so curious about what it must be like up there, in company heaven,' said Janey.

'Erm. Yes. Well. I guess, well, we'll find out tomorrow won't we?'

'I'm still not sure about becoming your assistant, you know. It'll look like nepotism.'

'Balls to what people think, Janey. I need you with me otherwise I won't know what I am doing. You are essential to me.'

'Yeah ... thanks, but ...'

'No buts. It will be the first announcement as director.'

Janey chopsticked the tail off a king prawn with a blink of an eye, chewed, and swallowed the sushi. I knew her well enough to know that she felt awkward about her impending promotion but it was going to happen regardless. I had made up my mind.

'This is your card for the eighth floor,' said the receptionist, handing me a grey card with the number 8 stenciled on it. 'This is your hand towel for the eighth floor.'

It was grey with a large 8 printed on it.

'And remember to hang your coat on the appropriate designated hook otherwise it will be removed and destroyed.'

I didn't say anything. I just accepted what was being said and given to me. Freddy had either missed changing the rules for the eighth floor or had not been authorised to do so.

'This is your welcome pack to the eighth floor.'

A grey folder with an 8 stenciled on it.

'And this is your eighth floor cup. Please do not use this for anything other than tea or coffee.'

Grey. 8.

'You will also be required to watch an induction video to the eighth floor and I would suggest that you view that today before your meeting with the CEO.'

I wondered if the video was going to be presented by a grey person filmed against a grey background with 8s painted on it.

'And what about Janey's eighth floor access?' I asked.

'You are referring to Janey McDonald who works for the new media department?'

'Yes. Janey McDonald who worked - *worked* - for the new media department. She is my assistant.'

'To my knowledge and company records, she works as a Social Media Initiator. She is not a Directorial Assistant.'

'Yes. I know that, but I thought I could take the liberty of collecting her access card on her behalf.'

'No, Mr Gallachi, you can't. It is against company policy to ...'

'Yes. Yes. I know - to have possession of other employees' identities. It's ok. You don't have to repeat yourself. I'll just go up to the eighth floor then - that is if there is nothing else that I should know.'

The receptionist looked perturbed at my annoyance. I wanted Janey by my side as we moved to the eighth floor, but it seemed the gatekeeper wanted to stick to the company rulebook.

I clasped my grey eighth floor merchandise in my hands, headed out of the office and towards the same lift that had entrapped myself and Janey before. I now held an access card in my hand as if it was the key to the universe and life itself. I would now find out what the eighth floor was all about and why it was such an enigma. I entered the lift and the door shut behind me. The same multi-coloured lights reflected off the mirrors and my body.

'Attention employee 79503. You have been granted access to the eighth floor.'

The lift began to move upwards with a smooth slow action as if it had been designed for a person carrying a pyramid of champagne glasses on a silver tray. What would I see when the doors opened? I imagined it to be a semi-paradise, filled with colourful decorations, exotic pot plants, maybe several large fish aquariums that contained lion fish or puffer fish, automatic doors that opened with a *swish* like *Star Trek,* and chairs that didn't need castors and hovered like jet packs.

The doors opened.

'Attention employee 79503. Attention employee 79503. You may now disembark.'

The lack of colour shocked me to such an extent that I remained static in the lift, hoping it would swallow me again and spit me back out on the ground floor. It was as grey as my pass-card and towel. Grey carpets. Grey walls. Grey lights. Not a hover seat in sight. Grey offices containing grey desks. Fake plastic pot plants, also grey and black, that didn't need to be shown any love. No lion fish. No puffer fish. Grey.

'Attention employee 79503. Loitering is considered a company offence. If you remain immobile, you will be reprimanded.'

I stepped out of the lift and took my first steps onto the eighth floor's nondescript carpet. I could feel the fibres of the carpet twist into the soles of my shoes as I walked forwards and it felt as if it had been laid just for my arrival. A row of small offices lined the wall to my left. A row of small offices lined the wall to the right. As I looked ahead, I could see an office in the distance, on its own and in the middle. I assumed it was the CEO's office. A cloakroom, toilet and coffee machine were situated a turn to my right. I turned towards the cloakroom to hang my coat and then looked at the coffee machine. It served nothing but black coffee. Where was my *Weiner Mélange*? I was about to hang my coat when a figure, running towards me in the distance, distracted me. He or she was carrying a piece of paper in their hand and approaching the lift at some speed.

The lift doors shut behind me and travelled back down to the ground floor. I felt trapped.

'Mr Gallachi?' said the man, wheezing.

'Yes?'

'I, sir ...' the man coughed, '... would like to welcome ...' the man took a breath, '... you, sir, to the eighth floor, sir.'

The man was chubby and overweight and had the physique of an ex-football player that had eaten too many hamburgers. His face was lit up and beetroot red. He waved the piece of paper into my face, making a subtle request that I grab it from his mitts.

'This, sir ...' said the man taking a deep breath, '... is your certificate to certify ... sir, that you are now an eighth floor worker, sir. Your office number, sir ... is #745344.' The man could barely speak.

'And can I ask where that is?'

'To the left, sir.'

The man placed his hands on his knees and bent over, trying to get air into his lungs. It looked as if he was going to keel over and die.

'Are you ok? Do you need some help?' I asked with concern.

'No, sir. Thanks, sir. This always happens when ... when a new person joins the eighth floor.'

The man stood up. The redness in his face had started to fade and be replaced by his normal skin tone.

'There is a hook for your towel, sir. Please allow me to guide you to it.'

The man shuffled his feet to the right and pointed

to the row of towels and an empty hook I assumed were mine.

'Here, sir. You receive a fresh towel automatically every day, sir. Please allow me to show you to your office, sir, where you can relieve yourself, sir, of that welcome pack file you are carrying.'

The man turned away from the hooks, walked down the middle of the hallway, and towards the office I could see far away in the distance. When we had walked for a short while, the man stopped dead in front of me and pivoted himself around on one foot.

'Here, sir.'

The man pointed to an empty office that contained a desk, a laptop and a cabinet.

'Do I watch ...'

The man had vanished.

'Hello? Hello?' I said.

My voice echoed down the hallway. The people in the offices to the right and left of my office didn't look up. They weren't even aware that I existed and were concentrating on whatever it was they were doing. I opened the door to my office and walked in. The overpowering smell of toxic plastic fumes from the new items in the room wafted up my nostrils. There wasn't an ounce of dust to be seen anywhere. The desk had not been touched. No cup ring marks. The chair looked as if it had never been sat in. The carpet was brand new and the filing cabinet that lined the wall also seemed to be devoid of any knocks or scratches. But it wasn't the smell of the new merchandise that bothered me. Everything was grey. Grey desk. A grey hoverless chair. A grey cabinet. Grey carpet. Grey laptop. Even the supplied company mug was grey with an 8 drawn on it. The only element in the room that wasn't grey was the window and even that reflected back the rainy grey clouds lining the sky. I should have listened to Freddy, taken his advice, and steered clear of this drab bleak existence. I sat down at my desk, tapped my fingers on its surface, and opened my laptop.

'Hello and welcome to the eighth floor and your new position as director within *the* company.'

An automatic video on my laptop had started playing. The door to my office shut and locked itself.

'As an eighth floor member and director of *the* company, you will be expected to perform many tasks, but before I talk about them, there is one golden rule you must obey: Do not talk about specific details of the eighth floor to non eighth floor employees. Do not talk about specific details of the eighth floor to non-eighth floor employees. Do not talk about specific details of the eighth floor to non eighth floor employees.'

Do not talk about specific details of the eighth floor to non-eighth floor employees. The phrase entered my head and started to repeat itself as the video had done. The odd deep voice of the narrator continued to repeat the phrase until she finally moved on to the next subject. Was there something wrong with her throat?

'Now that you are a director of the company, you are expected to work overtime without extra pay. This is, of course, should be obvious to you and be unconditionally accepted. You work for *the* company and any work you complete for us should be regarded as a privilege.'

I recognised the woman in the video. It was an old TV presenter from a quiz show from at least ten years ago. She had aged and had skin like old worn shoe leather.

'You have recognised me. Good. I am Carol Penny. I am a spokeswoman for *the* company and one of the biggest shareholders. I will overlook your opinion that states that I look old and sound odd. It is immaterial. The fact that you are sitting in that seat and listening to this video is a reminder of how important you are to *the* company and myself. Together we must love and nurture *the* company as if it was a baby sucking at our teats. You must love *the* company as if it were your own child. You must love *the* company as if it were your own child. You must love *the* company as if it were your own child. You must be willing to put your life on the line for *the* company. You must be willing to put your life on the line for *the* company. You must be willing to put your life on the line for *the* company.'

I must love the company like my own child.

I must be willing to put my life on the line for the company.

I shook my head and looked at the laptop screen. The video had stopped and Carol Penny could no longer be heard or seen. Instead, the operating system, featuring grey wallpaper and an 8, stared back at me. My office door unlocked itself.

I must love the company like my own child.

I must be willing to put my life on the line for the company.

Do not talk about specific details of the eighth floor to non-eighth floor employees.

I couldn't get the lines out of my head. The sentences kept repeating like a broken record. I felt confused. I felt trapped. Alone. I didn't even know what my tasks as a director were. What was expected of me apart from working overtime and dying for *the* company? Where was Janey? If I was going to survive a day on the eighth floor, I needed her by my side. I felt lost without her and my frightening first impressions of the eighth floor only proved that I needed her more than ever.

My phone rang. Red buttons flicked on and off. I feared to answer it. Maybe it was Carol Penny again. Maybe she was going to swear at me for thinking that she sounded odd and looked ancient. In any case, how could she know that? The phone continued to ring. Maybe it was the CEO. Maybe it was Janey. I reached forwards, placed my shaky hand on the receiver and picked it up. I reeled in my arm with a slow lethargic motion and dreaded the voice on the other end.

'Gordon?'

I breathed out a sigh of relief. The sweat started to dry on my forehead and I started to feel like a human again. It was Freddy.

'Freddy. I'm glad to hear your voice. How are you?' I asked, regaining my composure.

'Ah, ya know. I'm awight, son. I'm awight. I was just wondering if ya wanted to fit a rand in. I'm all on me Todd 'ere at 'ome with the missus. I wanted to get aht in the air, ya know. Howz me Uncle Bob? Did you get an office on the eighth floor?'

I had never been so relieved to hear anybody's voice before, but for some reason, I wasn't sure what to say back. I had a nagging feeling at the back of my brain that told me that I was either missing something, forgetting something, or violating a rule.

'Ah well, Freddy. I would love to play golf but *the* company needs my presence at the moment. It's all go. I'm sure you understand.'

A brief silence fell between us before Freddy spoke again.

'I getcha, son. I getcha. Maybe some other time, eh?'

Freddy hung up, returning me to the world of the grey eighth floor, a place I now wished I had not been so curious about.

20.

Lisa is fantastic. I don't know what I would do without her. She taps away on her laptop and prepares speeches, letters and, now, this book. I find her to be professional. I find her to be at the top of her job. I find her attractive. There's nothing wrong with that.

Anyway.

I need to focus on the book that will inspire all company employees and give them something to aspire to. It will be the best Christmas present they could ever have imagined. How could anybody not be inspired by a story of a man starting on the bottom rungs of a company and working his way up to the top? My story makes it possible for anybody to become a CEO or take control of their own destiny. It is a rags to riches story but without the rags.

I look at my watch and we have three hours until my meeting with the chairman and the subs.

'I will have to edit out your descriptions of the eighth floor. This book violates the rule—'

I glance at Lisa and we say together:

'—do not talk about specific details of the eighth

floor to non eighth floor employees.'

We stare at each other during an awkward pause until I speak.

'Yes. I am aware of that, but I am sure, as with everything else you do, that you will write the perfect morale-boosting book. You'll edit the details. Smooth out my notes and streamline it into a tale of inspiration.'

'I'll also adjust the parts where you mention that you didn't know what your duties were.'

'Oh. Yes. Good example of streamlining. Yes. Yes. Fix all of that. Change whatever you have to change to make it sound fantastic.'

I hadn't realised that I had been been so blasé with my confessions to Lisa. She knows me inside and out, what my inner feelings are, how I felt about *the* company, and how I felt about people I worked with. She knows the truth. She isn't going to tell anybody. I trust her.

Lisa picks up the menu by her laptop and flips through the pages.

'Are you hungry? You can choose whatever you want. I'm paying. Whatever the price is - it doesn't matter. You can choose anything. Anything on that menu. Anything at all.'

Lisa rotates her eyes up from the page and back down again. Lisa orders and continues to take down my notes.

After working as a director for six months, I still hadn't had a one on one meeting with the CEO. We may have worked on the same floor, but to be honest, I never saw him. His office was situated right at the end of the eighth floor and had been the office I had spotted far away in the distance. A meeting had been booked into my diary by Janey who was now my assistant. I was glad that she was by my side. I often wondered where I would have been without her.

'Your meeting is in five minutes. I think you should make a move now,' said Janey.

Janey was good at reminding me about meetings and deadlines. I was so intent on focusing on the finance and new media departments that I usually forgot everything. I spent my time researching and finding examples of what other companies did to improve their sales and services. I took this research and converted it into glorified PowerPoint presentations and urged the departments to follow the examples. My tactics had proved successful and the results of raised profit spoke for me.

I stood up and put my jacket on. The sweaty man, who I still didn't have a name for, walked into my office.

'Sir ... you have a meeting with the CEO ...' the man coughed, '... in office #616.'

'Yes. I know. I am getting ready for it.'

'Good. Good.' The man sneezed. 'Ms Snow wanted me to remind you about it.'

'Relay my thanks to her but Janey has already reminded me of the meeting.'

'Very good, sir ...', the man caught a breath. 'Will you be needing a reminder of the reminder? That can be arranged in case you forget the meeting, sir.'

'I don't need a reminder. As you can see, I am getting ready to make my way to the CEO's office now.'

'Very good, sir. I will let Ms Snow know that you are on your way.'

The sweaty man coughed, and had disappeared through my office door by the time I had walked across to Janey, kissed her on the forehead, and stepped out into the main corridor. It was a long walk to the CEO's office, and I had some understanding of the sweaty man's tiredness and breathlessness. When I arrived, Angela Snow, the CEO's assistant, showed me into the office.

'The CEO is expecting you. Please come in.'

The CEO stood up from his desk, raised his thin arm in my direction, and wanted me to shake his bony hand made up of pointy chipolata fingers. I shook his hand without exerting a strong grip in fear of breaking it.

'Yes. Mark Gallacchi. Come in and please take a seat. Do you want a coffee? Tea? Water?'

The CEO seemed to be as enthusiastic in his office as he was on stage and in meetings. It was my first personal meeting with the man who was the face of *the* company. I had not exchanged so much as two words with him before this. Hello. Goodbye. A nod of the head. The top heads of *the* company had been enigmas to me up until this point. I didn't know who any of them were as people. I only knew their faces.

The CEO's office was larger than mine and had

more wall space to fill up with commercial posters of happy families, dogs and flowers. His desk was larger than mine and was filled up with gadgets, half of which I assumed he would have no reason to use. There wasn't a speck of dust to be seen anywhere on his desk. Not a speck. He sat and pressed a button on the arm of his chair. He leant back and shut his eyes for a brief moment whilst the robotic whir of the massage mechanism kicked in. After half a minute, he switched off the massage function, opened his eyes, and stared at me. I wanted a chair like that.

'Mark Gallacchi, you are here today, sitting in my office, and in that chair, to share *the* company's vision of a brighter tomorrow.'

I twitched.

'As with the great circle of life, things have to give. Insects are eaten by spiders, spiders are eaten by birds, and so on and so on. Freddy Hardcastle had to go. He had to retire. Not because he was tired of *the* company. Not because he disliked *the* company. He left so that new fresh blood could take over and catapult *the* company into future successes.'

I twitched again. The man was a walking speech machine.

'And part of that future success is you, Mark Gallacchi. Together, we will bring *the* company up to date. We will bring *the* company into the 21st century, and screaming into the 22nd and beyond, to give our children something to admire.'

I was half expecting him to break into Winston

Churchill quotes.

'How would it feel? How would it feel, Mark, if your children came up to you and said: "Father. You have been *the* influence in my life. You have taught me that working hard and studying hard creates a life worth leading. You are my true inspiration."?'

'I guess that would be fantastic,' I said.

The CEO halted his speech stared at me as if I had said something wrong. He got up from his seat, walked over to an impressive water cooler in the corner of the office, and fetched a cup. He seemed taller and larger in his office but maybe it was just an illusion. His limbs were thinner than drainpipes and there was a distinct lack of meat on them. His trouser legs and jacket arms flapped around in the air as he moved. His hair was immaculate as if it had been styled by a professional.

'I feel that we need to do some work, Mark Gallacchi. I know you are new to the eighth floor, but we need to do some work. Are you with me?'

The CEO put his cup down on the desk and raised his arms up in front of him. He wanted me to stand up and do *the* company wave. I raised myself to my feet and raised my arms up in front of me.

'Wooooo ... ahhhhh! Wooooo ... ... ahhhh! WOOOO ... ... AHHHH! WOOOO ... ... AHHHH!'

We were both doing the corporate company wave together in tandem. I could feel a bond forming between us as we stood facing each other, taking part in the ritual that I thought was only reserved for large corporate occasions. It was just myself and the CEO, alone, in his office, doing *the* company wave. I felt a tremendous sense of self-pride and importance as we climaxed.

'YEAAAAAAAHHHHH!'

The wave was over and it left me feeling exhilarated, ecstatic and euphoric. The CEO smiled, picked up his cup of water and sipped. After he had swallowed, he offered the cup to me.

'You look as if you need some refreshment.'

I took the cup and gulped down the remaining water, which was at room temperature and tasted odd and stale. It had a tang that I couldn't place or define. I put the cup down on the CEO's desk and waited for further instructions.

'Please. Sit,' said the CEO, pointing to a chair.

I sat and remained as still as one of Janey's plastic action figures.

'Now. I don't need to remind you of the unfortunate situation regarding Anita Fox.'

Anita Fox. The name jabbed my brain like a needle piercing a balloon. It had been some time since she had been fired. I started to picture her in my mind and it brought back bad memories.

'As you are aware, she is no longer working for *the* company after her display of negativity towards you. The reason I bring this is up is because we cannot tolerate negativity at *the* company, which is why you have been chosen to take over her responsibilities as well as maintain a watchful eye on the new media department, which, I must add, has had a remarkable impact on *the* company. It's all due to your performance.'

I had been doing both these jobs anyway.

'We only envisage this to be temporary whilst we find someone else to fill her role, which we have failed to do. I must reiterate that her attitude was negative and this is not tolerated by *the* company. You will adopt a positive mental attitude at all times. You will adopt a positive mental attitude at all times. You will adopt a positive mental attitude at all times.'

I will adopt a positive mental attitude at all times.

'On a personal note, and as this is our first personal meeting, I wanted to welcome you onboard, Mark Gallacchi. You have proven yourself already, but I expect more from you.'

I shook the CEO's outstretched bony hand again and left his office, feeling as if I had a clearer vision of *the* company's expectations of me.

When I returned to my office, Janey was waiting for me.

'What is this place, Mark?' she asked.

'What do you mean?' I asked back.

'I mean. What is this place? What is this floor? What the hell is it, Mark? It's lifeless and has no soul. I'm getting tired of it. I mean, there's not a spot of colour anywhere. If I threw up over your desk, it would be an improvement.'

'Don't say hell and don't bite the hand that feeds, Janey,' I said.

'What's that supposed to mean?'

Janey frowned and squinted.

'It means the company has made this possible for us. We are on the eighth floor, Janey. The eighth floor. We've made it!'

'What have we made exactly?'

'Ok. So it's a little drab, but we can live well on what they are paying us. *The* company has made it all possible.'

Janey panned the room. She hated it. I could tell. I knew when she was displeased. The eighth floor wouldn't allow us to bring in any of our own ornaments to adorn the office and they wouldn't allow us to redecorate. This was it. Grey. I didn't like it any more than Janey did, but I couldn't admit how much I didn't like it. My tongue was being held and I was astonished that the word "drab" had fallen out of my mouth.

'Drab? This is worse than drab, Mark. After a year of working here, you'll probably need antidepressants or worse.'

'It's not that bad. It's neutral and uninfluenced by anything. It won't distract me from doing my job.'

'You can keep on convincing yourself of that. I'm not buying it. I won't be here very long anyway.'

I froze. Was she going to leave me? Was she leaving the company? And if so, why hadn't she told me before now? Had she found someone else? Was she two-timing me? No. I couldn't believe that.

'Won't be here? What are you saying?' I asked.

Janey beamed a smile that ran from ear to ear and looked at me with a raised eyebrow, coaxing me to make a guess.

'I'm pregnant.'

I rushed forward and gave Janey a hug and a kiss. I was now going to be a father and have my own family. We would have to get married as soon as possible. No expense spared. *The* company had made it all possible for us to move into a larger house, provide for our impending baby, and have a life of complete wedded bliss. And then a realisation hit me. The one person I needed to complete my working days would no longer be here. A tear fell from my left eye, travelled down my face, and dripped onto Janey's shoulder.

'That's great news,' I said.

I unlocked myself from the embrace and wiped the tears away from my eyes. Janey wasn't crying, but continued smiling a smile that never looked as if it was going to sag.

'Gordon! Awight me ol' china? I thought we could squidge in some fishin' again.'

'Gordon! Howzabout we shoot a rand today.'

'Gordon! I've used me loaf and baked some bread. Ha! Ha! Did you like me pun? Anyways, I thought I could nip rand and give ya some.'

'Gordon! I thought youz and me could start doin' some DIY together. Ya know, fixing 'ouses like they do on the box.'

Three weeks had gone by and there was no end to Freddy's phone calls. Once a day at least. Twice a day was average. Three times wasn't close enough. Four was normal. We were both getting tired of it, Janey more so. She was the one that answered the phone.

'No. Mark is really busy right now. Maybe some other time.'

'No. Mark is still really busy as he was when you rang the first time.'

'Can you ring back sometime, in the future?'

Sometimes she let the phone ring until it stopped. He just wasn't getting the message and we didn't want to offend him by being blunt. While I was looking at Anita's logo project, I came up with an idea.

'Janey. I've got it. Do you think you'd be able to track down Gordon?' I asked.

'As in Gordon Hardcastle?'

'Yep. The one and only. I'm thinking if we can get Gordon to talk to his dad again, he'll stop calling us. We'd be doing a good deed too. Everybody wins.'

'Maybe Gordon doesn't wanna be found,' said Janey.

'Probably, but I think it's the only way to stop Freddy from distracting us from the important work needed to be done here at *the* company. As far as I know, Freddy mentioned something about him being in Dubai and sand.'

Janey nodded, opened her laptop and started to tap the keys. I, however, had turned my attention to the logo project, left behind by Anita Fox. I opened the folder and clicked on the PDF entitled final logo. I couldn't believe it when the file opened and displayed the blue oval with the double black lined border plus italic lettering. It was the old logo that I disliked and had said a four year old could have designed. Was a cruel joke being played on me or was there another file marked final logo 2? I couldn't find one. Instead, I opened a word file of correspondence between Anita and the subs:

> The subs: *We find the rectangular logo features too many right angles. So we are dismissing all of the square designs. We, however, liked the blue oval design featuring curves. We feel this is the best logo to represent the company.*
> Fox: *I am delighted that you like the oval design. We have worked hard on this project, and we value your essential and valuable input. We will move forward with the oval design and send a final version by PDF to you.*

Anita annoyed me from her dead career's grave. It had all been a waste of time changing and designing multiple versions of different logos, and it had been a waste of time bouncing them all off the subs. In my role as director, new rules had to be drawn up and implemented to stop them wasting company time. I opened my email inbox, hit compose, and started to write my first authoritative message:

> *Dear ...*

I stopped and thought about a recipient's name but realised that I couldn't find a mention of anybody anywhere in any of Anita's old emails and documents.

I breathed a despondent sigh and carried on tapping the keys:

Dear Sub-Directors,

It has come to my attention that you are keen on the blue oval design logo that Anita sent you as part of her logo design project. As Anita is no longer with us and not in charge of this project anymore, I will finalise the logo project. I would urge the sub-directors to reassess your current evaluation of the logo and consider the other choices available on the PDF. If we are to read into current trends; ovals, curves, and Times New Roman fonts are out; squares, rectangles, and Bank Gothic fonts are in. I do not believe that the oval logo represents the *company moving forward, which leads me to the issue of moving forward. I also believe that time management is a problem. We can not afford to spend a large amount of time weighing up a range of different options in future projects. Time is money and the more we waste, the further we lag behind our competitors. As a director, I will take the initiative and suggest that, in the future, we do not let the same thing happen again.*

Best regards,

Mark Gallacchi
Director

I clicked on send without spell checking, without

pausing for thought, and without any regrets. The subs could say what they wanted, but at the end of the day, *the* company headquarters, of which I was now a major player, had the final say. Or at least that was my impression. They could argue all they wanted with me. I was in control.

The company was going to use the blue oval logo. Thesubs had had words with the CEO and he agreed that it was to be the company's new logo much to my horror. I had been outmaneuvered, outranked, outvoted, and anything else that started with out. I twiddled a pen in my fingers and looked at the grey wall featuring a generic black and white picture of a dog and some flowers. I stared at one of the white petals, fell into a trance, and started to drift away. I was wiping my mind clean like a computer's hard drive. Ctrl + Alt + Del. Reboot. Restart. It was better than focusing on my disappointment, or how much I had come to hate the subs after working with them for just six months.

'I got him.'

Janey's remark made me drop my pen on my desk and jolted my body back into my comfortable executive chair. I observed a slight tummy bulge showing through her top.

'I'm sorry. Did I make you jump? Sorry. Look. I got him.'

'You got him? Oh! You mean, you found Gordon? You found the real Gordon Hardcastle? As in *Gordon* Gordon?'

'Yep.'

Janey looked as satisfied as the cat that got the cream and had licked its whiskers. It was good news. Freddy needed to stop calling me over five times a day and stop calling me Gordon. I was now Mark Gallacchi, a Director of *the* company - not to be mistaken for anybody else.

'What did he say?'

'Well, what we expected. He doesn't have a father, etc, etc. He said he won't call him but I think he will.'

'What makes you say that?'

Janey paused. 'I said that Freddy was dying.'

'You told him what?'

'I had to do something otherwise he wasn't going to call him.'

After Janey had told me about her white lie, and that there were no guarantees that Gordon would call his father, I started to worry that my phone would be the first number Freddy would call for the foreseeable future. If Gordon called Freddy, he would find out that he was not at death's door and still his usual self. If they talked, they **had** to work things out for my sake, if not their own. Freddy was distracting me and would have to be quashed for good if I was going to become the best director the company had ever seen.

21.

The phone calls stopped. We no longer had to pretend that we were not in the office, or out at lunch, or too busy to answer the phone. Janey had done it. She had found Gordon and served him up to Freddy. I wondered what conversation had transpired between them. Maybe Freddy had done all the talking. Maybe Gordon had hung up on him. Maybe nothing was going to happen at all. In any case, the phone calls had stopped for the time being.

Over the next month, or maybe even two months, I had got used to the eighth floor's greyscale colour scheme. I had got used to wiping my hands dry on my very own grey hand towel with my name on it. I had got used to the grey mug I used to carry my tea, the grey carpets, and the slightly overweight man who rushed about between offices, delivering various pieces of paper. I felt I could reach my goals without being distracted.

But my goals were being threatened.

Threatened by the sub-directors.

The subs.

I had come to loathe them after being in the director's chair for almost a year. They had signed off on the oval logo that I hated, and the CEO, who also loved the oval logo, had overruled me. It wasn't just the logo. A meeting had been arranged, between them, myself, other directors and the CEO, to discuss a new service *the* company was introducing. I had been in the office since 7 a.m., and the meeting room had been prepared by the sweaty overweight man for 9 a.m. sharp. I walked into the meeting room at 8.30 a.m. and sat down in one of the comfortable conference room seats.

'I'm sorry ... sir,' the man gasped, '... but I thought this meeting was due to start at 9 a.m. sharp.'

The overweight man placed a decanter of water on the shiny black table in front of me and looked at me.

'I like to be early,' I said.

'Early. Yes, sir. I see, sir. Very well, sir. I shall ...' the man wheezed, '... have to work around you, sir. I'm sorry for any inconvenience.'

'You do what you have to do, my good man. You won't even know I am here.'

'Oh, sir. But I will know you are there. You work on the eighth floor. You are a V.I.P and, therefore ...' the man sneezed, '... one of my V.I.Ps.'

'Bless you.'

'Thank you, sir. And bless you too, sir.'

I watched the man run out of the conference room, into the kitchen area, grab a silver tray, and run back into the conference room again. The tray contained a number of snack items all coloured to match the greyscale theme. Grey bread rolls, blackberries, white chocolate finger biscuits, licorice sweets, sugar cubes for the tea or coffee.

'Is there any milk?'

'Milk, sir? That all depends, sir.'

'Depends on?'

'What you plan to do with it, sir.'

I was stumped. I didn't understand what he meant. I wasn't going to start spraying milk around the room.

'If you plan to drink a glass of milk ... then I can certainly supply you with a glass of milk, sir,' the man coughed, '... but it is strictly forbidden to use the milk to soften the bitterness of your tea or coffee beverages, sir.'

'Oh, really? Nobody has told me that before.'

'Yes, sir. It is in the rulebook, sir. Any tea or coffee that changes its colour ... due to the addition of milk by an employee working on the eight floor ...' the man coughed, '... will not be tolerated. It is subject to disciplinary action, sir.'

'I see. Well, I would like a glass of milk in that case then.'

'Yes, sir. Very good, sir. I have read you your rights with regards to the aforementioned milk beverage ...' the man paused and sneezed, '... and the matter will be out of my hands once I serve you the milk, sir.'

I had never had such a long conversation about a glass of milk before. The eighth floor was still full of little surprises and rules that I still had to abide by.

I made a decision to study the rulebook further for the following day. As the overweight man continued to bring in tray after tray of monotone snacks and nibbles, I looked at my reflection in the glossy black conference table's surface. There wasn't a hair out of place. No stubble. My tie was crooked. I straightened it. I was ready for the meeting.

The other directors filtered into the room at precisely 8.59, sat down, and stared at me. I looked around the table. Every one of them was wearing the same suit, had the same haircut, the same tie, the same pen and notepad, and the same mug as me.

'We will ignore the fact that you entered the room early, as usual, Mr Gallacchi. I admire your keenness, but it's still considered a waste of twenty-nine minutes of company time.'

I had the same argument with the CEO every time I came to the conference room early. I liked to collect my thoughts before a major meeting such as this one. They didn't seem to understand my mindset. Today, I didn't feel like arguing and I nodded my head in agreement. The CEO didn't like me "wasting" company time and I didn't like "wasting" my breath.

'Now we are gathered here to discuss the new service *the* company is offering consumers. I think we will all agree that it is needed in our portfolio. Our competitors are all offering the same service to their consumers and it's about time that we did the same.'

The CEO pressed a button on a console in front of him and displayed a slide behind him that projected onto a huge screen that filled up the whole wall. I couldn't understand what it was displaying. There was a pie chart, a bar graph, some horrible clip art, and some percentages that read over 100% accompanied by arrows. Not even Jackson Pollock could have painted something as abstract as this seemed to be.

'As you can see, this model represents maximum ROI, has good ROE, good ROA prospects, and research has shown keen EPS as well. In short - it's a winner.'

The other directors hummed and they harred and made all other kinds of encouraging noises that I didn't understand. Based on what I saw on the slide, I was amazed anybody knew anything about the new product - if it was a product.

'This product is both innovative and aspirational and will lift *the* company upwards into the third sector.'

The CEO pointed to the up arrows and the high percentages. It made all the others nod and agree with some outcries of the word "yes". I wasn't sure what I was supposed to do on this occasion so I smiled and nodded too, looked at the screen, and then at my peers. Yes. Yes. Wonderful. Hum. Har.

'What do you think, Mark, as you are the latest addition to the eighth floor, what do you think of this new product?'

The CEO waved his hand in my direction and all the other V.I.Ps turned and looked at me. I had only just finished nodding and yessing and now he wanted my opinion on something I knew nothing about.

'I agree with you. I think it is a way forward for *the* company. It is a great product and will surely be a surefire hit with our investors and, likewise, our customers.'

I didn't know where the words had come from. I wasn't even sure what I was agreeing to. I was shocked. It was if a ghost of a former CEO had possessed me and made me speak like a puppet. A few moments of silence fell over the room, and I didn't know where to look. At first, I looked down at my reflection on the table. I could see the pained expression on my face that wished I could be rescued; that a hole could open up in the floor and swallow me through the grey plastic carpet fibres. What was happening? Claps. I heard claps. I looked up and the CEO was clapping.

'Yes. Mark. You are quite right to agree because this—this is what this product represents for us.'

The CEO pointed to a badly drawn bag of money pulled straight from a clip art collection. Hum. Har. Guffaw. Yes. Yes. I couldn't help thinking that I had passed some kind of test automatically; the scribbles on the presentation had been some kind of test. Maybe it wasn't a product after all. Maybe it was just a test. The CEO stood by the slide and looked at it, admiring the work that had gone into creating it before turning around.

'Now. Moving on to another issue, we need to talk about our logo.'

The CEO pressed a button and displayed the awful oval logo that I had tried so hard to get rejected.

'The sub-directors have chosen this to be the new corporate logo for *the* company. I think you'll agree, they have made a good choice.'

Hum. Har. Guffaw. Yes. Yes. This time, I couldn't agree with the room. There wasn't a fibre in my soul that had any affection for that awful logo. The clip art of the moneybag was better than this and *the* company had paid a fortune to develop it. So much for looking after our expenditure.

'I plan to send this final design to the chairman today for final approval, and after he approves, we will reveal it at the next company meeting in two weeks. And I must give special thanks to Mark Gallacchi for his input on this project. As some of you might know, he took this project over and saw it through to its completion.'

The others looked at me again and started to clap. I was seething on the inside, but my tongue was being held and clamped by an invisible force. I couldn't have spoken out against the new logo if I had tried my hardest. The logo shone bold on the projector screen behind the CEO. This was it. This was the new company logo and there was nothing I could do about it. What was happening? The CEO looked at me and started waving his hands up and down. The others stood to attention and started to do the same. I was one of them.

'Woooooo ... ahhhhhh! Woooooo ... ... ahhhhh! WOOOOO ... ... AHHHHH! WOOOOO ... ... AHHHHH! ... ... YEAAAAAAAHHHHHH!'

After the wave had finished, we all sat back down in

our seats and looked at the CEO.

'That concludes the meeting. We will meet again next week in the same room and at the same time. Thank you everybody.'

What had just happened?

When I returned to my office, Janey was sitting at my desk with her face buried in a laptop. I wanted to tell her how odd I was feeling, but the same tongue clamping sensation that I had experienced in the meeting room started to take hold again. She knew all about my dislike towards the oval logo from our time discussing it with Anita Fox, but now it felt as if I couldn't talk about it. Janey looked up from the screen and raised a smile. I placed the black coffee I had collected from the coffee machine on my desk.

'How did it go?' asked Janey.

'Great. We have a new product launch coming up, which is exciting, and the new logo is going to be announced soon too.'

'Oh. So they went with your rectangular design?'

'N ... n ... no. They ... they ...'

I couldn't speak my mind. I tried to spit out the words of hatred that I had for the logo but they wouldn't come out. The harder I tried, the more my mouth and mind resisted. I couldn't fight against it.

'... they went with the oval design.'

'What? The oval design? The crap logo? Are you kidding me?'

I shuddered. I felt like a piston that had jammed

with steam building up inside.

'But, you hate that design. Why didn't you try and get your logo approved? It's much better than ... than ... that thing.'

'Thelogorepresentsthefutureof*the*companyandwillmoveusforwardgoingintothethirdquarter.'

The words fired from my mouth like bullets. I sat down on the seat opposite my desk.

'Are you ok?' asked Janey.

'Sorry. Sorry. It must be the pressure I am under or something. I'm ok. I'm ok.'

I took a sip of my black coffee and raised my hand to my forehead. I felt warm. Janey looked at me and fetched a cup of water from the water cooler.

'Here. Drink this. I don't know why you drink that coffee. It's probably not good for you.'

'Thanks.' I took a sip from the cup. 'The CEO believes that the logo is the right for *the* company and I agree.'

I had given up resisting.

'You do?'

'Yes. Now I do.'

'I see.'

Janey raised her eyebrows, turned around, and walked away from my chair. She seemed confused by my responses, and I couldn't blame her. I was confused myself. I followed her with my eyes as she sat down; her jet-black hair; her striking eyes; luscious lips; her curvy body; the bump that represented our immediate future. I loved her. I loved the bump. I was sure about that.

'I love you.'

The three little words left my mouth without any restriction.

'Me too.'

I grinned but, at the same time, felt worried about the future. There wasn't a person in the world that could replace her even on a temporary basis.

'I'm sorry. I don't mean to offend you but you know how it is.'

I try to reassure Lisa that what I just said wasn't an insult. Janey is my wife and, therefore, irreplaceable. I hope that Lisa sees this the same way I do.

'It's ok. I understand. I need to go to the bathroom. I'll be right back,' says Lisa, leaving the table.

Lisa is a gem. I knew she would understand and not be offended. There isn't anybody I would rather have as Janey's replacement than Lisa. I remember that there was a time when I would have frowned at the idea of replacing Janey. I remembered the interviews for the job. Janey had filled up my diary with hopeful candidates that I didn't look forward to meeting.

No.

Inexperienced.

No. No.

Over experienced.

Too qualified.

He spoke too soft.

She spoke too loud.

He was wearing the wrong kind of shoes.

I made every little excuse not to hire a replacement. Janey was irreplaceable as my assistant, that was, until Lisa walked into the meeting room on the fifth floor. She was tall, wore a tailored power suit and looked professional. She was Swedish but I wouldn't have known. Her English was perfect and I couldn't detect an accent. She didn't move the air as she walked into the room, the air moved for her.

'Yes. This is Lisa Johansson,' said Janey.

Janey's abrupt and snappy introduction made her sound as if she didn't like the candidate from the outset. Lisa had not even spoken a word and I felt sorry for her.

'Yoo-hans-son,' said Lisa, correcting Janey's pronunciation.

Janey glared at her. She never appreciated being corrected when she was wrong.

'Thanks, Janey,' I said.

I was as subtle as I could have been in suggesting that Janey should leave the room. Lisa had made Janey stiffen up and spit out her introduction like an insult. Janey left the room and slammed the door behind her harder than she had done with any of the other applicants. When I think back to how I used to act when I first joined *the* company, I am repulsed. I can't believe I said the things I have said and acted the way I acted. This kind of attitude on the eighth floor would not be tolerated and it is an attitude I am glad I don't have anymore. I have an image to uphold and I am going to do my upmost to do it.

Lisa returns to the table after her toilet pause and looks at her watch.

'We have only a few hours left before your meeting with the chairman.'

'That should be more than enough time. Let's move on. I'm almost finished.'

I sip my glass of water, clear my throat, and continue to tell Lisa the rest of my story.

22.

'What the hell is this? I mean, really, what the hell is this?'

It was my first exchange of words with the chairman who was doing most of the exchanging. It was rare for anybody to hear direct from the chairman. When I started working for *the* company, work colleagues had described him as a crusty grey old man who had a perpetual grin on his face. His teeth were yellow and resembled a double yellow line on a road; dust blew off his hairpiece when there was a breeze; he slept in a coffin and only came out at night. I couldn't verify any of the rumours. I hadn't seen him. I hadn't heard his voice up until now and it was angry.

'What the hell is the CEO playing at? Is this really the best logo we could come up with?' said the chairman, on the phone. I couldn't get a word in edgeways. 'You. You were the one responsible for this weren't you? You were the one who drew up this logo with the help of some agency somewhere that I paid a ransom for, I bet. Here we are, in the middle of a company crisis, and you want to go and blow all my profits. Everything. What is wrong with you? What the hell is this anyway? You still haven't answered my question.'

'If I could, I would like to explain,' I said, managing to slip in some words.

'Explain? It'd better be good. I mean, really good.'

I wanted to tell the chairman that I hated the logo as much as he did, but I couldn't get the truth out.

'I ... thin ... thin ...'

'What the hell is wrong with you? Where did you go to school to be able to talk gibberish? You'd better give me an explanation or—'

'Thelogorepresentsthefutureof*the*companyandwillmoveusforwardgoingintothethirdquarter.'

Where did that come from? It was the same spiel I had spat at Janey. I couldn't hold it back. It was involuntary. Robotic.

The chairman fell silent and breathed heavy into the phone receiver. I gulped. I wasn't sure what he was going to do next. Was he going to fire me? I couldn't even defend myself.

'Ah ha. Ok. I understand.'

The chairman's tone had softened, and the anger had vanished from his voice.

'I give you permission to give me your honest opinion. Do you understand?' he asked.

A huge weight lifted from my shoulders, my brain unlocked itself, and my mouth could speak what my mind wanted to say.

'I don't like the logo. I think it is cheap, nasty and a looks as if a child drew it,' I said with calmness.

A small, almost creepy, laugh echoed through the phone. It sounded as if the chairman *did* live in a vault surrounded by candles and bats. I imagined him sleeping in a coffin.

'Good. Good. Speak your mind. You're safe with me.'

I didn't feel reassured by the chairman's vow of security.

'I'm guessing that you had other logo designs that were rejected.'

'Yes.'

'Can you send me them?'

'Yes.'

'Good. I will have words with the CEO about this matter, but just so that you know, I understand what has happened. Do you understand?'

I wasn't sure how to answer. I was too busy trying to deal with my confusion. What was it that he understood? What did I understand? I understood nothing.

'Do you understand?' the chairman asked again.

I had to lie.

'Yes.'

It was the best answer I had. It was short and required little effort to say. I think I understood where the chairman was coming from but I wasn't sure. I only knew that he had made me feel like Mark Gallacchi again; the man who wasn't afraid to speak his mind; the man whose backbone had been placed back into his body.

'I don't know what he's been playing at. The share

prices continue to drop, we don't seem to be putting out any new groundbreaking products or services, and if we carry on like this, I will lose the company to some American organisation that will come along, pay a pittance to buy us out, and then shut us down. I will have words with him. I will have words. Anyway, send me the other logo or logos, and I'll sort the rest out.'

The chairman hung up. I placed my phone down on my desk and picked up my grey mug that still had a drop of lukewarm coffee in the bottom of it. I took a swig and tried to relax. My heart was thumping fast and I needed to calm down. I had voiced my opinion, and the restrictions that had prevented me from voicing them were no longer holding me back. The old Mark had returned. I opened my laptop, sent the chairman the logo PDF, and finished my black coffee. As soon as the empty cup had made contact with the desk's surface, the sweaty overweight man dashed into my office.

'Very good, sir, you have finished your coffee, sir.' The man wheezed, and sounded as if he had coughed up some phlegm. 'Was it a good cup of coffee sir? Was its taste to your satisfaction, sir?'

'It was adequate.'

'Adequate, sir? Oh dear. That won't do. Adequate is another way of saying that it didn't ...' the man sneezed, '... reach your expectations. A standard has been violated.'

'It was better than average. Don't worry about it. It was perfectly ok.'

The chubby man reached forward, snatched my empty mug off my desk and sniffed it. He raised his eyes to the ceiling whilst his rosy red complexion seemed to fade into pastel peach. He looked mortified.

'Oh dear, oh dear, sir. Oh dear, oh dear—oh dear oh dear oh dear.'

I looked at the man with astonishment.

'Ohdearohdearohdearohdear ...'

'What is the matter?'

'You were right. I can tell this black coffee was just simply adequate and not perfect as it should be.' The man paused and hacked up a wet cough. 'I will fetch you a new coffee that will match your requirements. Black coffee again, sir?'

'Look. It doesn't matter. I don't want another coffee. Why don't you take a rest? You'll do yourself a mischief.'

'Oh no, sir. Mischief is not a word with use here, sir.'

The overweight rosy-cheeked man left my office and returned almost as fast as he had left.

'Here, sir. This will meet your requirements.'

The overweight man placed the mug in the same position as he had picked it up from and then left my office. The cup's steam rose and hit my nostrils in the same way fresh baked bread fumes did from a bakery. A smell of cocoa intoxicated my senses. I picked the mug up from my desk and was about to sip it when Janey walked in with Lisa.

'We have finished the induction.'

Janey grimaced. It was a sad day. We both knew

that after Lisa's induction and training had finished, she was ready to take over as my assistant. Janey would go on maternity leave, and we would become a family. It would be the start of our perfect life together. I raised the black coffee to my lips and sipped at the piping hot drink, allowing myself to inhale the fumes through my nose.

'I don't know how you can drink that stuff. It tastes awful,' said Janey.

I had never seen Janey drink any of the company's hot beverages. I had never convinced her to try the coffee.

'It is not that bad,' said Lisa. 'I quite like it.'

'Well, whatever.'

I placed the mug back down on my desk and swallowed the coffee. It hit the spot. Janey and Lisa looked at me for further instructions.

'Why don't we go through my calendar for the following months and prepare for the key meetings that are coming up?'

'If you don't mind, I really need to sit down and take it easy,' replied Janey.

Janey rubbed her convex belly and tried to appeal to my sense of sympathy. She batted her eyelids and gave the smile that had won me over to her side a countless number of times.

'Oh. Yes. Sure. If you are not feeling good, you can always go home and come back if you want to,' I said.

Janey's smile faded away, her eyes stopped fluttering and opened wide. I wasn't about to drop everything to take her home. *The* company needed me to be at the helm, in times, of what the chairman called "crisis".

'I can call a taxi to take you home,' I said.

'A taxi. I see. Don't worry about me. I'll make it home by myself. I'll be ok. Don't worry yourself at all,' said Janey.

Janey turned away and stomped out of my office leaving myself and Lisa alone. I didn't want Janey to go home by herself, but by refusing my offer of a taxi, she had made that decision herself. I felt bad but there was nothing I could do about it. I couldn't take time off from *the* company. Lisa looked at me as if she was ready to get into the job - being my assistant.

'I don't know what he is playing at. The rectangular logo is clearly the best logo of the bunch. It's the sub-directors, I bet. I bet it's the sub-directors. No. In fact, I know it is them. They stick their nose in at every turn and what happens? He caves in. He always caves in. If there was a cave in the building, he'd be in it, hiding. I mean, what the hell is he playing at?'

Again, I stayed silent, unable to get a word in through the gaps in the chairman's rage.

'I don't know what is happening, Mark. The share prices are spiraling downwards, the CEO can't make his own decisions, and the sub-directors seem to have more power than I have. How did it happen, Mark? It's outrageous and something will have to be done about it. Something I should have done quite some time ago before we got in this state.'

The chairman's voice had started to break up and sound husky through all of his shouting. It was peculiar to receive a phone call from him once a month let alone twice a week, but then again, these were peculiar times for *the* company. An economic crisis had forced *the* company to take a look at itself and try to adjust to the growing and evolving consumer and corporate markets. It was failing. I knew it, the chairman knew it, and, probably, the CEO knew it but seemed powerless to do anything about it.

'I want us all to meet. You, myself, the CEO and the sub-directors. I make the decisions around here and I will thrash it out with everyone. I won't have *my* company flushed down the toilet before I retire. Not over my old and not so feeble body. I'll set up a meeting and we'll see who has the last word on this.'

The chairman hung up without me even uttering a word into my phone. I looked forward to the meeting as it signalled change and progress. I had faith in the chairman to sort the problems out, move *the* company forwards, and get it back to where it used to be - at the top and looking down at all the other inferior competitors. The chairman would cut through the subs like a knife through butter. He would slice them up into pieces and feed them through a shredder. I pointed the accusing finger straight at them for most of *the* company's problems. They never compromised. They never entertained our point of view. They got their way for the most part.

They never made themselves known.

I had worked for *the* company for over a year, and I had never met one person from the subs. They sent emails and sent conference call requests both over the phone and the net, but I had never met anyone. They worked in the building but were question marks. They were shadows. I didn't even know if they were 'they'. I never caught any of their names either, which made me ask questions. It didn't matter to the CEO, who bent over backwards at the drop of a hat for them, him, her, it, and agreed with anything they said. There was nothing I could do either despite being a director. I had my opinions and views, but I couldn't express them no matter how much I wanted to. The chairman was the only person I could express myself to and I couldn't work out why. Not even Janey was allowed to know how I felt about company matters and she was the light of my life that I shared all my innermost thoughts with.

'I have called this meeting to discuss the current crisis. Now, what the bloody hell is going on? When I appointed you as CEO, I believed in you. I believed in your ability to sail the ship through stormy conditions and that includes typhoons. We are in a typhoon and the ship is sinking. What the bloody hell is going on?'

The chairman had started the meeting in an emphatic way. I admired his style even though he was old and dusty. He still had all of his own teeth. His grey silver hair, that stretched around the side of his head and formed a border between his bald scalp and ears, had been trimmed to perfection. He was taller than I expected him to be. His shoes had been polished to to such an extent that they looked like ceramic dishes. He wore a bow tie and it looked real. He had spent some time perfecting its symmetrical shape.

The CEO looked worried. The sweat on his forehead glistened in the meeting room's lamps that seemed to beam down on him like he was being interrogated. The subs had yet to join the meeting through a conference call, and this gave the chairman time to grill the CEO.

'I assure you that I can steer the ship. We are sailing into stormy economic times as I am sure you are well aware of and ...' said the CEO, sweating.

'Who do you think you are? Do you believe you are the captain? Let me just state something right here and now, you are not.'

The chairman's face had turned red and his voice had become louder. I sat in my seat and remained quiet. I wanted to reach out and pour myself a coffee from the canister in front of me, but I was afraid to even move. The fumes from the coffee combinedwith the small pastry items on the dishes made me hungry. They made my stomach growl. I refrained from moving and could only look at the tantalising snacks in front of me.

'Hello? Hello? Can you hear us? We are here now.'

The subs' voices pumped through a speaker in the middle of the conference room table.

'Yes. We can hear you. Now that we are all here, I can tell you that I have made some decisions, some big decisions that will affect everyone.'

The chairman walked around the table and stood

next to the speaker to be heard better. He owned the room. A short uncomfortable silence fell and, for a split second, I thought I heard the CEO gulp.

'First, I am dead against this oval monstrosity you call our new logo. It looks cheap and nasty and looks as if a child has drawn it.'

They were my words. My words! The chairman had agreed with me and liked my input. I smiled and felt an immediate sense of pride.

'Erm, before we really get into this, can I offer everyone a cup of coffee?" asked the CEO.

The CEO grabbed the canister from the centre of the table along with three cups and started to pour. He was so eager that he overfilled one cup, spilling coffee onto the conference room table.

'What are you doing, man? Coffee? That coffee? What? Are you kidding me? I haven't touched company coffee since I was at the helm. I don't want to drink any of that poison. That's another item on my list that I will get to after this logo malarkey.'

The CEO tentatively placed the canister back on the centre of the desk, grabbed a serviette, and dabbed at the coffee slick.

'What is wrong with the logo? I mean, we all liked it here, I mean, we think it looks good, I mean, we thought it was the best one,' said an anonymous sub.

'Well, I don't think so. I am the chairman of *the* company, and what I say in this meeting, as well as all other meetings, goes.'

I looked at the chairman with admiration. Here was

a man who could say what he wanted, when he wanted, and could get things done with one sentence, maybe even one word. I aspired to be like him as I sat in my chair, silent and still, watching him in action.

'This logo is hideous. It's old fashioned and staid. I propose, in fact, I have chosen the rectangular logo to be *the* company's new logo.'

'But, but, wait, please. You need to hear our opinions,' said the CEO with a timid nervous voice.

'I already know all your opinions, and I can say, right here, that I disagree with them and I frankly don't care for them. I am the chairman.'

The CEO leant back in his seat. He looked like a hurdler who had tripped over the first hurdle.

'I agree with the CEO. You should hear our side and ...' said the subs.

'You don't have the authority to order me to hear your side. I've been taking a back seat for too long, and now look what has happened. *The* company is in treacherous waters everybody. The water is seeping in through the portholes, and if we don't do something, we'll be swimming with the fishes, heading for Davy Jones's locker.'

I liked the chairman's references to the sea and its sea life. I made a mental note to use this style more.

'The rectangular logo will be the new company logo. Second, I want to replace all the coffee, tea and water machines with new machines.'

The CEO jolted forward and spoke out albeit with some hesitation and loose amounts of stutter.

'Now, just wait here. Do you know how much that will cost? Do, do, you know people on the eighth floor do not like change? Do, do, do you know that we all really like the taste of the coffee and tea here? Do, do, do, do ...'

'De Do Do Do! De Da Da Da! I think you've all been drinking it for so long that you've forgotten what good coffee tastes like. I import coffee beans direct from Brazil, and you know what? I've never felt better for it. I don't care how much it costs because I will pay for it personally out of my own money.'

I didn't think there was a problem with the coffee machines, but then again, I had been drinking the company coffee since I started working for *the* company. Maybe the chairman was right. I had become used to it.

'The coffee machines plus water coolers are gone as from today,' said the chairman.

The buzz of static from the subs' conference call echoed in the room.

'Third, and probably the biggest change I will make––I am relieving you of your duties,' said the chairman, and pointed in the CEO's direction.

The room fell silent.

One of the directors, stopped chewing on a biscuit and held the remaining portion in the air. The CEO was stunned. He sat in his chair and didn't move an inch. The words had gone in one ear, rested, and exited out through the other. The CEO wiped away the sweat on his forehead with the back of his hand. I remained quiet. I had never been in a meeting as intense as this before and I found it to be exhilarating.

'I'm sorry. Say that again. Who are you relieving of their duties? Is Mark Gallachi leaving us?' asked the subs.

The subs' poor connection had made them miss the Earth shattering news.

'No. I am, with immediate effect, relieving the CEO of his duties. He is no longer the captain of this sinking ship.'

'Now, now, now, hold on, now, I, I, this is outrageous. You can't just do this. I have been loyal to the company for years,' said the CEO.

The CEO stood up and started waving his thin arms around. His suit sleeves flapped around in the breeze as he moved. A long thin boney finger was being pointed. Sweat was flying.

'Loyal. Yes. Effective. No,' said the chairman.

The static buzz from the conference call became worse until the line broke down, cutting the subs off from the conversation.

'No. No. No. Listen ...' said the CEO.

'No. YOU listen. Since you took over, the share prices have dropped, there have not been any new products or services, you have no idea when it comes to moving *my* company forward and the logo is a good example of that. You have no idea. You have no bloody idea and that is why, in the best interests of *my* company, I have chosen to replace you.'

'But, but, replace me? With who?'

The chairman looked at me and smiled. I remained

calm and smiled back.

'With him? Are you kidding?'

'Who do you think I mean? He is the only one who can do your job, pull us out of our spiralling whirlpool of corporate destruction, and move *my* company forward.'

'This jumped up little upstart? Are you kidding me? You can't do this to me. I refuse to leave.'

The CEO sat down, crossed his arms and sat firm in his seat. He reminded me of a protestor sitting outside the city's hall, waiting for the police to drag him away.

'Security is already on their way. You can either leave with dignity, or they'll drag you out of the building. It's your choice. You can take your assistant, that Angela Snow woman with you too. There will be no need for her now that you are gone.'

The CEO shook his head, uncrossed his arms, and stood up, raising his slender frame to its full height.

'You won't get away with this. I'll see you in court,' said the CEO.

The CEO chose the dignified walk, or, maybe, undignified stomp out of the building. I had not said a word during the meeting and I didn't have to. The chairman had said it all. The other directors sat in silence and watched the events unfold.

'Well. That takes care of that,' said the chairman.

The chairman brushed his hands together and mimicked throwing trash into the bin. He walked across to my side of the table and stared down at me.

'Congratulations. We'll finalise and talk about

everything I expect from you. Welcome to the helm, Mark.'

The chairman extended his hand, and I extended mine for a handshake. His grip made my knuckles crack like someone popping bubble wrap, and his vigorous shake felt as if he wanted to separate my hand from my arm.

The subs remained quiet and were about to speak when the chairman hung up the conference call.

It was too late.

Meeting adjourned.

23.

'So, I think that is really it. Through hard work and determination, I climbed the corporate ladder from temporary contract to CEO.'

I pick up a rice cracker from my plate and nibble it. I swallow the morsel of healthy food, and I feel pleased about the information I have relayed to my excellent assistant, Lisa. She will be rewarded for her work on the book amongst other things. *Employee of the year* will be hers for sure.

'Is that everything?' asks Lisa.

I rub my mouth and chin clear of rice cracker crumbs. Was that everything?

'No, actually. Maybe I should mention, as a closing statement, how *the* company has grown since my two and a half years in charge, just to finish off with a vision of the future. What do you think?'

'It is up to you. I am more than happy to write it all down. The more information the better.'

'Yes. I think I will. It needs to be wrapped up, and the book needs to have the message that anything can be achieved within *the* company. *The* company is the environment that supports human development through its employees, it supports the immediate community through charity work, and it supports the world through being more thoughtful with green issues. Yes, say something about all of that. Really try to emphasis what *the* company is doing for everybody and everything, and how everything and anything can be achieved.'

Lisa taps down some notes on her laptop. I can't help but admire the way she touch-types. She is the assistant that every CEO should have and she is mine. I think about ways of keeping her on after Janey returns to work. I will have to convince Janey to stay at home for a while longer; make up some other job title for Lisa; have two assistants. I will have to think of something.

'I'll just wrap up the story by describing the last two years or so, and then we can head off to the office.'

After I had come to terms with being promoted to CEO, I remembered rushing home (after a particular hard day's work + overtime) to tell Janey the good news.

'They made me the CEO. I've been promoted!"

Janey did not start jumping up and down for joy. I wondered why she did not seem enthusiastic. Her mouth flinched a wry smile.

'That's great news but ...'

'But?'

Janey started to cry. '... I will see less of you. We will see less of you.'

I gave Janey a hug and reassured her that everything would be ok.

I had no choice. *The* company needed me more than ever.

I had, almost single handed, reversed the share prices and made them shoot towards the sky. They had shot up from the day my appointment as CEO was announced and continued to soar. The chairman was pleased. The whole of the eighth floor was pleased. I was ecstatic. I was now the most important cog in the machine that was getting things done, and sailing, as the chairman put it, the ship into calmer waters. The new rectangular company logo had proved to be a success and many consumers and corporate clients said they recognised it to be the modern equivalent of the *Coca-Cola* logo. New products and services were being rolled out month after month and each one sold by the bucket load. The subs followed my decisions and my rules. Of course, I let them have their way, now and again, just to give them some feeling of importance, but I always found a way of getting what I wanted. Everything concerning the subs would go round in a circle until they felt dizzy and hopped off, returning to the original concepts I had planned all along. They were predictable and I had them sussed and under control. Conventions and conferences always ended in rapturous applause and standing ovations. I spent hours perfecting the speeches with the help of Lisa. I was pleased with my extension of maritime metaphors. I had improved on the chairman's usual phrases by coming up with quips like: "*The* company used to be the Titanic heading for the iceberg" and "this boat is no longer sinking. The leak has been plugged and we are sailing to land" and "the share prices may have taken a dive in the past but now they are coming up for air". The deafening cheers and claps meant that everyone appreciated my hard work, my abundance of enthusiasm, and my sheer diligence. I couldn't believe the person I had been when I first started working for *the* company. I was rude, obstinate, and maybe even ignorant. *The* company had turned me around, and there wasn't any way of going back to the old Mark Gallacchi. No. My dad had been right all along.

Although Janey hated the fact that I was not at home for most of the time, she understood that there was nothing I could do about it, and our lifestyle had changed to such an extent that I felt a sense to provide. We had a large house that some called a mansion. Three executive vehicles. A gym. Swimming pool. Acres of land. It all cost money for upkeep but we could now afford it. And besides, money wasn't the reason for everything. *The* company needed me and I needed them. I wanted to do my best for them and I was doing my best. The results spoke for themselves. Even the replacement of old vending machines with new, hi-tech coffee machines seemed to boost the morale of the employees. Everybody seemed to walk with more bounce in their steps after the coffee machines were introduced. I, for one, was glad of the change. The chairman had been right. The old company coffee, tea, and water had tasted foul. My *Wiener Melange* had never tasted so good.

'That's it. I think. Just do your magic and turn the information into the best morale boosting book that's ever existed.'

I finish off the rice cracker and lick my lips clean. Lisa presses save, closes her word processor, and shuts her laptop.

'I will.'

'How much time do we have before my meeting with the chairman?' I ask.

'Thirty minutes.'

'Ok. Well, we'd better head for the office.'

I am still perplexed about why the chairman wants to see me, and why the subs wants to speak to me. There are a number of new products in the pipeline that need their, or, in the end, my approval, but there isn't anything outstanding to talk about. Everything is running smooth and on schedule. I have made sure to assign the best employees to each project to ensure that everything gets done and on time.

There isn't anything to discuss.

I hold down the switch on the water cooler, collect a cup of refreshing mineral water, and sit down at my desk. A photograph of Janey holding our newborn daughter greets me. My life can't be any better. When I reflect back on my life, there aren't many aspects that I would change. I have achieved it all. Success. Glory. The top job. The CEO. *The* company is fantastic, and I'm glad I didn't resign or get laid off. I love *the* company.

'Mark? The chairman is here. Shall I show him in?' asks Lisa.

'Yes. Yes. By all means.'

The chairman walks in and shakes my hand with the same strong grip that inflicts pain. I wonder if he works out and concentrates only on hand exercises.

'Hello, Mark. Nice to see you. Are the sub-directors on the line?' he asks.

'Not yet.'

The chairman hangs his coat on the stand, strides to the empty visitor's seat opposite me, and sits down. He looks calm and not his usual outlandish self. He hasn't complained about anything, or used the phrase *what the bloody hell is going on?* I feel at ease. I assume he wants to talk to me and commend me for doing the best job any CEO has done and beyond.

'Hello? Hello? Can you hear us?' says a sub's voice, crackling through the static of the speakerphone.

'Yes. We can hear you. Shall we get going?' says the chairman.

He seems unusually calm. I shrug my shoulders.

'Yes,' I reply.

'Now. Mark. I don't have to speak for myself when I say this, but we all think you are great. You're a great person and you get along with everybody. We admire your work ethics and your hard work. Not sure about all these references to the sea in your speeches, but I won't hold that against you.'

The chairman gives out a small dusty laugh that sounds as if his throat has been irritated by swallowing gravel. The meeting is how I imagined it. He is praising me for my hard work. Nothing more. I deserve it after all the hours of overtime I have done and the results I have achieved.

'Since you took control, the share prices have gone through the roof, we're making more money than we know what to do with, and our products have won numerous awards. This is why what I have to say is more difficult, but I have to say it—Mark, we would like you to step down from your CEO position.'

Speechless. Numb. Shock. A sledgehammer has smacked me on the forehead and I can't see straight. For a moment, I thought he said he didn't want me to be CEO anymore.

'We appreciate all you have done for us, and we want you to know that your legacy will remain with us for years to come.'

It was what he said. They are getting rid of me? Why? I am the best CEO the company has ever had. I have done my job well and better than anybody else. Did the overtime mean nothing to them? Did the results mean nothing to them? Did the exuberant profits mean nothing to them? Did I mean nothing to them? I am stunned and speechless.

'You were the one that came up with our theme song *Making Miracles Materialise*. You were the one who endorsed the ultra successful rectangle logo. You will go down in *the* company's history as one of the best,

Mark. This isn't personal and we don't want you to take it that way.'

Not personal? In what way am I supposed to take it? There has to be a reason why they want me to step down but I was buggered if I knew what it was.

'We've decided to replace you with that Lisa Johansson. After all she is going to win *employee of the year* and rightly so.'

What? Lisa? But she's only been my assistant for a few months. Lisa? What the hell was this? Was she the reason I was being shafted, kicked out, and let go?

'Yes. We feel the same way.' One of the subs' voices splutters through the speaker and every word sounds as if bites have been taken out of them. '*The* company has always thrived on change and we believe it is in our best interests to change now. Lisa is the best person for the job in our qualified opinion.'

Qualified? What was qualified about the subs? They don't even know her or what she does. I remain tight lipped and angry. Change? What did they know about change? They always did what was predictable like they based their information and actions on a bad soap opera.

'But I do want to make you an attractive offer, Mark ,and please, hear me out on this. I have a smaller company on the side that deals in sand,' said the chairman.

Sand? What was he talking about? It didn't sound like an attractive offer to me. I wanted to tell the chairman to stick his sand where the desert sun didn't shine.

'They sell sand to the Arab market.'

Was this a joke? It almost sounded like something Freddy Hardcastle would have said or made up to get a laugh. I look at the chairman's face. He isn't smiling. He isn't laughing. His face remains still and motionless while he speaks. He is being serious.

'I know what you are thinking but it's true. I suck up the sand from the bottom of the ocean and sell it to the Arabs. Their desert sand is bloody useless and they can't use it in construction. That's where I come in. I have my work cut out with the fucking environmentalists who say "you're destroying the environment" and "you're destroying the planet" and "you're destroying sea life's habitat' but fuck all that. What's a few dead starfish compared to a big bank account full of cash?'

Now I don't know what to say. I agree with the environmentalists, but then again, I do sit in a building made out of concrete, which, I guess, makes me a hypocrite. A job working with sand? I start to think of my future. I think of the worst case scenario: my mansion has a "for sale" sign out in front of it; someone is buying one of my cars; Janey is divorcing me and taking our kid away with her. Everything is going to fall apart if I step down from *the* company, but what is the alternative? Work for a company that is destroying the environment for the sake of a few new skyscrapers? I can't do that.

'You'll be on roughly the same wage as you are now but working less. I would like to hear a yes.'

The chairman rubs his hands together in a similar

way to an evil *James Bond* villain. All that is missing is a cat on his lap.

Same wage but working less.

Now, can I do it?

I imagine the best case scenario: the "for sale" sign being thrown on a bonfire whilst myself, Janey and Jane watch it burn; the person who assumed my sports car is for sale is being thrown off my property by security; Divorce? Janey and I are in love and that is never going to happen (plus we have the nipper to consider); Lisa wins the *employee of the year* award, which I will probably have to present to her, and she will become *the* company's new CEO. I can't get over that. She must have dropped me in it. No, surely not. I put the negative thoughts of Lisa to one side, and I think about the chairman's offer. I would still be earning a good wage, working less, and I would be able to spend more time with my family. That's how everything should be. In fact, that's better than it should be – more time with Janey and Jane. I can live with the fact only a miniscule number of starfish would die. At least I think I can live it. I'm not sure Janey can, but what choice do I have? I have to accept.

'Yes. I accept.'

I make a snap decision.

'Perfect. Are we happy?' asks the chairman.

'Yes. We're happy,' reply the subs.

'Are you happy?' the chairman asks me.

'Yes. Of course. 100%," I say.

My reply is spoken through gritted teeth. The

chairman did not offer me a choice.

The following day I start to pack away my belongings into a box. I really want to have a word with Lisa but I have not seen her today. In fact, I haven't seen her since yesterday. As most of the items belong to the company, I leave most of the office equipment behind. I pack the photo of Janey and Jane into the box last of all and smile at them as they smile back at me. As I close the box, the phone rings. I don't know if I should answer it as I am no longer the CEO but I do anyway.

'Gordon?'

'No, this is Mark Galla—Freddy, is that you?'

I hadn't heard Freddy's voice for a long time, well over two years. I welcome it as if he is a long lost uncle.

'Ah Gordon! I woz just checkin' to see if ya wanted to shoot a rand. Ya know. The full eigh'een like.'

'You know what, Freddy? I think that would be great.'

I don't ask any questions about Gordon Hardcastle. I don't ask if they have patched things up and are now father and son again. I walk out of the office and drive straight to the golf course. On my journey there, I wonder if I have made the right decision to accept the new CEO job, but when I consider all things, I know I can turn the sand company around. I will make them see sense. I will make them respect the environment without bankrupting them. There has to be a way of turning it into the best sand supplying company the world has ever seen. I know I can do it. After all, I am going to be their CEO starting in a week's time.

24.

I love this company.